Books by Clare Weze

The Lightning Catcher
The Storm Swimmer

THE
STORM
SWIMMER

CLARE WEZE

BLOOMSBURY
CHILDREN'S BOOKS

LONDON OXFORD NEW YORK NEW DELHI SYDNEY

BLOOMSBURY CHILDREN'S BOOKS
Bloomsbury Publishing Plc
50 Bedford Square, London WC1B 3DP, UK
29 Earlsfort Terrace, Dublin 2, Ireland

BLOOMSBURY, BLOOMSBURY CHILDREN'S BOOKS and the Diana logo
are trademarks of Bloomsbury Publishing Plc

First published in Great Britain in 2023 by Bloomsbury Publishing Plc

A catalogue record for this book is available from the British Library

ISBN: PB: 978-1-5266-2221-1; eBook: 978-1-5266-2220-4;
ePDF: 978-1-5266-5295-9

2 4 6 8 10 9 7 5 3 1

Typeset by RefineCatch Limited, Bungay, Suffolk

Printed and bound in Great Britain by CPI Group (UK) Ltd, Croydon
CR0 4YY

To find out more about our authors and books visit www.bloomsbury.com
and sign up for our newsletters

For Annette and Vernon Waterhouse

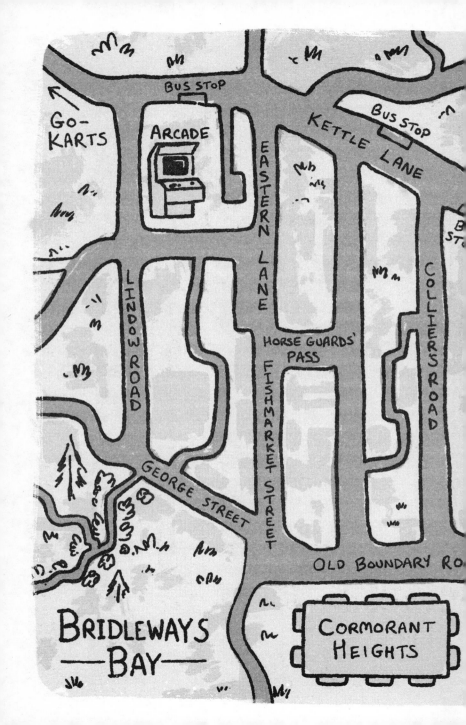

WOODLAND ROAD
DUNES
SHORE STREET
SHORE STREET
SHORE STREET
BACKMAN ALLEY
SEAGROVE PASSAGE
BUS STOP
CAR PARK
CARAVAN PARK

Chapter 1

Ginika wouldn't have chosen this spot for their goodbye picnic tea, but Dad kept changing his mind. There had been a nice wide street not far from their old flat. She could have stood there and looked up at her old bedroom window, but Mum said she couldn't get near the place without coming out in a rash. Then there had been the road right next to her favourite train line, but a wailing man holding his head in his hands spoilt it for Dad.

But after Kingsland Road, Dad had snaked and jerked the rattling campervan down clever side roads to give her a view straight through to a distant Tower Bridge and glittering skyscrapers. She'd glimpsed the river, seen silhouettes of boats and buses. She'd been part of a roaring surge of traffic, so that now, sitting at the campervan's little

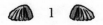 1

picnic table, she felt powerful and brave enough to do this: persuade her parents to let her carry on living with them.

In this campervan, on these London streets.

She put down her fork, swallowed her mouthful of jollof rice and started soft and easy, repeating what she'd rehearsed to perfection. 'You know, I really don't mind being squashed up in here. I don't need space at all, or a bedroom of my own. I'm so much smaller than you that you've probably forgotten how tiny a space I can fit into …' Her words ran into the usual expression on Dad's face whenever she raised the subject: fed up. Tired. Mum had looked down at her hands as soon as she'd started speaking.

Ginika took an extra-deep breath and tried to keep her mind on the prize: life in a campervan! She'd be the only one of her friends to live like this, and they would be *so* jealous. 'I know you think I need a proper house, but I really don't—'

Dad held up his hand. 'Ginki – I know what you're going to say and we've been through this. You can't live in here with us.'

'I *so* can!' Even if the campervan was small, it had to be better than moving hundreds of miles away.

'Darling,' Mum said, 'you've been as brave as anything about the move and we're proud of you. All this mess is nothing to do with you – there's no need for you to be

squashed up and slumming it with us. You can have all that healthy space and normality by the sea.'

'But why *right now?*' Ginika said. 'We've got loads of stuff planned for the last summer holiday before big school. *Everyone's* coming. And the end-of-summer show – how can I miss that?'

Mum stared into her jollof bowl and sighed. 'There will be other dance shows—'

'Not ones I've rehearsed so *perfectly*. Everything's in it. Every move I've ever learned.'

Mum shook her head. 'It has to be now. And you *love* Grandma and Grandpa! It'll be so nice for you up in Cumbria. The fresh air! The beach! Sea! Jellyfish!' She glanced between Ginika and Dad as if she had to give them equal eyeballing. 'And Clawdy-puss. He *loves* you. It's going to be a treat.'

'Why don't you just talk to me like you talk to each other?'

'We do,' Mum said. 'We are.'

'You're not. It's all fairy stories.'

'Ginika—'

'It's all *you'll love it, such a treat*. If it was so fantastic, you'd be coming with me.'

'We have to work.'

'There are jobs around Grandma and Grandpa's.'

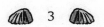

'No there aren't, Ginika!'

That made no sense.

'Yes there are,' Ginika said. 'Grandma and Grandpa work really hard in their boarding house. They never stop. You've told me that.'

'Yes, but there aren't jobs for *us*. You don't understand.'

Ginika looked from Mum to Dad, but neither spoke. 'I don't *want* to live there without you,' she said into the silence. 'I don't want to leave my friends, or miss the show, or miss … everything. I live *here*. If you're staying, why can't I?'

'Look,' Dad said. 'Neither of us is going to be here enough to take care of you. It's going to be non-stop work. It's as simple as that.' He took a sip of tea and a huge bite from his yam croquette, as though the subject was closed.

'But I don't mind you being busy,' Ginika said. 'Mum, I could go to Alisha's after school and when you do the sleeping-over-at-work thing—'

'Ginika, I'm going to be doing sleep-ins practically every other night,' Mum said. Her voice was getting higher and louder. 'And anyway, we can't all fit in here.' She wiggled her shoulders and pulled away from the cupboard she was leaning against. 'Not comfortably. Not in everyday life. Dad can't go on sleeping on the floor. Can he?'

Ginika shook her head. 'But—'

'There isn't room for three in this bed.'

 4

'So why don't we just rent another flat with room for all of us—'

'Because the campervan solution is the obvious one,' Mum and Dad said together, as though they'd been rehearsing too. As soon as they spoke, something clattered outside and three or four boys' voices suddenly rippled into laughter, close by, just under the window next to the bed.

Everyone looked at the window. Clip-cloppy footsteps faded away.

Beads of sweat were forming on the dark brown skin of Dad's forehead. 'We have some serious debts to repay, Ginika. We hung on and tried to make the rent for much longer than we should have. We've got nothing for a deposit.' He made *one-potato*, *two-potatoes* with his fists on the table with every word, like he was stacking all the reasons on top of each other, thinking he was explaining everything, but really, he was crushing it. And he looked like he had more reasons, spare reasons, piles of them.

'But if you sold this,' Ginika said, drained now, her voice close to a whine, 'wouldn't you have a bit of money for a new flat?'

Dad laughed. 'Sweet, this van's a *wreck*!'

'It isn't worth more than a couple of months' rent, and anyway, then what?' Mum said. 'Keeping the van means

paying no rent for a while. No rent means the difference between surviving and going under.'

She made it sound like they were drowning.

'Perhaps I could stay at Alisha's quite a lot then,' Ginika said. 'And just live in here with you at weekends!'

Dad shook his head. 'We need to get you far, far away, where you'll be safe.'

Mum's little finger touched Dad's, and pushed it slightly. If Ginika hadn't been hyper and focused, she wouldn't even have noticed. It was *so* subtle. The hairs on the back of her neck tingled. There was definitely more to know than they were telling her. And last week, just before the last of their belongings were taken away from their flat, there had been a quiet struggle going on between the two of them. They were very discreet and clever about it, but not clever enough for Ginika.

'Safe from what?' she asked. 'What aren't you telling me?'

Mum closed her eyes for a few seconds, as though fighting to stop herself from speaking. She was cross with Dad. He must have done something. But what?

'Safe by the sea. Comfy, with space all around you,' Dad said, but he looked hot and edgy, as though he had a spring coiled in his spine and was ready to leap.

There was definitely some kind of extra trouble going on. Ginika could tell that from the way they looked at each other, *and* from the times they tried *not* to look at each other.

And Dad's face had been weird since the eviction. Whenever Ginika saw him before he knew she was there, before he'd had time to make sure he looked 'cheerful', his face was pinched, like he was thinking of horrible things. And he was restless, as if he was expecting someone to jump on his back. He always managed to pull himself together, but she could see him doing it – it was like a curtain coming down. His legs would relax, and then his arms, but his neck stayed hunched and stiff and ready for action. It was as though he thought someone was hunting him.

Were they? Why? What had he done?

'We'll build up again and be back on our feet in no time,' Dad said. 'But for now, Mum and I need to just squash in the campervan while you stay healthy and spacious by the sea. With you up there, Mum can take more shifts at the care home and I can do unlimited hours in the delivery van, and it'll all come good much faster.'

Ginika pushed her fork around her bowl and took a deep breath. 'But what if I didn't even have any grandparents here?' she said. 'Where would you have sent me then? Would I be going to Nigeria, to live with Grandma and Grandpa Orendu?'

Both of them looked at her. Dad didn't gasp, and neither did Mum, but the air around the little table now felt gaspy and shocked and knotted.

'Ah, Ginki, Ginki … not good,' Dad said, shaking his head. 'Grandma and Grandpa Orendu would love to have you, but you *do* have grandparents here, who are also lovely, and that means you can have a nice, comfortable home with them by the seaside, out of the way of this ridiculous mess we're in, because why should you go through this rubbish too?'

Mum's shoulders were getting lower. So was her head. She looked like she would disappear completely under her blonde fringe if she could.

'You haven't even said how long it's going to be *for*,' Ginika said.

They looked at each other again.

Dad said, 'We're not sure just yet…'

Dad's knees bumped Ginika's under the table again. It happened every time he moved even the smallest amount. Everyone's breath was too close. Normally, this campervan smelt of ink and oil and summer. Tonight, it smelt of rice and yams and people.

'See, darling?' Mum said. 'It's just too much of a squeeze. We'd all get bad-tempered with each other if we tried to move you in here. It's bad enough with just me and Dad.

Come on, it's nearly five thirty. Let's get to the park. Message Alisha to meet up. You'll feel so much better when you've said goodbye properly and made some plans for video-calling each other. You could do dance routines together that way!'

There was another silence. A heavy one, full of deep and uneasy thoughts.

'Please be brave, sweet,' Dad said. 'I know you can.'

Chapter 2

Two days and three hundred miles later, Ginika sprawled on her stomach facing the sea, arms outstretched, chin on the soft, damp sand. The tideline, with its knots of seaweed and bones and crabs and rope and an orange welly, was just behind her. She might easily never leave this spot. Ever. Not just because it was nice listening to the waves *slap-slop-sloshing* in, but because everything she loved was now hundreds of miles away: Mum, Dad, her best friend, her bedroom (the best), its view of the Docklands Light Railway (the *absolute* best). So, apart from her grandparents, this patch of beach was the only decent thing in her whole universe.

They still weren't telling her the whole truth. Not Mum, not Dad, not Grandma Gabriella or Grandpa Will. So the whole truth must be something really bad indeed. She should try – even harder – to find out what it was. Then her thoughts started going round in circles. Perhaps she *shouldn't* find out what it was. Perhaps that would be too terrifying.

Ginika felt furious tears pressing behind her eyes – yet again. Suddenly, she wanted to hurl something into the sea. She could get on one of those trains sitting in Bridleways Bay station *right now* and go *right back* to London … then they'd *have* to let her stay at Alisha's house. They couldn't keep on sending her away … could they?

She didn't get up. She didn't throw anything. She clenched her teeth and turned her face to the sand.

Grandpa's footsteps startled her as they *cruuunched* over the pebbles. She must have gone into a bit of a dream.

'Playing dead, Gini? I've never seen anyone lie so still.'

She didn't reply.

'Well, well. We've been texting you, and Grandma has even called. Is your phone on?'

Ginika turned her head so that she could see him with one eye. 'Sorry,' she said. 'Muted it. Wanted to listen to the sea.'

'I see. Understandable, but not very helpful.'

Ginika said nothing. From this angle, his nose looked very long and his moustache seemed to be clinging to it on a crazy slant that didn't make sense. She was just thinking how nice it would be to see the world like this all the time when Grandpa said, 'Are you OK, Gini? It's a good job the tide's going out.'

'Yep,' she said. 'Fine.'

Grandpa was on one knee now. A smell of oranges seeped from his trouser pocket. His best trousers, so he must be on his way back from band practice. But where was his guitar? His head was slightly tilted to meet her eyes more easily, but his hat looked ready to fall off. He chatted light-heartedly but firmly about Ginika keeping her word, about being trusted near the sea alone, and about staying in touch by phone, always. Then he said, 'Why don't you come back to Cormorant Heights with me now? We'll do something with all your suitcases.'

Ginika turned her head again, forehead down this time, and spoke directly into the sand itself. 'I'll come back when my feelings matter to anyone.'

'Gini, your feelings and your well-being are at the heart of everything. Your mum and dad's plans fell to pieces.'

'The campervan is the plan. That's a great plan, but why aren't I part of it?'

Grandpa sighed. 'We've been through all this a hundred times, Gini.'

'Not being a bit squashed isn't a good enough reason to make me lose everything. There's more, and they won't tell me what it is.'

'Everything? You've lost a lot, but you still have quite a few things left.'

She growled into the sand with frustration, then felt bad. It wasn't Grandpa's fault. Without lifting her head, she went over everything she'd lost, running all the words into each other so Grandpa couldn't interrupt. 'And Alisha …' she finished.

'You haven't lost Alisha. You've just whizzed four or five hours away from her. You'll be whizzing back again.'

Ginika returned to her silence. A few spots of rain began to fall.

Grandpa was quiet too, until he suddenly said, 'Fish don't know what water is. Did you know that, Gini? How would they, when it's all they've ever known?'

Ginika tilted her head sideways again. 'You can't distract me just like that, being – like – so obvious about it.'

Grandpa sucked his cheeks. 'There's sand in your hair.'

'Anyway,' she said, 'how do you know that's true? Nobody knows what a fish thinks.'

'Not sure it's healthy to dwell on it all, Gini,' Grandpa said, straightening up and turning to go.

'I'm not dwelling.'

'You're OK? Really?'

She nodded. 'I'm chilling. I'm not dwelling.' She would *not* think of her old bedroom, which she'd never see again.

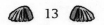

Ever. Or Mum's smell when she hugged her goodnight – she put that out of her mind. Dad too, taking her all over the place as queen of the world, just because he was there – no. Closed.

'You're going to get wet,' Grandpa said. 'And your phone, Gini! The spray will hit it – look!'

She reached around to sling her phone further behind, beyond the tips of her toes.

'Come home with me.'

Ginika sighed. 'In a minute. Just need to watch the waves for a bit longer.'

Alone again, Ginika folded her arms beneath her chin and returned to perfect stillness, like something dead. It suited her mood. She didn't move a muscle, not even when she noticed something in the water moving towards her.

It was a *person*. A boy.

He arrived inside a wave, totally invisible unless you were specially looking. He rode the middle of the surf, head just underwater, eyes brighter gleams of green-grey, like the sea. When he reached the water's edge he was already sitting upright, but Ginika didn't see how he made that move – it was completely fluid. The water slid away from his top half like oil; the rest of him stayed in the waves.

He wore seaweed, cleverly draped and tied. His hair was

the colour of the sea, and she couldn't make sense of it. How was that possible? And his skin had a greenish tinge – or was that just a trick of the light?

Behind him, a few clumps of dark, floaty seaweed suddenly moved off, one after the other, and her mind jolted with shock. That wasn't seaweed – it was people! More people in the sea, about five or six of them, but unlike the boy's, their hair was *exactly* like seaweed. A burst of heat flooded her face and head and she let out a shaky breath.

Ginika and the boy stared at each other through the fine, gentle drizzle. She tried to calm herself and nodded at him – gently, in case he got scared and swam away – but her thudding heartbeat was surely making her entire body pop and jump. He looked over his shoulder to see where the others were going, hesitated, then turned back to Ginika, plainly amazed. He looked around her, beyond her then back to her, as if he too could not believe what he was seeing. Then their eyes locked again. His mouth turned upwards into a tiny shy smile, and Ginika grinned. His smile widened. She kept staring, even when a trickle of salty spray flicked into her face as he whipped back into the water as fast as he'd arrived.

His legs surfaced once – a neat, expert flip – and he disappeared. Those legs! So close together, they looked and acted exactly like a fish-tail in the water.

She jumped to her feet, heart thumping hard.

He didn't come up.

She held her breath and waited. There was only the *slap-slop-slap* of the waves.

He must be drowning. She had to get help … Where were the others? There was no sign of them. *He was drowning!*

No. He wasn't. He popped up much further out to sea, all silvery in the sunshine, but his movements were so much like a seal – or a dolphin or something – that her heart kept right on racing. It was the dipping he did, over and over, as if his body weighed nothing and he was part of each wave, just folding with it. And when he floated, he didn't bob like most people. He rippled with the water as if it was melting him.

Further and further out now, and getting smaller. He wasn't like a boy any more at all; he was like a sea creature. A zippy, stretchy sea creature.

Ginika sank to her knees on the sand. She went over and over what she'd just seen. She pinched herself. She slapped her arm. It was all real.

Ginika danced across the wet sand and over the pebble line to the car park without stopping, feeling invincible, as though she was bringing the foamy sea home in her stomach. She knew she was pretty wet, but it didn't seem to matter. Every dance move she'd abandoned since moving here came back to her in one super-speedy tangle, and she performed them all.

That boy! What was he doing, living in the sea? Because that's what it looked like. But that was ultra-impossible, surely? And the others – were they his family? Did they all belong to the sea? Just, *how*?

It stopped raining. All the way along Shore Street, she felt like a sea creature too. She invented an octopus move and put it with a slide step, which made an old lady stop walking and stare after Ginika with a huge smile on her face. Perhaps she was thinking: *The dancing girl is back.*

She skipped, spun and kicked her way up Old Boundary Road, and every single move from the summer dance show she was going to miss lifted her higher and higher. Each spiral, each turn, each slide, until her excitement felt like a volcano ready to burst from the top of her head. When Cormorant Heights came into view she speeded up for a final blast.

It was a stern house. From here, the triangular roof boards that jutted over the attic windows looked exactly like black eyebrows, frowning. The trim above the porch looked like two arms, folded in disapproval. She skidded to a halt and dived up the front steps. It would be better if there were actual cormorants around here, but she'd never seen one yet. The cormorant picture on the house sign was cool, but there should be a nest for them on the roof too—

She slammed into one of her grandparents' lodgers, a man she'd seen twice now, usually from behind as he disappeared up the stairs to his room. He was eating from a carton of chips and one of them popped out and fell on the pavement, because he was also trying to manage a bulging bag.

'Oh no! I'm really sorry—'

'OK, no sweat,' he said. 'Not a disaster, not this time.' And he flattened himself against the wall to let her pass. Ginika felt her cheeks heat up as she scooted inside. Sharing the house with strangers was so weird, even a house as big as Cormorant Heights.

Then, from nowhere, Clawd the cat arrived. He took his usual soft, soundless steps around everyone's legs and was almost trodden on, but stopped and stared at the lodger for a long time. The lodger looked ultra-panicked. Maybe he didn't like cats.

Ginika galloped upstairs to change and phone Alisha, but her mind was still racing. *A boy from the sea!* Sea people! Maybe they were lost. The others had seemed so different – their seaweedy hair! She'd only caught tantalising glimpses of them, but they'd seemed bigger, so perhaps they were adults. Perhaps sea people's hair grew like seaweed when they got older. And he'd been just as shocked to see her. Why was that?

Alisha wasn't answering her phone. Ginika ended up putting everything on an instant message from her bed, almost upside down with her feet on the window sill. The phone rested on her pillow, which sat on her chest so that the whole job felt a little like mountaineering.

Her mind wouldn't stop racing. If you lived in the sea, how did you sleep? If they came ashore, somebody would have discovered them by now.

But how did *any* sea creature sleep? She started to look it up on her phone, but got sidetracked by a picture of a fish in a coral reef that burped out a cocoon of mucus to sleep in, down on the ocean floor. She tried to imagine the boy doing that, but it was too weird. And anyway, he had a nose, and his chest had looked ordinary, and she was sure he'd been breathing. So maybe he managed like a dolphin or a whale – although she hadn't seen any blowhole. But how did whales sleep?

She carried on searching and found that sperm whales probably sleep with only one half of their brain at a time so they can stay at the surface to breathe. A picture showed a circle of sleepy whales hanging together, with their blowholes just above the water, tails pointing down into the deep.

It was magical. Her heart raced. Had the boy seen whales do this? Would he be there again tomorrow?

Chapter 3

Morning. The sound of a seagull. Pattering rain. For a moment, Ginika forgot she wasn't in her old bedroom and jumped up to watch the train that always stopped outside her London window. Then she remembered the boy from the sea.

She did her hair in quick, fat braids. He'd looked about her age. Maybe a tiny bit older? But no older than someone in Year Eight. Although something told her he didn't go to any kind of school.

By the time she burst into the kitchen and breathed in the smell of toast and coffee, she'd invented a whole day in the life of her sea boy. She'd imagined him swimming across to Bridleways Bay from the horizon, where the moon glittered silvery white on the sea, with the flying fishes. He must have touched the silky soft hairs on velvet swimming crabs, and looked into their red jewel eyes. He'd *know* dolphins. And seahorses. It was all so amazing. The tales he'd tell!

But would they even be able to understand each other's language? The thought gave her a tingling feeling. She couldn't stop moving to the rhythm in her head, she was so excited. She dropped the spoon into her bowl of cereal and was told to calm down by Grandma.

Grandpa had been sitting in a stripe of sunshine, but now he took his plate and cup to the sink and winked at Ginika. 'That's put some roses in your cheeks.'

'What has?' Ginika asked.

'Your beach time last night. Was playing dead the answer after all? Or have you made a new friend?'

Ginika flushed and covered it up by doing intricate hand movements from an Indian dance she half remembered from her many routines, copying the coiled pattern of Grandpa's left ear exactly. 'No,' she said. It was true – she hadn't actually been *introduced* to the boy from the sea. Not yet. She let her hands follow Grandpa as he sat down. He covered his ears and closed his eyes as if in pain.

Grandma had been pinning her grey-blonde curls into one of her famously elaborate buns, but she stopped to laugh. 'More octopus than dancer today, I think. But not *too* much bimbling on the beach this morning, please, because I need you to help me here.'

Grandpa opened his eyes. 'I've found you the perfect solution,' he said. 'And I knew it would come in handy one day.' He reached under the table and pulled out a bright orange bag from a spare chair. 'This is a swim buoy. It will keep all your things dry – especially your *phone*! One of the lodgers left it last year. You attach it to yourself, see?'

'But I'm not going swimming,' Ginika said.

'No, but you're close to the sea,' he said, 'and sooner or later you're going to be in the shallows paddling.'

Ginika shuddered.

'Great for your lunch and snacks too, Ginika,' Grandma said. 'Here, let's put this notebook in there.'

As Ginika watched them fussing, she twisted the ends of her hair and thought. It was nice to have a secret. And she'd never had one quite like this before. 'Can people live in the sea?' she asked.

Grandpa stopped adjusting the bag's belt and looked at her. Grandma said, 'How would they breathe?'

Ginika shrugged.

Grandma glanced at both of them in turn. 'There's your answer. Anyway, why would anyone want to? *Brrr!* Cold.'

Ginika sat down. 'What if there are ways of doing it that nobody's heard of?'

'How would those ways have been kept secret?' Grandma asked.

Grandpa frowned, opened his mouth, then closed it again.

Ginika pursed her lips. 'Well …'

Grandma smirked. 'Have you ever tried to keep a secret, cherub?'

Ginika grinned.

'If there were ways for people to live and breathe in the sea,' Grandma said, 'they'd have found them and broadcast them from here to kingdom come. And beyond.'

'And yet,' Grandpa said, 'when I was small, my grandmother talked about the legend of the sea people. They were only ever seen in Bridleways Bay – way out in the seagrass meadows – and they came here at certain seasons. You could set your calendar by them.' His eyes were faraway. He got up, ready to go out.

Ginika was rapt. 'Sea people?'

Grandma snorted. 'There's no such thing as mermaids!' she said, and sneezed one of her squashed, closed-mouth sneezes that always sounded like cat laughter, if cats could laugh.

'No, *not* mermaids,' Grandpa said firmly, pausing in the kitchen doorway. 'The legend is clear on that. No fish-tails. They're sea people, and they never stop moving. That part of the legend always reminded me of whales and dolphins. It makes sense to keep moving on.'

Shivery excitement fizzed at the back of Ginika's neck and she gripped her cup. 'Wow, what? Did your grandma actually see them?'

'No, but *her* grandmother talked about them so convincingly that my granny swore she'd almost known them. That's how legends keep going, I suppose. And once, I thought I ...' He stopped and smiled. 'It's fun to speculate. To imagine how it could be possible. Because it could, if you had the right body specialisms.'

And then Grandpa was up and running like a talking book. A book about how whales store air in special spaces in their heads so that they can dive for hours without coming up. The boy had stayed down for ages ... but he hadn't looked as if he had extra spaces in his head. His head looked pretty ordinary.

'But that's *whales* though,' Ginika said. 'What about the *sea people*? If they're true – just pretend – how would they keep moving all the time? And why?'

'Hah, yes, why! I've been pondering that for decades. *I* think it must be because they live on the high seas, where there's no land, and that's what you have to do there. You either keep moving to dodge the predators, or you just drift, like a jellyfish. Better to keep moving.'

'*Well!*' Grandma said to Grandpa. 'All those years of reading about sea life and now you're getting fact and fiction properly mangled up. Take no notice, Ginika. It's a load of old bittle-bottle.'

Ginika giggled and mouthed '*bittle-bottle*' at Grandpa, but he shook his head, put on his jacket and left. And then Grandma started. Where was she going? It mustn't be any further than the wind turbines. What would she be doing in this drizzle? And how close to the sea would she be getting, because there were white horses on the waves today, which meant a rough sea, strong winds …

'Be very careful, Ginika. I know you love it stormy, but don't go too near the waves in case there's a surge that snatches you away.' She held up her hands as Ginika started to protest. 'Yes, you don't *want* to go in, I know that, but those giant Atlantic rollers just swell up from nowhere, and they could *take* you in—'

'I *know*.'

'OK, missus, I know you know, but I'm here to protect you. That's my job.'

'I don't need protecting. I'd never get too close – and I'm not a baby any more.'

The beach was busy near the car park, but thinned out the further she walked. She headed back to the last place she'd seen the boy before he'd disappeared. She'd marked it in her mind: a thin strip of beach where the pebble line was low and the wind turbines far out at sea began directly opposite.

She made her way to the sand dunes, then positioned herself in the tall grasses where she was invisible, and flatter than a stalking cat. Then she waited. The rain had dribbled away to a bit of fine spitting, but the sky still looked angry and stormy. When he came, she would say hello, maybe ask him his name, and then she'd find out if he could speak. And if he could – that would be mind-blowing. Maybe she'd take a photo … but then again, maybe not. He might get upset, or even angry. And anyway, how would he know what a photo was? It might be scary if you'd never seen yourself on a screen.

She searched down the rest of the beach as far as her eyes could see. When she was little, she couldn't believe a beach could still go on after you'd been walking on it for an hour. She drifted with that thought, turned back to the sea and there was the boy.

He definitely hadn't been there a few seconds ago. He sat in the smallest waves at the very edge of the sea, and he was eating, taking bites from something in his hands – something too small for her to see, but from the look on his face, it was delicious. He carried no bag – this wasn't a picnic. It was as if he'd magicked the food from nowhere, or plucked it straight out of the sea, just like his seaweed clothes.

Grandpa's legend. The sea people ... always moving on. But this boy wasn't moving on, was he? And he wasn't up at the seagrass meadows, which you couldn't even see from here.

Watching this boy was never going to get boring, because he didn't do the things most people did. She hadn't seen him stand or walk at all. He was kneeling now, and stretching to reach for something in the sand, and his legs were quite slack. His feet looked a bit too big for him. Then he rolled along the wet sand speedily, with his legs in the water. She took a deep, trembly, excited breath. What a great way to get around! He wasn't using his legs to walk though – not at all. Maybe they weren't meant for walking.

He spat something out of his mouth and wrinkled his nose, and she giggled. She wanted to run across to him, and took a deep breath to prepare herself ... But now he half leaped, like the mudskippers she'd read about, dipped beneath the waves and resurfaced with a long ribbon of seaweed. He mud-skipped along with it rippling and tumbling out behind him. It should have been clumsy and impossible and hilarious, but it wasn't any of those things. It was spellbinding.

Slowly, carefully, Ginika got to her feet.

Took a step forward.

One foot in front of the other, delicately, smoothly.

Closer ... gentle raindrops dib-dabbed on her forehead and the world stood still.

The sun came out.

And just as she found her stride, her phone vibrated and he vanished with a *plop*.

She kicked the sand in temper. Hoping it was Alisha, she took her eyes off the spot where he'd just been, but it was only a text from Grandma reminding her not to be too long.

Alisha should have answered by now. They were supposed to be messaging every day to stay best friends so that the three hundred miles between them wouldn't matter. And Alisha should have been *so excited* and curious about the boy from the sea. What was happening?

But whatever, she was right. This boy *definitely* lived in the sea. She needed to entice him back somehow. With a gift of ... what?

She looked around her. What did the beach offer? Glass – brown and green, or clear, sometimes worn smooth, often still jagged and sharp. There was none today, not yet, not here. On the luckiest days there might be clean white bones from a bird, or even – she liked to think – a whale. But not today.

She wondered how often he actually came out of the water and on to the shore, and what he liked or needed here. Cockles? But they were further out to sea. What lived right on the shore that was good to eat? Maybe he ate things that she'd find completely gross. Like lugworms. But weren't they poisonous? Or was that the sand mason worm? She'd never seen one of those, but the cute little houses they built out of sand stuck up all over the place at the shoreline near sunset. Maybe he could tolerate worm poison … The thought made her feel wobbly and strange. Then again, maybe our food would make him ill, so that wouldn't be any good as a gift.

If Alisha were here, she would know what to give him. Alisha would be diving into the sea right now to find the boy – which Ginika could never do, not in that deep, dark water, not since the boat accident on holiday in Cornwall. She shuddered. She tried a video call, but Alisha didn't pick up.

A message arrived. Alisha: *No time! Rehearsing!*

It was only just ten o'clock – they must be doing extra rehearsals for the show. She pictured Alisha going through the whole thing without her. But Alisha wouldn't be alone. Lola or Keisha would fill in the gap she'd left. That gave her a funny feeling in her chest.

Ginika: *It's total truth about the boy. He really lives in the sea.*

Alisha didn't reply.

She picked her way towards the car park again slowly, doing giant steps to avoid droppings from the horses that were always galloping here. A child skipped by waving a brightly coloured windmill. There used to be one of those in a box of her old toys in one of the attic rooms. It had kaleidoscope colours …

That was it! The perfect gift.

Chapter 4

Back at Cormorant Heights, Ginika found the windmill in the first box she opened. But just as she reached the bottom of the stairs, Grandma caught her.

'You're here! Right, let's make a start.' She took hold of Ginika by the waist and gently walked her to the kitchen sink. 'There's the dishwasher to empty and fill again to start with, then you can bozzle over to the shop for a few things—'

'But I'm busy—'

'Doing what?' Grandma started to scrape leftovers into the bin.

'Just beach stuff. It's … interesting.'

'Well, I'm glad you're getting over your fear of water, Ginika, but keep your guard up. We're trusting you to be sensible.'

'I *will*.'

'And you can't have things all your own way. I need you to fold the sheets with me too afterwards. It's a two-person job, otherwise the sheets end up all skew-whiff.'

Grandpa was coming down the stairs. It was definitely him because he always speeded up on the last three steps. Ginika said, 'Couldn't Grandpa … ?'

Out of Grandma's sight, and wearing his guitar on his back, Grandpa opened the front door with extreme and silent care, giving a look to Ginika alone. A look that clearly said, *You haven't seen me.* He slid out into the street.

'Never mind,' Ginika said. 'I'll start doing the dishwasher.'

By the time Ginika escaped from Cormorant Heights, she'd lost three hours – hours in which the boy might have reappeared and left again. So much wasted time. She trailed a stick through the sand right from the car park end of the beach, which had a few dog walkers, down to where the wind turbines began, which was deserted. The pattern she made there was big and bold and, almost without her realising, turned into the map of the Docklands Light Railway. The stations between Limehouse and West Silvertown were piles of pebbles. She wrote her name in the sand. After that, it took her half an hour to fix stick extensions on to the windmill and plant it in the ground. He'd surely see it when he poked his head out of the waves?

Maybe it should have been a kite.

Ginika scanned the sea for signs of seaweed that wasn't seaweed. Then she took off her shoes, walked to the very edge of the water and lowered her stomach on to the sand. It was cool and shivery and delicious. She propped herself on her elbows, looked into the sea and waited. He might have thought she was something dead last time – hadn't Grandpa said she was 'playing dead'? Her arms had been outstretched, and she'd kept perfectly still, like a beached whale. But he wouldn't be fooled twice. He kind of, almost, knew her now.

Keeping still was hard. She shivered. A tiny crab raced sideways along a stream of water, then realised she was there and buried itself in the sand.

Nothing happened.

The sky was a deep greyish blue, like the slates on the roof of Cormorant Heights. The wind got up and blew the more powdery sand behind her into her creation. And now some annoying dog walkers made their slow, stick-throwing way down the beach, which wasn't going to help the chances of the boy showing up. Their heads swivelled her way as they passed. The man stuck his hands in his pockets and scrabbled for coins until his wife nudged him to stop looking, told him, *no*, this wasn't a young artist showing off her sand sculptures and waiting for money. The windmill blew and they smiled at Ginika, chuckling as they walked away.

This was pathetic and stupid and hopeless, but she suddenly realised something huge: ever since seeing that strange boy, she'd forgotten to wish she was home. And there was something else too, something quite funny: back home in London, *sometimes* she used to wish she was here by the sea with Grandma and Grandpa.

A lot of time passed, but he didn't come, and the waves were retreating. The tide was going out. She'd dozed off for a few minutes, and a lady walking a poodle had asked if she was OK.

She stood up, still feeling a little woozy from her sleep, fastened the swim buoy around her waist, tucked her shoes inside it and decided to follow the tide. She took the wind-mill with her and left its stick extensions behind. As she walked, the water remained ankle-deep and began to feel warmer. The wind blew that special oily-sugar seaweed scent into her face and she giggled. No need to be brave here, because she'd only need to stop walking for a few minutes and the sea would be *miles* away! She slowed right down and watched the sea getting further away from her.

The wet sand felt good on her feet. She plonked each heel down firmly, making strong prints. A small amount of water tickled through her toes and she tapped the swim buoy and smiled. Good old Grandpa; she was getting braver, and the water out there was warm enough to at least lie down in …

After she had been walking again for what felt like a long, long time, Ginika stopped beside an elongated bank of the softest, smoothest sand that poked out to sea at an angle. This had to be the sandbar Grandpa had warned her to keep away from. She heard his voice: *The water can come in under the sand. You think you can wade through, but it creeps in from the edges. Don't ever get caught on the sandbar, Ginika!*

Well, she wouldn't get caught – the tide was going out. This was just a great resting place: a long, thin, dry area, like her own personal island. She stuck the windmill in the centre of it and sat down, scanning the sea for the boy. He'd surely see these gently turning sails more easily now that she was miles from anywhere. In fact, there was only the windmill, Ginika and the sandbar in sight.

It was almost four thirty. She vowed to stay there until the boy arrived, even if night had to fall all around her.

She looked behind at the distant pebbles. The sun came out suddenly enough to make her laugh, and the world was now a place full of jewels. Quartz shimmered in the pebbles. The sun was like gold on the sand. Even the seagulls cutting through the sky glinted with silver, and the Ferris wheel glittered brilliantly. She picked up the windmill and let its colours catch the light. It looked fantastic. She played its reflection over the waves ahead like she was conducting an orchestra.

Then, smoothly and definitely, one of the waves wasn't just a wave, and there he was again. He looked terrifically curious, but also nervous – ready to disappear in an instant.

Grandpa's meaningful look from this morning came back to her: *You haven't seen me.*

She whispered, 'It's OK.'

Slowly, she offered the windmill to him. Arm's length. Holding her breath. Helpfully, the wind started to gently spin it, and the patterns shifted together like a kaleidoscope. Blue shiny dots fell into pink and silver triangles, round and round, attracting the boy's amazed eyes.

Above them the clouds were darkening again, and lowering. Heading for the sea. She ignored them as he came closer and sniffed the air around the windmill cautiously. Like a bird alert for danger, his eyes constantly darting around and behind her as he crept forward, slowly, towards the windmill. She had time to notice the long blond sweep of his eyelashes against brown cheeks that were tinged with green before his eyes settled on her properly. And those eyes glistened, as if the tears that bathed them were made of oil. They shone with faint rainbow colours, like a starling's feather.

In the distance, dark, shadowy figures moved just below the surface. If Ginika hadn't known, she might have thought they were sleek, graceful seals … No, that long dark-green seaweedy hair made them more like underwater *cormorants*. So different to the boy's ever-changing hair, which was now a pale and beautiful green. Her eyes kept flicking back to the others, but they didn't come any closer. If a boat went past and they kept still, all anyone would see was floaty seaweed.

The boy also looked behind him at his family, and shuffled himself on to the far edge of the sandbar. He took the windmill, and at exactly the same time, they smiled at each other. Her heart jumped and skipped. The moment stretched out. His eyes scanned her up and down, and she did the same to him, studying his legs the most – her eyes were drawn to them. They bent in a different way to hers, a way she couldn't understand, which made them fit together very closely. His feet were quite big, and his toes – yes: his toes were webbed. The smooth, shiny skin on the soles of his feet looked as if they'd never touched the ground. Her toes were wrinkling in the water already.

But his knees had scabs, just like hers. And, kneeling on the sandbar as she was, the two of them were exactly the same height.

Warm, heavy rain fell, and Ginika ignored that too.

And then he opened his mouth and spoke words she didn't understand, something that sounded like, *Gaaaippeeu*.

His voice echoed.

His voice was like silvery thrumming strings, folding over and over.

His voice seemed to double up in places – it split into two tones. Even three. There were clicks too, scattered here and there. And she didn't understand a word.

Ginika felt dizzy. She might faint. Her heart galloped, her chest tingled, and her head seemed to contain no words.

He waited for her to reply. In the silence, the sea changed direction and crept closer, but Ginika didn't notice, because the boy spoke again.

His voice was the strangest thing Ginika had ever heard in her life.

Chapter 5

A sudden breeze almost took the windmill out of the boy's hand. Above their heads, dark grey clouds fattened and churned.

Ginika felt water tickling the edges of her knees, and she looked down. The tide was coming in, and quickly. She looked behind her – water was already there. The tide had crept around the sandbar and was filling it up from the other side, just as Grandpa had warned. Her way back to the beach was disappearing.

'*No!*' The word came out of her mouth in a wail that the wind took instantly. Panic rose in her chest, but then everything happened at once: there was a crack of thunder; lightning flashed out at sea; the wind and rain rushed at them, churning the water, gathering it into the storm; and the boy's sea family were suddenly closer. A head came out of the water – still not close enough for Ginika to see much more than eyes and nose – then an arm, flashing an urgent, unmistakeable hand signal at the boy. *Come! Now!*

The boy saw this, but turned back to Ginika, who – breathless, panicking – whimpered as the waves closed in and slapped the sides of the sandbar, higher … still higher. She shifted, looked around wildly and saw the sea people surging away through the storm, climbing up to the crest of each swell and plunging down the other side. They were leaving.

Suddenly the solid wet sand beneath Ginika melted and she found herself in the water up to her neck. Her toes glanced across the sandy bottom, then she lost touch with the ground entirely and slipped under the dark, lethally surging waves. Sudden muted underwater sounds filled her ears: rushing; bubbling. The swim buoy at her waist pulled and bobbed. Then a swell brought her to the surface and she gasped, snatched for the boy's arm and missed.

The boy's reaction was faster than Ginika's brain could calculate. He flipped fully under the water like a fish, scooped her up from below and the world fell away. She travelled through the water, zoomed by the boy, who kept her head above the waves, somehow knowing that she needed to breathe, that she had none of his underwater skills. Sky and sea rushed by in a blur, and with a faceful of spray every other second, there was no way for Ginika to tell which was which. He propelled them through the water with the same movements she'd seen the other sea people use, riding each wave as if it was a magic carpet, and during the dips, rippling with a strength that was more than a match for the turbulence of the storm.

Minutes later, hair dripping, eyes stinging with salt, Ginika was back on the main beach. There her Docklands Light Railway; the pebble stations were all submerged, and a can of cola skimmed the surface above them. She checked her phone. The swim buoy had kept everything miraculously dry.

It took a lot of effort, because she knew he wouldn't be able to understand her language if she couldn't understand his, but Ginika finally found her voice again, and said, 'Thank you.' The words wobbled together. She lifted her hands to her face, and they were shaking too. Her eyes were sore from the saltwater. She rubbed them, then tried to tell the boy how grateful she was using only her eyes, but as memories of the boat accident crowded in, a bluish, freezing mist seemed to descend inside her mind and she could only put her head in her hands and get herself as low to the ground as possible so she wouldn't buckle over from the waist.

Breathe, Ginika – Dad had always been able to calm her

down when this happened. She focused on her breath, imagining him by her side. *Breathe*.

When she stopped feeling dizzy and sat up, the boy was blinking at her shaking hands. His eyes seemed to follow each shake, and she put her hands down and sat on them to keep them still. She tried to smile, wanting so badly to explain, but of course, he wouldn't understand. How the boat had flipped upside down. The pain of saltwater up her nose. Mum's arms pulling her to the surface, away from the never-ending deep. And afterwards, the look on the face of the skipper who'd promised them the boat would be perfectly safe even though the sea was rough; his face as Ginika coughed up water on the deck of the rescue boat; the faces of the others who'd passed her from hand to hand.

The boy held up one finger for a couple of seconds – as though telling her to stay put – disappeared into the waves, and reappeared a few minutes later with his hands full of tiny purple snails.

'Ha-*click*-duuu,' he said, holding the snails out to her, palms flat, eyes darting anxiously to where Ginika's hands disappeared beneath her knees.

She took one and examined it – delicate and so pretty – but he put another to his lips, sucked it out of its shell and chewed. Ginika's stomach clenched and her eyes widened.

He held another snail next to her mouth and she moved her head away. A salty, tree-bark smell wafted from it. It wasn't too nice. *People* do *eat snails*, she told herself ... Dad would say the snails just needed seasoning.

'Baaaaiiii-*click*,' he said solemnly, and made his other hand tremble just as Ginika's had. 'Baaaaiiii-*click*.'

Ginika shook her head. Were the snails supposed to make her better? A cure for shaking? 'No, thank you,' she said with a smile. 'I'm OK.' She held her hands up to her face and showed him that they were getting better.

He stared at her for a moment, then tossed the snails back into the water, glancing out to sea all the time, as if he was expecting his family. Ginika looked for them too, but there was no sign of anyone yet. They must have swum out beyond the storm. The sea was still rolling, and travelling up the beach, but the thunderstorm had moved out towards the horizon.

She patted her chest and said, 'Ginika.'

The boy seemed to understand, because he patted his chest too, and with his doubled-up voice, said, 'Eee-*click*-peri.'

'Ginika,' she repeated.

'Gnka,' he said, with a trilling sound on the G. He rolled it on his tongue, like some people roll their *R*s. 'Gnka,' he said again.

It would do. In fact, it was pretty good. But she couldn't say Eee-peri with a click in the middle.

His skin was the colour of sand now – the greenish tinge had almost gone. And now they were closer, she could see his hair properly: *so* shiny and smooth. Almost like delicate strands of glass. It changed when he moved, one minute reflecting the grey storm sky, the next reflecting the sand. Mum would have *adored* it. And his velvety seaweed clothes. His breath smelt like celery and seawater and snails.

'I'll call you Peri,' she said. Mum's birthstone was peridot, she wore a piece of it in a necklace, and that was the same pale green she'd seen in his hair earlier. His camouflage hair ... 'Peri,' she said again. 'Hope that's OK – it's the best I can do.'

All those words must have overwhelmed him, because he went quiet and sat still, observing her, nostrils flaring to sniff every so often. Ginika wondered when his family would arrive. And that thought led to a horrible realisation: he'd rescued her, and because of that, he wasn't with his family any more. Would he catch up with them? What if they didn't come back for him? But of course they would, wouldn't they?

Where are you from? She wanted to ask that so badly. And, *Where will your parents be? Won't they be worried? Shouldn't you go now?*

She shifted so that she was closer to him and tried to use gestures, pointing to him and to the sea, miming swimming away. His response was confusing. He turned his back on the sea completely and stared towards town. It was only a few minutes to six, but the storm had darkened the sky so much that the street lights had come on, and their glow lit the rooftops of the houses, like a thousand tangerines had spilt there. Peri focused on that scene. He looked spell-bound, and pointed wildly, but his pointing was different to any Ginika had seen before: he used his whole hand.

He clearly loved those lights. But did he even know what they were?

'Lights,' she said.

'Liii,' he replied. In his mouth, the half-word sounded like chalk crumbling in a damp cave.

'Ligh-tttt,' she said, to help him get it right.

'Tttttttttt,' he said, his lips tripping and trilling the *T*s, and they both collapsed into squeals of laughter.

Ginika shivered with shock at the sound of his laugh. It was like split bells, as though two people were laughing, one inside the other. It was a wet laugh, but it wasn't phlegmy – it was bubbly. And when he threw back his head to laugh harder, she saw membranes far up in his nostrils that opened and closed. They must be there to stop seawater going in.

They calmed down and Ginika grinned, easily, heartily, and every bad and sad feeling oozed straight out of her.

'Gnka,' he trilled.

'Peri,' she said, and they spent two minutes saying each other's name and giggling.

Ginika knew, from a few rare occasions at school, that this laughter could catch fire. She realised, with giddy glee in her heart, that Peri was someone who might never stop laughing, and might even collapse from laughter. And she knew that because she was one of those people too.

Then Peri suddenly whipped his head towards the sea. A patch of darker, dipping water was not just water. The sea people were back, just two of them this time, and Peri was electrified. He glanced rapidly between the lights of the town and the people in the sea. They stayed distant and low, but Ginika got a sense of strength, of the bendy, athletic bodies hiding beneath their amazing floating hair. Her heart leaped. Her blood pulsed loudly in her ears.

There was that urgent gesture again – *Come! Now!* – but Peri ignored it.

Then came an underwater sound. There were two tones to it: a rushing rustling, like reeds underwater, and a fierce *boom* that seemed to lie on top of it. The booming part was loud and got inside your head like an alarm – Ginika felt herself almost being sucked into the sea by it, towards the sea people – and Peri left, pummelling through the water as if it weighed no more than air. They'd summoned him.

And now Ginika witnessed an argument she knew as well as she knew her own family. A child asking to stay longer. Parents saying, *No*. Peri gazed longingly at the twinkly lights and, although from this distance, she could see his lips moving but hear no words, it was easy to guess what he was asking for. More time. He'd like to explore those lights. Now. Tonight!

But his parents didn't look like they were simply explaining that it was time to go – they looked horrified. They looked like they were warning him off. Their heads were above the water surface from the chin up, and their hands only emerged to gesture towards the lights, but it was easy to read their responses. So, although sea people must be able to hold their breath for a long time, it didn't look as though they could actually breathe underwater. She should have listened more carefully when Grandpa was going on about whales.

They shook their heads, they looked very, very cross and – Ginika was reminded of a really strict teacher she'd once had – they dealt with Peri in a scarily stern way. Their heads jerked a lot, as though the part of them that was underwater was moving, busy and just as exasperated as the rest of their bodies. They weren't going to change their minds *at all*.

And then all of them were gone – Peri too. He looked back at her once – his face was miserable, and quite sulky – and then it was as if they'd never existed. All three of them sped away to invisibility.

Ginika didn't move. She was shaky, amazed and almost breathless, but her mouth creased into a smile because the whole thing reminded her of how Mum and Dad had been in the campervan. *Parents want stuff that we don't want.* Was Peri a little bit like her, disagreeing with his parents' weird decisions? She knew how that felt.

It was chilly now, but her heart began to race. Would he ever come back?

Chapter 6

The following morning, Ginika hurried out of Cormorant Heights like a tornado – which felt good. Being here and doing this felt almost like flying free. She could do things that just couldn't happen in London. When she reached the right place on the beach, she was going to skid to a kneeling position on that wet sand and—

'Ginika*aaaaaaa!*'

She was suddenly surrounded by four girls on scooters, giggly screams and flying hair. They swept her through the bottom of Shore Street, bouncing shrieks and buzzing words over her head, and spiralling in figure-of-eight scooter tricks.

Her name had been called by the bossy person she'd hung out with last year, the one who'd followed her home from the beach one day and then stuck. 'Oh yes,' Grandma had said. 'I know her family – they own the caravan park.

She'll be a nice friend for you.' And it was set. Which would have been great, but Scarlett's pushiness could be annoying.

Scarlett cupped her hands over her mouth and shouted as if she was still metres away. 'Mum said you were baaack!'

Everyone laughed, but Ginika's ears hurt.

Scarlett stopped giggling and swished her hair out of her eyes. 'Why didn't you call round for me? Where have you been? Come to the bike-pump track with us!'

'I'm already going … somewhere.' Ginika felt disappointment all over her face and tried to cover it with smiles. 'See you later!'

She carried on walking and didn't look back, but Scarlett's voice followed like a witch's curse. 'Yay! Pump track later – let's *all* hit the beach!'

No, Ginika thought. *Not right now!*

Scarlett looked the same as she had last summer, but her hair was much longer. Ginika now remembered something pretty unusual – all three of Scarlett's friends had the same name: Olivia. They were nice – summer holiday friends, just like Ginika had been last year – but they were staying at Scarlett's parents' caravan park, and always did what Scarlett wanted.

Scarlett skipped ahead, and turned back to the Olivias to say, 'Ginika's *living* here now! All the time!'

Two of the Olivias made their mouths into Os, as if this was amazing, if not impossible. The third gave Ginika a serious stare and continued walking, looking at the ground.

It was impossible to change direction without looking weird and furtive. Ginika's brain whirred frantically. If Peri came back now, and she missed him ... Worse, if Scarlett saw him ... She was far too loud and bossy for someone like Peri. She might scare him away altogether, which was a terrible thought. Ginika swallowed hard.

On the beach, Scarlett gave orders even while they crunched over the pebbles – 'Find the smoothest sand to sit on ... not the wet bit – find the edge where it's still dry ... not there – too close to that dead crab. Ugh!' And now Ginika found herself digging wet sand with a pencil when she should have been half a mile down the beach, hopefully with a boy who lived in the sea.

In and out of the waves they skipped, all four of them snorting with laughter, never deeper than their ankles, but Ginika stayed on the sand next to their abandoned scooters. They talked about people and places Ginika had never known, roller-skating parks as big as this beach, ice-cream parlours, funfairs, prizes won in places that were so much better than here. Twice, Scarlett ignored Ginika and whispered things into the other girls' ears. And although two of the Olivias were giggly and lively, even with their elbows and legs flying at angles everywhere, Scarlett's presence took over the whole space. When her mouth wasn't talking, her hair was swishing.

Sometimes she was funny. When the Olivia with big round eyes and pale hair gave her a pretty pebble she'd been rolling her toes over, Scarlett said, 'Ugh, no, it might have your feet juices on it now. Give it to this Olivia.' She pointed to the smallest Olivia with the cheeky grin. Everyone laughed, but Ginika's face must have kept its incredulous expression for longer, because Scarlett reached out a finger and pointed it centimetres from Ginika's chin.

'See, I told you she was like that,' she said to the others.

Heat flooded Ginika's face. 'Like what?'

Scarlett smiled. 'You always look like you're about to burst out laughing at something really funny.'

Ginika tried to work out if this was good or bad, but they all laughed. The starey Olivia's eyes were full of questions.

'Look at her face!' shrieked Scarlett. 'Chill, Ginika, it's brilliant! It feels like if we stick with you, fun stuff will happen.'

But time was dribbling away. It was a hot day now. Kids squealed near the water; the sky was so bright that staring into the blue hurt. Ginika squinted out to sea. There were surely too many people around for Peri to come back. They filled the beach right down to where the wind turbines began. The day was ruined, but still she stared at the horizon, hoping for a sign. Hoping to see the sea people hiding, waiting, camouflaged, so that she would be the only one who knew they were there. But if Grandpa was right and they had to keep moving on because of predators ... then his family might have taken him away. For now.

'What have you seen?' Scarlett asked.

'Nothing,' Ginika said in a rush. Scarlett narrowed her eyes. All three Olivias stared.

Then there was a commotion down the beach and everyone looked at that instead. Ginika's heart calmed down.

A group of people had been laying a portable path for people using wheelchairs and pushchairs along the beach and, before they were properly finished, a blond boy zoomed along it in his wheelchair and looked like he wasn't going to stop when the path ran out. He was shouted at, but took no notice. Once the path was built and he was close to the water's edge, he stared out to sea. His shoulders went down quickly, as if he'd just sighed. He looked like Ginika felt.

Scarlett and the Olivias were now squabbling. The

Olivias wanted to go back to the caravan park, but Scarlett didn't. Hair and voices flew around, and then one by one, the Olivias picked up their scooters.

Scarlett let out a long, loud sigh. 'You're allowed on the pump track without me anyway – my dad won't mind, as long as you stick to the rules. So, go. Go on! … They're getting on my nerves anyway,' Scarlett said, once the girls were out of earshot. She undid her long brown ponytail, stretching the band that tied it over her fingers as if she *wanted* it to snap. 'Sometimes they just won't leave me alone.'

Ginika tried to care, but couldn't. The sea was flat. She buried her bare toes in the cool, wet sand, but still felt empty inside.

Then Scarlett jumped to her feet. 'Hey – genius idea! I'll get my mum to supervise so we can go in the sea! Run back and get your swimming stuff.'

Ginika shook her head.

'What's up? You can swim, can't you?'

'Course I can,' Ginika said. Her face was clammy and a droplet of sweat rolled down her back. The thought of being in the sea with Scarlett made her stomach turn over.

'Oh.' Scarlett lowered her voice to a whisper. 'It's because your mum and dad are missing, isn't it?'

'They're not miss—'

'Well, they've left you here,' Scarlett said, narrowing her eyes. 'They're *kind of* missing.'

Ginika returned to her digging. The pencil was splintering and caked in wet sand. It looked like it could never be a pencil again. 'They're just working hard for a while and sorting stuff out,' she said, trying to sound light.

'*Sorting stuff aaat*,' Scarlett repeated. 'I love how you say *out* – say it again!'

Ginika managed to shake her head a little, but there didn't seem to be any way to object without looking like a toddler. Or a troublemaker. She sighed.

'You sigh down your nose,' Scarlett said. 'You do!' she added when Ginika frowned. 'Most people sigh out of their mouths, but you do it down your nose.' Then she did an amazing impression of a crab for no reason, forcing Ginika to smile, and said, 'Oh well, if you don't want to go in the water, we don't have to.' The words were smothered in layers of kindness.

Ginika didn't know what to say. She dug and dug.

'Mum says I have to look after you extra often this summer,' Scarlett said, 'because she feels so sorry for you. And you're definitely quieter this year. You're not the same.'

Ginika was too surprised to react. She felt like a snail, and Scarlett was tap-tap-tapping at her shell.

'So how come you can't all live together in the same house? Your mum and dad must be living somewhere.'

'It's just easiest and nicest for me to be here while Mum's sleeping-in at her extra job and Dad's driving all the time,' she said, and it came out of her mouth in exactly the same way it always came out of Mum's.

'I'd hate it. My mum says she'd sooner live in a tent than lose me.' Scarlett shuddered and reassembled her ponytail. 'So yeah – sorry for you, she is.' She gave Ginika's arm a quick, gentle stroke and smiled kindly. 'So where *are* they living now?'

'Near where Mum works.'

'Where's that?' Scarlett asked.

'You wouldn't know it. It's in East London. Limehouse.'

'Limehouse sounds nice,' Scarlett said. 'Do they live in a flat or a house?'

Somehow Scarlett knew. Ginika's heart thrummed. Scarlett was testing her, to see if she would lie. She thought about the campervan. She could make it sound nice, because it didn't look quite as old and scuzzy any more. You could lie on the double bed and look at the stars through the roof window ... then she thought about Mum's cheeks, and how pink they turned whenever anyone asked about the campervan.

Or it could be a perfectly innocent question.

'They've got a nice place, it's just tiny. Only big enough for the two of them.' Ginika's mouth was so dry that her tongue stuck to her teeth. 'It's only for the time being.' The words sounded sticky and strange, wrongly shaped and tight.

Scarlett just smiled. Then she leaned forward, as though getting ready to tell Ginika a fabulous secret. 'When we start at Ashcroft Academy in September, everyone will think your gran and grandad are your parents.' She studied Ginika from her curly, coily hair to her bare brown toes. 'There won't be anyone else like you at school. Hmm. Woo. That's going to be just … sheesh.'

Ginika's heart was beating far too fast. Did Scarlett mean that Ginika would be the only Black person at school, and so she'd stand out? Was that even possible? She'd only ever seen white people in Bridleways Bay, but surely Ashcroft Academy would be big and full of all kinds of people. Wouldn't it? Not that she'd be going there anyway. 'I won't be staying here long enough to start school,' she said quickly. 'Everything should be sorted before September. I'll be going to secondary school in London.'

Scarlett blew a bubbly, disbelieving raspberry. 'Ha! Don't you know how long adults take to sort the tiniest thing? You'll be here years.'

You'll be here years. The problem was, those words matched some of the things she'd overheard the night Mum and Dad sold all their belongings. To some stranger with a huge van.

He was called the House Clearance Man and he took *all* their furniture away, even Ginika's sleigh bed. Even her dark blue chest of drawers with the Docklands Light Railway tracks stencilled on in silver.

And when he didn't pay the price that had been agreed, things got stressed. Dad started shouting, so they sent Ginika back into the flat ... but she didn't actually go. Instead of climbing the stairs, she had listened in and overheard everything – including some things that made sense and some things that definitely did not.

Apparently they were being EVICTED, which meant they had to leave the flat. There was a PROPERTY LADDER, and they hadn't been able to get on it. If they had got on this ladder, they could have stayed in their home because then they'd have had something called EQUITY, which must be some weird protective thing involving money. All this had happened because of ZERO-HOURS CONTRACTS and something the boss gave Dad called REDUNDANCY, which she now knew was just another word for losing your job.

'Have a heart,' Dad had said, right at the end.

She heard the House Clearance Man bang the van doors shut and get ready to drive away. 'Not my problem.'

'This stuff is all we own in the world.'

'Not my problem.'

Dad's voice got louder then. 'Keep your word, man! You know this isn't what we agreed ... It could take years to climb back to where we were.'

Years. Maybe Scarlett was right.

Ginika felt sick. And not just at the thought of being stuck here for years. Scarlett was staring at her as if she was an experiment that was going well.

Chapter 7

Ginika raced home, scraping her arm against the stone wall of narrow Backman Alley, and only slowed down when she tripped over a loose kerbstone. The alley was empty. At night, this shortcut was noisy, but now there was only Dixon the Border collie sheepdog, who was too ancient to move from his patch of squashed grass on the verge. Everybody on the street stroked him as they went past, and since Grandpa had introduced them last year, so did Ginika.

He nuzzled her hand and then angled his head to get his favourite spot stroked. Ginika felt better for seeing him, even though he panted stinkily in her face. And even though Scarlett's words still boomed in her head: *You'll be here years*.

Grandpa was standing on top of the wheelie bin in the back yard. The shock of this sight knocked Scarlett and the eviction out of Ginika's mind – but only for a moment.

He put a finger to his lips and shook his head. 'Not a word to anyone.'

'But what are you doing?'

'Just weighing down the lid. The binmen won't take it unless it's flat.'

He wasn't supposed to climb. Grandma would be hopping mad if she could see this. She said, 'But Grandma—'

'Let's not worry Grandma,' he said, feeling his way down with one foot. Despite the bin-climbing, he smelt of freshly cut wood and newspapers. 'She thinks I'm too old to fall safely, but I'm sure I could still fall nicely. I'm sure.'

'How long is it since you *actually* fell?' Ginika asked, eyes wide, because she last fell properly mere days ago.

'A long time,' he said sheepishly. 'Decades, probably. Not since before you were born.'

Ginika's eyes grew even wider. She thought about all those years that Grandpa stayed steady and a grin spread across her face, but faded when the echo of Scarlett's words hit her all over again. *Everyone will think your gran and grandad are your parents.* She told Grandpa all about Scarlett.

'She said I'll be stuck here for months and months ... I mean, not stuck, but – you know what I mean.'

'I do, Gini. I do.' He chewed his lip and tried to keep his

expression plain, but Grandpa's face wasn't very good at hiding anything. 'Has Scarlett always been so tactless?'

'Yeah … she says things that aren't nice, but covers them up with jokes and smiling. And sometimes she's fun, but …'

'Ah, tricky. Slippery stuff. And living on the caravan park gives her a fresh crop of playmates each year,' he said. 'I see.'

Ginika waited, but he didn't explain what he saw.

'What are the other girls like?' he asked.

'Nice, but she talks about them behind their backs.'

'Huh.' He shook his head and lowered his fantastic caterpillar eyebrows. 'Any chance that you could walk off into the sunset with them instead? If not, pretend it's all just weather.'

'*Weather?*'

'Yes. It's raining, so you have to shelter. It's windy, so you have to be extra careful, watch for flying branches. Or think of her as an obstacle you can't change. You need to go around her somehow.'

'But what about secondary school? What about my real friends?'

'Try to think further ahead,' he said. 'One day you'll be back in London and there'll be another nice flat—'

'But it won't have a view of the Docklands Light Railway.'

Grandpa pursed his lips. 'How do you know? It might have an even better view.'

'There couldn't be a better one.'

'Well then, how lucky are you, Miss Ginika Orendu, to have achieved the ultimate in views by the age of eleven? You'll go on to do great things.'

She looked at him. It was often hard to tell when he was joking. 'Why do you think it's funny?'

'I don't, Gini. But there are several ways to look at it, not just the one.'

When Ginika shrugged, he threw a cardboard box on to a collapsing heap of others and said, 'You've scraped your arm. Go inside and get it cleaned up properly.'

So he wasn't denying anything Scarlett had actually said about starting school at Ashcroft Academy. She was about to ask why when Grandma called to say that tea was ready.

But while they ate, the atmosphere was tense and knotty. Grandma also deflected all questions about the worrying secondary school possibility and shot secret looks at Grandpa – clever, minuscule ones that Ginika wasn't completely sure she'd seen – and soon afterwards, they started talking about all the lodgers who had oddities, as if she hadn't heard about most of them last summer. Probably even the summer before.

Grandpa focused on the lodger who often made his

floor vibrate. He kept some kind of printing machinery in his room, which he wasn't supposed to have, but Grandpa let it pass. Everyone at the table knew this already. Grandma thought he should be stopped because the corridor was starting to buzz and hum. It was old news, but Grandma said it again.

'You only let him off because he's got such apologetic eyes. But he isn't being apologetic at all! Lordy, imagine being stuck with that expression all your life.'

And Grandpa stuck up for the buzzy man – again – and said he had his machine on the wrong setting and he'd soon figure it out. Then there was the floaty girl in Room Four who drifted around like a ghost because she was troubled, and when Grandma got on to her, Ginika couldn't take it any more.

'Stop pretending! Tell me the *truth*! Am I going to start school here or NOT?'

Grandma's eyes widened. She stood up, and a silky curl escaped from its complicated clasp and flopped over one eye. 'Well, I'm sorry, Ginika, but I just don't *know*. There's your answer, and that's the end of it.'

Clawd clattered through the cat flap and made straight for Grandma's leg to lean against until she fed him, because it was teatime for him too, but he misjudged. Grandma trod on his tail and he yowled. '*Clawd!* Must you *always* loiter?'

But she couldn't keep up the crossness and stretched over to squeeze Ginika's hand. 'Think of some of your favourite things instead, my darling,' she said. 'Mine are hares. And Clawd when he's lying on his back with his paws curled up. The sea when the waves have white horses on top. You could write them into your notebook.' She rummaged in her bag. 'Here, have this lovely smooth new pen to do it with.'

Ginika stared at the pen for a few seconds, and then she couldn't help it – everything bubbled over and came out of her mouth. 'Mine are all the things I can't have any more! The dance show! Trains! Starting secondary school with – just – all my *proper*, actual friends.' It was much louder than she'd intended.

There was a shocked silence. Grandpa stopped chewing the mouthful he'd just taken, and Grandma came over to hug Ginika, leaving Clawd to stand in the middle of the floor with his tail straight up in the air, making everything look urgent.

'Let's just finish eating,' Grandma soothed, pulling her closer, 'and have a nice long drink of water, shall we? Then we'll see where we are.'

But Ginika stood up too, as dramatically and defiantly as she could, pulled out her phone and tapped in Mum's number.

It rang out and out.

The time was right – between Mum's receptionist job and her care-home shift. Ginika cut the call and tried Dad. The room was quiet as that call rang out too.

'Why aren't they answering?' she asked nobody and everybody. 'It's the right time. And Mum hasn't even answered my message from the day before yesterday.'

'Your dad's having an absolute week of it at the moment,' Grandma said. 'He's driving *all* the time.'

Well, Grandma could only know that because Mum or Dad had told her. So they *did* answer their phones sometimes … just not to Ginika. Huh.

'Yes, think how he must feel, Gini,' Grandpa said. 'You're not the only one who's lost things.'

'I *know*.'

'One minute he's a maintenance engineer; the next, all gone! Poof!' Grandpa's blue eyes gleamed with an angry excitement.

'What aren't you telling me?'

'Nothing, Ginika – there's really no need to work yourself into such a froth,' Grandma said, placing her hands on the table as flat as they would go. 'But you do need to understand something: whatever your parents are going through that makes it hard for them to keep in touch, they love you beyond anything on this planet.'

'I *know* that! *Argh!* That's nothing to do with any of this. It's all the *secret* stuff. It's not fair to shut me out, I need to know, I'm old enough to—'

'These are adult problems, Ginika,' Grandpa said. 'It's to do with money and debt and I doubt you'd understand it properly anyway.'

'Is Dad in trouble? Is that it?'

'No!' they both said at once.

There was a moment of silence. Ginika was sure someone was going to reveal the truth and mend the crackly atmosphere, but Grandma started clearing the table.

Ginika stayed on her feet, but didn't help with the plates. Grandpa got up quickly and ran hot water into the pans in the sink. 'Slam some doors if it would make you feel better, Gini,' he said. 'But watch your fingers.'

'No!' Grandma said quickly. 'Lodgers, remember?'

'Oh, forget the lodgers for once!' Grandpa said to her.

'But why can't they just, even … *talk?*' Ginika said. 'Talking's easy.'

Grandma didn't turn round.

Grandpa looked across at Ginika. 'Sometimes it's the hardest thing of all.'

Chapter 8

Ginika had an idea. Grandma's phone could often be found in places where Grandma was not: on the sideboard in the sitting room; on Grandma's dressing table. Ginika stood up; she was going to find that phone and try ringing Dad from it …

Ten minutes later, Ginika sat on the stairs between the first and second landings. A lodger stepped past her delicately, without looking back. She had swiped Grandma's phone from the top of the microwave and was now calling Dad.

'All right, Gabriella?' Dad said.

'It's me.'

'Ginki?'

'You didn't answer *me*, but when you thought it was Grandma, you picked up. Why?'

There was a pause. Then he got clever. 'Ah, sorry I missed you, sweet – it's these crazy hours. Don't know which way is up – been noodling around catching a break while waiting for the next load and stupidly left my phone on the dashboard.'

She'd felt like a spy for a moment, but that crumbled at the sound of his untouchable voice on its own, without the rest of him …

'Ginki?'

'Mmm.'

'Look, just relax into this thing that we're all doing, yeah? Let Grandma and Grandpa Delaney look after you, and try to make some nice friends.'

'But it's hard up here. There's a bossy girl who always wants to be friends, but I don't even like her.'

'Give it a bit more time. Make the most of it. Think of all those funny old words of your grandma's. You'll get such a fantastic vocabulary!'

Ginika sighed. 'You sound so far away. Why don't you video-call me instead?'

'Not allowed. Especially in work hours.'

'But how would they know?'

'This is a work phone, sweetheart. They monitor all usage.'

She didn't reply.

'Silly them, eh?' Dad said.

'How long am I going to be here? Will I have to start secondary school here and everything?'

'We'll have a better idea when one or two things come through. Be patient. We'll let you know just as soon as soon can be.'

Then he chitter-chatted about his deliveries, and his jam-packed, full-to-bursting van. He didn't sound real. Ginika couldn't think of much else to say. She watched sunlight filtering down through the jagged edges of the rooftops in soft greys and purples, and thought of the sea boy again.

'Sweetheart? You OK?'

'Mmm.'

'Just had the most magnificent New York-style stacked sandwich! Followed by a white chocolate cheesecake. With cherries. And all free! The supermarket I delivered to was clearing out their short-dated stock. Mm-mm.'

'Oh. Yum.'

'And just seen the Docklands Light Railway doing that thing it does at Poplar.'

'Mmm,' Ginika said, on a sigh.

'Dips down? Then sails away down its rollercoaster tracks in a perfect balancing act – Ginki?'

'Lit up like a city ship. Yeah.'

When she was little, Dad had taken her to meet Mum off the Docklands Light Railway every night just before bed. They waited on the platform as the train came to a stop, predictable every time, and always bringing its own little wind. He'd told her some of its special engineering secrets in language too complicated to understand, but it didn't matter, because his words – *electric traction motor*, *inductive loop cable*, *transformer* – painted strange and magical pictures in her mind. Then Mum would get off and Ginika would watch the train getting smaller and smaller until it looked like a toy train that was going to *all-the-places*, *all-the-places*, *all-the-places*. So now, Mum, Dad, home and the Docklands Light Railway were all mixed up in her head and she couldn't really separate them.

'What are you doing?' he asked.

'Sitting on the stairs.'

'Nice. OK, gotta go in a minute, Ginki, but can you put your grandma on for me now, please? See you soon, sweet one!'

'OK.' Ginika tried pounding down to the kitchen with the firm, fearless steps of a firefighter. Facing the terror. She put a stern, no-nonsense expression on her face, and it worked. She mustered the courage to ask, 'Are you in trouble, Dad?'

'What? Course not!'

But she didn't believe him. There had been a note of fear in that *what*.

She took a deep breath and dug further.

'Mum said she can't even go past the end of our old street because it gives her "chills and hatred". That's what she said.'

'She said *that* to you?'

'No. I overheard her.'

'Ginki ... I've warned you about that. You don't understand—'

'I understand what *chills* and *hatred* mean. Something horrible must have happened.'

'Yes,' Dad snapped. 'We got *evicted*. That's horrible enough for anyone.' He sounded cross now. And cold. Ginika felt tears begin to prickle behind her eyes. Then he sighed and said, 'Remember what we're all doing, Ginki – we're pulling together, aren't we?'

'Yes,' she whispered.

'We're each doing our bit. Your bit is to stay up there and be cool.'

After passing the phone to Grandma, Ginika ran upstairs, letting her feet clatter loudly on the wood, then took off her shoes and waited two full minutes. A door closed quietly in the corridor behind her, as though one of the lodgers was trying not to be there. Creeping back down the stairs delicately was difficult but worthwhile: these were exactly the right conditions for information gathering.

Except that they were talking about *her*, not Dad.

'She's not quite so nattery now,' Grandma was saying. 'Will thinks she's got a new friend, but it's a bit of a secret. Yes. He's keeping an eye on her. On the beach. Well, you had that freedom, Tara!'

Mum! She was talking to Mum! Why hadn't Ginika got to talk to Mum?

'She's sensible, and she's so terrified of water still. There couldn't be a safer child to play near the sea. But she's much quieter than usual. Some of her zip has gone. The dancing part is fading.'

A long silence.

'Is he? Still? Well, why doesn't he report them?' Silence. 'No, OK, but ...' Grandma stopped and sighed. Then things went muffled and mumbly. Grandma said, 'Oh, love ...' and there was nothing else.

Ginika was confused. Maybe Dad was right: listening to one side of a conversation only gave you mangled weird-ness. Then Grandma told Grandpa – in a loud voice, a closer voice – that Mum was bone tired. Ginika leaped off her stair and got ready to pretend she was on her way down and had just taken her shoes off to do a little skidding. She wondered how it felt when the tiredness was actually in your bones.

And now Grandma and Grandpa were rowing. The call must have ended.

'Just leave it,' Grandpa said. 'Tara's got enough to worry about with Chidi.'

Dad!

'But those people will eat him alive!' Grandma said, but her voice faded out at the end – she was on her way somewhere else, and it was all over. Just when they'd almost-but-not-quite got to the point, which was: trouble. But what kind? Something bad enough to keep her out of the way.

Had Grandma really meant what she said about people eating Dad alive? Who would *do* that to Dad? Police? He'd never been in that kind of trouble. But maybe, secretly, lately … maybe food money got so low that he'd had to steal. Money must have been really, really low if they couldn't pay the rent. Police didn't eat people, but Grandma had her way with words … It meant something else, but something equally bad.

The emptiness inside her started to fill up with tears. What if Dad was in terrible danger? She felt herself slipping back to the sad, hard place she'd been the day she moved up here, where in the night she'd cry for Mum, miss Dad and want to crawl out of her room, over the rooftops and away, as if that could get her back to London. Stupid.

She climbed the stairs as though she could outrun her tears, but the higher she climbed, the heavier her feet landed and the more those tears pressed against her eyes. She speeded up on the second landing, hurtling past all those closed doors with people behind them.

At the bottom of the second flight of stairs, Ginika met the lodger with the bulgy bag, who was just about to climb them. He hovered, as if not sure whether to carry on or let her go first, so she hovered too, trying to do her friendliest smile. It was awkward. He went ahead, and as she followed, something inside the bag moved.

Chapter 9

She gaped at it, astonished. A wriggle. It was something alive. It moved again. It wasn't just a wriggle – it was more of a struggle.

Ginika went faster to keep the man in sight. Halfway up the stairs, a tiny dog's face popped out of the bag, saw Ginika and licked its lips nervously. *This* was why he carried that bag everywhere, and why he always looked so worried: pets weren't allowed in Cormorant Heights. Only Clawd.

Ginika and the dog locked eyes. She felt a giggle beginning, and squashed it down. At the top of the stairs, the dog wriggled again and turned its head to look where it was going. The man reached a hand around to feel what his dog was doing. So he knew, now, that its head was out. He must also surely know that Ginika was still behind him. He pressed the dog's head down gently, and it disappeared back into the bag.

He stepped up his pace noisily, because the floor was wonky just here and there was no carpet – Grandpa had stripped a piece ready for floor-mending. Everything echoed. Silently, the head popped out again and the bulgy eyes fixed on Ginika's. It had to be a chihuahua. That was the breed that fit best in a bag. Its fur was light brown, shining almost golden in the sunlight as they passed the window at the end of the third corridor. Twice, a little brown foot poked out too, and it trembled before disappearing back into the bag. Extreme cuteness. If Grandma could see this, surely she'd love it? Surely both grandparents would change their minds? But this man probably couldn't risk it.

Ginika carried on following, loving the dog, cheering up. Giggling had left her with a warm glow. And from now on, she'd never go anywhere without a biscuit in her pocket. They passed an empty room with its door wide open, and the dog's nose wrinkled in sudden interest. Ginika smiled again. Grandpa *never would* get round to fixing up this one – Grandma was always saying that. She also said it was developing some very odd smells. She was right, and this little dog knew.

Mr Chihuahua Man was brave. Nothing was going to

separate him from his dog. The thought made her heart beat a little faster – she should be brave too. If there were secret dogs and secret sea boys, then anything was possible, wasn't it?

Ginika's phone buzzed and chirruped and the screen lit up. A video call was coming in. Mr Chihuahua Man jumped, turned round and his dog began to bark. And now there was a jumble as he tried to shush the dog and turn his key in the lock of Room Eleven at the same time. Ginika, hot with embarrassment, squeaked 'Sorry!' and zoomed back down the stairs they had both just climbed.

She accepted the call as she went, ducking into her own room, hoping Grandma hadn't heard the dog …

'Ginika?'

'*Alisha!*'

After giggling for a couple of minutes at the sight of each other on-screen – 'You look medium-sized!' Alisha said, and Ginika shrieked, 'So do you!' – Ginika got straight into Peri, because that was the most awesome news she had.

'Has he got legs?' Alisha asked.

'Yes, but he doesn't use them for walking.'

Alisha looked at her doubtfully. 'He can't be a merman if he's got legs. Must just be someone really good at swimming and holding their breath.'

'No, he's someone who lives in the sea. He's not a merman.'

'Wait.' Alisha leaned sideways to reach something and all Ginika could see was half of one eye, an ear and a lot of hair. When she came back to the screen fully, with a packet of crisps in her hand, she was shaking her head. 'But how can someone live in the sea though, Ginika?'

'That's what I want to find out.'

Alisha continued to frown.

'I keep getting all these ideas,' Ginika said. 'He hasn't got gills, but neither have whales and dolphins. Maybe he pops up to breathe just like them.'

'It's probably just someone messing about.'

'No! He's definitely real. If you saw him you'd … understand.'

Alisha nodded quickly, then launched into dance talk. There were new routines at their old dance school, and she demonstrated one, skipping around her bedroom in and out of the screen. 'Miss Johnson is putting more ballet in it now,' she said. 'Look at this!'

Ginika smiled politely. She didn't know how Alisha even made one of those shapes.

'And this is what we're doing for the show.' Alisha disappeared off-screen again. Ginika saw a leg, lifted high. Something like a forward roll followed. Ginika's heart plummeted. She didn't feel like seeing any more, not today. Not until she'd had a chance to catch up. Although what was the point? The dance show was completely out of reach.

'OK, show me your cat now,' Alisha said.

'Um … I'm not sure where he is.'

'Could you find him?' Alisha fed crisps into her mouth without once looking down.

'OK.'

This was *so* stupid, Ginika thought as she trotted down one set of stairs, then another. Why was Alisha more interested in a cat she'd never seen than a boy who lived in the *sea*?

'How long's it taking you? How big is this house?'

'Way big,' Ginika said.

'Whoa. What's that?'

There was a hum in the air. They were going past the room of the man with the buzzing machine.

'It's just a lodger,' Ginika whispered. 'He does that.'

'*Whoa*, your house is *sooo weird*. How come people are just all over the place doing stuff?'

'They're not – they're all in their digs. That's what you call the rooms in a boarding house.' There was pride in Ginika's voice, but really, she wasn't sure if the rooms were the digs or the whole house was a dig. Or even a dug.

Clawd was asleep on the sitting room window sill.

'Ah, so fluffy!' Alisha crooned. 'Tiger-coloured! And what's going on with those cheeks! He's got *actual* cheeks!'

Clawd twitched and opened his eyes, looking slightly irritated. Ginika kept him on-screen while she told Alisha about Dad's probable trouble.

'Hmm,' Alisha said. 'Why don't you just ask them?'

'I have. They're not telling me everything.'

Alisha hugged her knees and didn't say anything. The sight of that familiar bedroom gave Ginika a pang of homesickness. There was Alisha's wardrobe and the dressing table next to it, with Alisha's frog collection gleaming all shades of green. And that rumble in the background – was that the Docklands Light Railway rattling by? Alisha didn't care about trains.

'Yeah … I don't know what you can do. Probably nothing.' Alisha sounded small and far away now.

To break up the miserable feelings she was getting, Ginika said, 'Hey, your hair! I like it!' Alisha's braids were gone and her loose hair formed a halo that touched her shoulders.

Alisha repeated part of the dance routine, then stopped and sighed.

'You could come up here and visit,' Ginika said. 'Do you think they'll let you?'

'Dunno. What would we do?'

'We could do loads. The beach is waaay long. It's got jellyfish, seaweed, every type of sea bird. And *both* pebbles and sand, in strips, like somebody arranged it. And people ride horses here because the sands go on for miles and miles – that's why it's called Bridleways Bay. But the main thing is the boy from the sea. You could see him!'

Alisha gave a thin little smile. 'I probably won't be allowed to come all that way anyway.'

The idea is dead in the water. That was one of Dad's phrases. It fitted.

Now Alisha jangled in a way that was nothing to do with dancing. 'Got to go,' she said, scratching and pulling at her ear. 'I'm supposed to be at this thing ...' She looked embarrassed. 'Sorry, I forgot. It's all arranged.'

The screen went dead. Ginika had just opened her mouth to say, 'Bye,' but the word hadn't come out. She knelt on the floor beneath the window and looked up at Clawd. His back was straight and his head was steady and still, as though he was the king of every cat. She reached up to stroke him, and his purr sounded like a small, ever-lasting engine.

'Everything's different,' she said aloud. 'And everyone. Absolutely. Every. One.'

Clawd stared down at her for a few more seconds, then slowly closed his eyes. He definitely agreed.

There was a thunderstorm in the night. A lightning flash woke Ginika, even through closed eyelids. She stood on her bed in a wobbly position and watched the storm rage over the sea. Horizontal lightning flashed across the sky, low down, almost tipping into the swollen waves that rolled in all directions, and she wondered where Peri and his family were. They'd looked *so* strong in those daytime storm waves, but how did they manage when the sea was raging and lurching all night like this? And where did they sleep? How? Wasn't it impossible?

CRASH. Thunder couldn't possibly move this house, but nevertheless Ginika *felt* that one. She crept back under her duvet.

Ginika wasn't scared of storms – not at all – but that crash was *big*. She was glad her bedroom was attached to her grandparents' in this private annexe away from the lodgers. Another lightning flash lit up Grandma's fully loaded dressing table, transforming it into a ghostly pirate ship. But the end of their bed was just visible too; their feet were comforting lumps of safety in the darkness.

Chapter 10

Ginika woke early, and her mind was still stuffed full of worries. Secondary school: where would she be going? Secrets: why wasn't anyone telling her the truth about important things? Peri and his family: had the storm harmed them? Her dreams had swirled with monsters and menace.

Nobody else in the house was awake. She crept through her grandparents' room, made some cereal without clattering anything and ate it sitting on the kitchen countertop, looking out at the small triangle of glittering sea visible from downstairs. Nobody stirred; not a single lodger, and not even Clawd.

After packing two small cheese and onion pies for lunch, she let herself out quietly and ran to the beach, formulating a bulletproof plan: once she found Peri again, she would work out a way of asking all about his life, and find out if it was really true about them moving on and on all the time. Perhaps she could even get another ride! He could actually *show* her where seahorses live in the seagrass meadows, because he'd know the best times and ways of shimmying close to them, unseen. She shivered, suddenly realising how much braver she was getting. And if she got braver still, maybe she could even meet a dolphin – or see an albatross skimming stormy waves.

She gazed out over the dark blue waves and grinned. She'd be able to forget about stupid schools and people's stubborn secrets then – because none of that stuff could possibly matter next to such wonders.

The sun warmed her bare arms. The tide was in, and the sea was flat. It shone silvery blue, and long-legged birds stalked its calm shallows. One of them had a chick! It might be a ringed plover. She focused on its downy head, then spotted a lone balloon attached to a post and wondered if Peri would like it. Chicks and seals and seahorses were just part of his everyday life – which was incredible – but things like balloons might amaze him.

Ginika settled on the smooth, damp sand not far from the water's edge, and waited, shining her phone's torch into the sea from time to time, because Peri liked light.

She was still waiting two hours later, when the beach

had filled with every type of person except one who came from the sea. She'd had to move beyond the wind turbines to get a quiet spot. Perhaps the sun was too bright for Peri to see her phone on a day like this; even scanning the waves to the horizon hurt her eyes.

Ginika angled her body to face both sea and beach, so that nobody could creep up on her. If Grandpa came, she'd see him first if she stayed alert ... or even Grandma! That would be something. But Grandma was large and her long bright skirts and scarves were unique enough to be seen from miles away. And she'd *probably* text first if it was chore time ...

But it wasn't her grandparents who arrived; the unmistakeable silhouettes of Scarlett and the Olivias made their way down the beach in a flurry of hair and screams and giggles. Ginika dived into a hollow in the sand dunes well before the silhouettes turned into clear figures, and kept her head down until she couldn't hear them any more. Her heart thudded. She wasn't in the mood for Scarlett's bossiness. And what were they doing this far down the beach?

After a few minutes, she peeked, slowly and carefully, but they were still there. They'd gone quiet because they were examining something the sea had washed up. Still and studious; ankle-deep, bodies crouched.

A head shot round. Ginika ducked. She remained motionless for what felt like ages, even when giggling started up again. She was too hot. Sticky. The chatter died away, but she didn't crawl to the tips of the marram grass and look out until they were well out of earshot. Heading back the way they had come, the girls veered into the sea, kicking water at each other, then tearing off across the sand again. Leaving. Ginika let out a long, sultry breath and climbed out of the dunes. The grass had killed her knees.

She sprawled on the sand and searched the internet. She was looking for information about sea people – for *any* hint of them, no matter how small or half-made-up – and for anything on Grandpa's legend.

But there was nothing on people like Peri. All she found was a babyish mermaid cartoon on the tourist information website: *Visit Bridleways Bay, land of mysterious watery legends. We can't promise you mermaids, but you might be lucky enough to spot a porpoise, or even a minke whale.*

By lunchtime, she'd moved to a patch of dry sand midway between the dunes and the sea to eat her pies. The wet stuff was no good for sitting still – her legs had got too itchy. Her whole body was now stiff from waiting around, even though she'd got up to run around every so often. The battery on her phone was running low.

Over the next couple of hours, her arms and legs grew spidery with restlessness. Thoughts of her two possible new schools began to push Peri from her mind again. They seemed more real. The idea of Ashcroft Academy made her sweaty and cross and scared. And heartbreaking little scraps of her old life kept sneaking back in: a fox in the park around the corner from their old flat. He'd started to get used to her. He came closer each day. Alisha said it wouldn't have been the same fox, but she knew it was. Then there was the bus to dance class that often kept pace with the Docklands Light Railway for twenty glorious seconds before the train curved round dramatically and dipped into a tunnel.

The heat was heavy now, and the sun looked like it would never move again, just burn at that same point in the sky forever. A feeling of hopelessness hovered at the back of Ginika's mind: Peri might never come back.

At ten to three, Ginika snatched up her swim buoy and trudged homewards.

The blond boy she'd noticed the other day was sitting by the sea again, but this time, he was on his own. His wheelchair was at the very end of the black portable path, which stretched from the car park to the water's edge. She wondered if he minded being at the car park section of the beach. As she approached, their eyes met, then both looked away at the same time. Ginika bit her lip; she wanted to ask him why he was alone, but didn't quite dare.

When she reached the car park, she looked back at him – just once. His head still faced the flat and glittering sea.

At Cormorant Heights, a lodger was leaving. It was the Floaty One from Room Four, and she looked like a bundle of angry bags. 'No way will everything go in one journey,' she was saying, and it sounded like she had something stuck in her throat. 'How am I going to manage on the train?' Not so floaty any more.

Grandpa sighed and his frown lines appeared. He took three of the bags from her gently and carried them over to a waiting taxi.

Ginika stared, transfixed. Leaving in a hurry. Leaving when you didn't really want to leave. At their London flat that day, nobody had been ready. Mum was in the middle of her shower. In the scramble to get everything out on the pavement for the House Clearance Man, Ginika hadn't even had time to take final photos, or say goodbye to her room. Broken off, that's what they all were.

The Floaty One crammed her bags into the boot, long straight hair falling forward like curtains, and still Ginika didn't move. Grandpa sent her messages with his eyebrows, but in the end, Grandma had to pull her away.

'But what's happened?' Ginika said, craning her neck for a final glimpse. 'Why is she leaving? Why's she so cross?'

'It's normal for people to come and go,' Grandma said, steering Ginika into the kitchen by her shoulders. 'Crystal's having to move to Newcastle for her job, and they want her straight away or not at all, the devils.'

Grandma sat Ginika down and put a bowl of fruit and a glass of mango juice in front of her, but Ginika didn't eat or drink. How certain was it that this kitchen wouldn't disappear too? She'd been sure the London one couldn't. Who knew what people might decide to do next?

When Grandma left the room to fuss the Floaty One a little more, Ginika felt as if something huge and dark had come and plonked itself on her shoulders. Her head pounded. The lingering cooking smells got up her nose and everywhere felt full of jagged edges.

When she was with Peri, she didn't have any of these horrible feelings. Ginika took a deep breath and wondered about that. Was it the excitement of finding someone so different? Or was it that the two of them made such easy daftness together? She smiled, remembering how they'd said each other's names, and how his lips had sounded wrapped around English words. He was so funny. They were funny together. He made her laugh properly in a way she'd thought she never would again.

She sat up straight. There had probably never been a pair like the two of them in all the history of the world, and that was funny too. It piled funny on top of funny and made super-hilarious ultra-funny.

And there were things he *longed* for too, on land – she'd seen that in his eyes. She needed to help him. Show him. Somehow, she just *had* to find him again. But how, if he wouldn't come to the beach? She'd have to get into the sea – that's where he was. But how could she … ? She shuddered. Her shoulders sagged again.

Should she just tell Grandpa after all? He was full of so much knowledge about wildlife – it was his favourite hobby. And he was interested in the legend. If he knew there were actual, real live sea people, then might he have fabulous brainwaves about how she could find hers again?

Ginika spent the next hour following Grandpa around the house as he did his mending and straightening. Plucking up courage was harder than she'd expected, especially when Grandpa decided to relocate an annoying fly from the second-floor bathroom. This was something he could only do when Grandma wasn't around, because it involved water spillage.

Ginika got her words together while Grandpa loaded his spray-cleaning bottle, now filled with fresh water, and perfected his aim.

'Why do you think those sea people your grandma saw decided to live in the sea?' she asked.

Grandpa ignored her. He squeezed his watery trigger, again and again. *Squirt squirt squirt.* Ginika watched his face in the bathroom mirror, creased in concentration, keeping up with every dodge the fly tried to make, just like a master marksman. The fly avoided the water for much longer than Ginika would have thought possible, then dropped to the floor, waterlogged.

Grandpa approached it sideways, like a crab, and then quickly – and extremely gently – wrapped it in a wad of tissue.

'It's been in here since yesterday,' he told Ginika, 'but clearly can't find this open window.' He stuck his hand out of the window and shook the tissue. 'Released! He flies off unharmed. Magic!'

The bathroom floor was awash. Ginika mopped it up, giggling. She had seen this operation before, but Grandpa's unique dedication amazed her every time. She repeated her question.

'Ah. Yes,' Grandpa said, moving back to the corridor and fumbling in his toolbox. 'The people of the sea.' She expected him to chuckle, but his expression was serious. He said nothing for a minute, just positioned his sanding tool against the doorframe of Room Seven. 'My granny was your great-great-grandmother, remember?' he said with a smile. 'But I doubt it was an actual decision, as such. It probably just happened to them.'

'What ... like a curse? Something supernatural?'

'Needn't have been,' Grandpa said. 'Could've been perfectly natural.'

'How do you mean?'

'Well, if a big piece of land got cut off by the ocean and there were pockets of people stranded, and then life in the sea started to take over ...' Grandpa switched on his sander and deafened them both for a minute. Then he turned it off and ran his thumb down the doorframe he was smoothing. 'I've no idea how they deal with all the salt, but ... it takes a *very* long time for bodies to change, so if the sea people diverged from us an awfully long time ago, then you never know. It might be possible.'

'Before boats and travelling and writing and stuff?'

'Yes, yes. Before all that.'

'Whoa.' Ginika stared at the tiny particles of wood dust building up on the floor. 'Why is there nothing about them on the internet then?'

Grandpa looked at her. He smiled, then frowned, and finally, extending his metal tape measure with a sharp flick, he shrugged. 'I can only think it's because the sea is the last great frontier. There's an awful lot left to discover there.'

A surge of pure wonder swept through Ginika and she held her lips together with her fingers to prevent a big grin from breaking out. Peri! The sea people!

She opened her mouth to tell Grandpa everything, but he let out a long, impatient sigh and shook his head. 'Trouble is,' he said, 'the pollution we've spewed out over the last fifty years might mean some species could be wiped out before we even discover them. Not to mention climate change.'

The thought of that pressed down on Ginika like something solid. She remembered her last glimpse of Peri plunging into the churning waves. She knew Grandpa meant the tiny pieces of plastic in the ocean – he was always going on about those. What might happen to Peri if he ate creatures loaded up with minuscule bits of plastic? No, she didn't want to know – it was too horrible.

And what if he *really* never came back? What if his strict parents had taken one look at the rubbish on the beach at high tide and taken him away from Bridleways Bay forever? She'd be left with just Ashcroft Academy, looming closer and closer … Ginika's bottom lip wobbled.

Then she remembered Peri's face the day she gave him the windmill: *You haven't seen me*. She couldn't tell Grandpa. She just couldn't. Her lip wobbled even more.

'Hey,' Grandpa said, 'don't worry, Gini.' He took the

grabby tool he used for pulling out nails and chased her with it, snapping it like a baby crocodile's mouth.

Ginika tried to smile for him, but it was a weak one. Then a new sound wheezed out into the corridor near the buzzy lodger's room on the second landing. Grandpa stopped, grabby tool poised in mid-air, and opened his mouth in mock horror. Another smile crept on to Ginika's lips. The buzzy lodger's new sound reminded her of the gasp of a train door sliding closed. It was so unexpected that it broke through her sadness and she started to chuckle.

Ten minutes later, Ginika was in her room writing all the new information about sea people into her notebook. She couldn't tell Grandpa about Peri, and she wasn't brave enough to just wade out into the sea with armbands on, so she'd just have to find out as much as she possibly could about ALL ways of life in the ocean. Maybe then she'd know how to find him again.

She clicked impatiently through pages and pages of things on the internet, things Grandpa had already told her, then stopped on a page about salmon. When it told her what happens when salmon reach a certain age, she slowed down and read properly: there was a colour change. *Newly silver, a salmon leaves its river and sets off to the sea for the very first time.* Peri wasn't a fish, but he *had* looked different from his parents … Perhaps he was in the middle of changing. Perhaps that was why he hadn't come back – he'd suddenly become a teenaged sea person, with hair like seaweed and even stronger storm-swimming powers. Maybe teen sea people weren't interested in small seaside towns—

'Ginika?' Grandma's voice called up the stairs. 'Scarlett's here for you.'

Chapter 11

Ginika froze. She heard Grandpa telling Grandma that Ginika was here just a minute ago so couldn't be far away. Her heart sank. She remembered Scarlett's face when she'd said, *You'll be here years*. She'd looked so satisfied, so clever and so sure she was right. Then she pictured Scarlett right here on the doorstep of Cormorant Heights, all the time, tracking her down, maybe even following her right to the beach. Day after day. Forever. Something clicked into place in her head: Peri wouldn't come to her if someone else was there. If he ever came back, she *had* to be alone.

Ginika switched her phone to silent, left her room and crept higher up the house, stepping only on the far edges of those stairs that could be trusted not to creak. She stopped to listen. Nobody was coming, so she bounded up another flight, moving beyond the smell of mashed potato that hung around the lower corridors, and into the world of the top attic rooms, where the air smelt less of food and more of old and interesting things.

Silently, she slipped through the open door of one of Grandpa's junk rooms, and squeezed behind a tall chest. The wood smelt of raisins and old, dusty polish. A clock ticked somewhere out of sight.

'GINIKA! SCARLETT IS WAITING!'

Their voices were still far below her, but Ginika wriggled between stacked chairs, broken tables, pieces of guitars and Grandpa's weird gadgets to where an old sofa on its side made a fabulous, velvet-sheltered hiding place, like half a tent.

There was a space at the other side of it, like a clearing in a forest, and Clawd lay there in a shaft of sunlight with one eye open, watching her. She grinned and crawled over to him on her elbows, and he angled his head towards her for a stroke, which made her grin widen. His fur smelt powdery and gorgeous, but he began to purr loudly.

'Shh,' she whispered, and stopped stroking. He rolled on to his back, twisted himself comfy and stopped purring with an abrupt cat snort.

His new position was one of his very best: every part of him faced a different direction. His head and ears lined up perfectly north. His feet pointed south. His neck stretched sideways towards the west, with his chest bending that way too, but his tummy faced the ceiling. Despite all that, he looked more comfortable and happy than anyone she'd ever seen.

'Ginika, where are you?' Grandma sounded closer now – she might have reached the floor beneath this one. Her heart thudded, but she felt safe in here. Grandma couldn't possibly fit very far into this room at all.

She kept still.

'You can't hide, Ginika!'

Hmm, Ginika thought, *it actually looks as if I can.*

Half an hour went by. Ginika's phone lit up with a message from Scarlett: *Don't know where you are, but we're going to the bike-pump track now.*

She let out a long breath of relief, pressed her phone back to black-screen and screwed her eyes shut. This space was like a timeless oasis where nobody could ever bother her, and where the smells were earthy and old and strange.

She opened her eyes when she felt Clawd tentatively preparing to sit on her head.

Downstairs in the kitchen, Grandma gave her a knowing look. 'Whatever were you playing at?' she said. 'You can't treat your friends like that!'

Ginika blinked a few times and scraped fingernails along the back of Grandpa's chair. 'She's not my friend.'

'Ginika!'

Ginika shrugged and pursed her lips, feeling cut off from everything she wanted.

'Speak, Ginika! Where's your voice gone?'

Ginika huffed a little, and tutted, then said, 'How in this world do you get rid of someone who's just not … nice?'

Grandma looked shocked. Grandpa turned around awkwardly and tried to look at her, but she was still looming over him. Ginika felt a thrill of danger run through her and wracked her brain for more, but Grandma got there first. 'You know, hiding from people, pretending you're not there – that's a kind of lying, Ginika.'

'No it isn't.'

Grandma said gently, 'It is, you know.'

Ginika went to the sink and poured herself a glass of water.

'And to make Scarlett feel better,' Grandma said, '*I* told a white lie. I said you must have slipped out without either of us realising.'

Ginika thought of Scarlett's face. A hot, uncomfortable feeling of doubt started around her stomach and crept upwards. She tried to cover it with thoughts of Peri, and fixed her eyes on the swirling water in her glass.

Grandma sighed. 'You're bored, Ginika. And you wouldn't be if you took advantage of people that come to

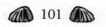

your doorstep, offering friendship …' She tailed off, and Grandpa appeared behind her. 'And aren't you keeping up with Alisha? What's happening with her?'

Ginika felt tears pricking her eyes. 'Nothing,' she said, as sulkily as possible, and that squashed the tears away.

'What do you mean, "nothing"? That makes no sense.'

'She's busy. Anyway, I don't even *want* anyone,' Ginika wailed, turning away from the sink and facing both of them. 'If I was on the Docklands Light Railway right now, or even if I could just see it, like I used to be able to, I'd be *perfectly* happy.'

Grandma narrowed her eyes. 'I don't remember you saying much about that train until this summer.'

'But …' Ginika blinked in surprise. 'It was always just … there. Right outside my bedroom window. I never thought it would ever not be there.'

The first thing she saw each morning. The last thing she saw before drawing her curtains at night. And when she was tiny, Mum had lifted her up to the window to wave goodnight to the passengers on their way home. Maybe it was babyish to hold on to that, but … she couldn't help it.

'I dare say it is still there,' Grandma said, nodding at the bangles on her wrist as though expecting them to agree.

Grandpa folded his arms and glanced between Ginika

and Grandma. 'The train means *home* to her,' he said. 'She's just homesick, Gabriella.'

The next morning brought perfect weather for an empty beach: exciting dark clouds with sunshine behind them, powered by a blustery wind. A dark, moody sea. But what was the point of even trying to find Peri again?

Ginika ate her breakfast with her head propped against her hand, elbows resting on the table, hunched and silent.

Grandma prodded one of her elbows gently. 'Oh, Ginika, you look absolutely hopeless! Drooping around the place … What is it? On one of your favourite white-horses days too.'

'Ah, white horses!' Grandpa said. 'My granny used to tell me to look out for the sea people on wild white-horses days. Apparently, they forage close to shore during storms – they use the white horses of disturbed seas as their cover.'

Ginika blurted, 'You didn't tell me that before!'

Grandpa put his knife down and looked at her. 'But … why … ?' He frowned, then shrugged. 'You might see some wild geese flying inland, as it's stormy.'

Hot in the face, Ginika tried to shrug casually and get on with her breakfast. But liquid seemed to slosh around all through the meal after that: the tea Grandpa poured, the milk in Ginika's cereal, the running tap. The sea and Peri both called to her.

She couldn't sit still. Grandma insisted that she clear the plates before getting ready to go out, and Ginika did ballet positions between table and sink, hoping, and whispering wishes under her breath about her boy from the sea.

On Shore Street, the wind dropped and the sun came out. Where was her storm? There *had* to be a storm.

But on the beach, things were different. Low clouds scurried across the sea towards town as if they were trying to outrun something. She ran to the edge of the wind turbines, feeling as if she was powered by a wave from the sea itself. Fresh air blew into her mouth and down to her lungs, and all the energy in the world seemed to grab hold of her. She giggled. She danced.

Then the rain began, fine and gently horizontal. She put on her coat, took off her shoes and squatted in front of the tideline not far from a seagull. It huddled against the wind, neck down, looking cosy.

She took out her phone and flashed it over the foamy waves, aiming below the white horses, but it quickly got wet, so she put it away. And then a darker wave grew bigger. Smoothly, silently, Peri flowed on to the wet sand in front of her. The shock made Ginika's heartbeat roar in her ears. She held out both hands and Peri took them in his wet ones. They giggled.

Chapter 12

Today, his clothes were made from the bubbly type of seaweed that looks like grapes.

He'd arrived carrying the windmill, but the spinner had fallen off, and now floated on the water, sadly. The sun still filtered through the see-through edges, but the poor blue dots were stiff and no longer sparkled.

'You found it!' Ginika said. 'Whoa!'

Peri held it upside down by the very end of its slimy, disintegrating wooden stick. He looked disappointed.

'It's OK,' she said. 'Not meant for water.' She shook her head, made her lips into a regretful shape and shrugged. 'Water.' She pointed to the windmill. 'No good.'

'No-god,' he said.

Ginika grinned. Everything felt brand new and thrilling. She studied him; did he look a teensy bit different? He did, but she couldn't quite pinpoint how. Maybe he'd grown a bit. His other hand was full of shells, which he handed to Ginika. Pale pink and delicate, almost like glass – these were Grandma's and Ginika's favourites.

'Thank you, Peri!'

He looked over his shoulder nervously, and Ginika scanned the sea too. Where were his family? And why was he so twitchy?

She pointed to the sea, raised her eyebrows in an exaggerated questioning way, and said, 'Where are the others?'

'Peehaw,' he said. He took her hand and led her into the water.

Ginika resisted. When the water reached her knees she shook her head furiously. 'Not good!' She attempted a drowning, floundering mime. 'Not again!'

Peri let go of her hand, made complicated hand signals that she guessed meant *follow me*, and shot off along the shoreline just under the water, visible only because he wanted her to see him.

Ginika grabbed her bag, shoes and the shells and sprinted along the beach beside him, out of breath, almost keeping up, bare feet making impressive speed, until he went on and on and she began to lag behind. This was further down the beach than she had ever been. Away from *all* the people.

Clever Peri, she thought, grinning.

The rain was slanting diagonally now, and it was heavier. It was hard to see properly. Peri stopped just beyond the spot where Grandpa said the very furthest night fishermen planted their rods. Behind them it was craggy and wild, and the tips of the rocks were bright green with algae. Here, the waves really did rise up like white horses before churning the smooth sand into clouds.

He sat in the water, poised, ready to escape in a microsecond if he had to, but it wasn't a tense way of being. It was completely part of him, just like the range of colours his hair reflected with every turn of his head. And just like the way he often dunked his face into the waves for a couple of seconds, as if his skin needed seawater. Or perhaps his eyes.

Ginika's toes had collected sand. The raindrops were bright now because sunshine glistened through them. She couldn't get much wetter, so she took off her coat and draped it on top of her swim buoy on a dry rock, next to her shoes, then lowered herself into the shallows – shorts, T-shirt, everything. The cold shock of the waves on her stomach took her breath away as she scoured the sea for his family again. Where were they? She pointed at the depths and raised her eyebrows at him, but he just looked puzzled.

This was so frustrating. There had to be a better way to communicate ...

She grabbed a handful of sand. 'Sand,' she said. He watched.

She scooped up some water and said, 'Water.'

He repeated the words – in a way. Then, legs close together and acting as one, he darted into the sea as fast as the tiny, super-speedy fishes that always swam close to the sand. He scooped up his own handfuls of sand and water and thrummed and trilled his own words for Ginika to copy.

Learning and teaching was hard. Then it was easy. Then hard again, but always fun, in a scary-shivery way. It was still only ten o'clock. They sat side by side at the very edge of the waves. The windmill, now fixed, was firmly and deeply planted and spun wildly in the wind behind them. Beneath it, the pink shells glistened. When the waves receded a little, they both stared at their pale, alien underwater toes, on the very edge of giggling, but still a bit shy. The shyness in his eyes looked like her own, but being rained on at the same time made everything sillier, and so much easier.

Everything in Peri's language came with lots of Ss and Es. Sometimes there were clicks in the middle; sometimes trills. His tongue had a yellow tinge to it. And his fingers, Ginika now noticed, were also slightly webbed.

She tried her best as the cool water swirled around their toes and lapped at their hands, but when 'sand' just sounded like *eeeee* and 'water' like a row of *K*s and trilling *G*s bunched together, that was all she could repeat. It was probably wrong. And he was staring at her pink tongue just as she'd stared at his yellow one.

He dipped into the sea, came back with a handful of tiny shrimp-like creatures and tried again, slowly, patiently. '*Kaaaadiiiii.*'

Ginika tried. '*Kaadiii.*'

He was doing something special with his breath – that had to be it, and it wasn't something her lips and tongue could manage. It was almost a whisper, but not like any whisper she could make. It was a balloon being blown up: big and echoey and impossible. There was something different happening at the back of his throat too. And she had a feeling there were sounds she wasn't hearing. Somewhere in her body, perhaps in the tiniest parts, extra bits of what he said vibrated.

Ginika was better at teaching than learning. Peri flipped here and there in the water and brought her things to name: 'shrimp' – he popped these in his mouth and chewed – 'shell', 'seaweed', 'fish'. There was no splash when he entered the water. Just a twist of an arm or a leg and his whole body changed direction, legs perfectly together. That was why he could do such streamlined, muscly flips. Even out on the sand, his mudskipper-style movements were much more bendy than Ginika's could ever be. His back and the tops of his arms looked waxy and very muscular.

By touching everything he wanted her to name – 'nose', 'ear', 'tongue', 'hair' – he learned fast. Sometimes their elbows bumped, and she noticed that his skin felt just as warm as hers. For every word he heard, he stroked the water and closed his eyes for a few seconds, and she saw that he was memorising. He leaped ahead of her, learning 'hello', 'goodbye', 'bird', 'face', 'eyes', 'hands', 'mouth', 'feet', 'wave', 'happy', 'sad', 'small', 'big', 'sun', 'sea', 'stomach' and 'hungry'. He was like a word sponge. There was a whooshing, fizzy feeling in the air: something new and unstoppable was happening.

His fingernails were short and thick, but looked sharp like claws, and they were a strange underwater shade of white. The delicate webbing between his fingers was also paler than the rest of his skin. All these mini-differences made the breath catch in her throat.

But one thing was the same between the two of them: when he asked for her word for 'seagull', he repeated the 'gull' part over and over to himself, giggling and snorting, as if it was side-splittingly hilarious. That word obviously sounded like something else in his language, something very funny indeed, and Ginika caught the fun infection, and snickered and gurgled with him. They touched hands accidentally and, after the seriousness of the learning, it brought on more giggling. They tangled their feet together on purpose and giggled even more.

When she tried naming 'home', he looked confused. There were no houses visible here, just rooftops behind the dunes. They stared at each other through the raindrops. This whole thing was even harder than she'd imagined. Asking him to show her the wonders of the sea didn't even feel possible ...

But then she had an idea, reached for her swim buoy, scrabbled inside it and smiled. Grandma *had* put it in, and ... yeah. Notebooks and pencils were quite useful things to have on beaches after all.

She tore out a page, pointed to the water and wrote the word for it, with a little drawing of waves. Peri traced the curves of the letters with a finger, as if the word was a rare work of art. Ginika did the same for the sky, with a bird in it, and then her hand, and her ear. His face was now all astonishment. Copying her pointing finger, he pointed to the pen and paper. Then, kicking a cracked yogurt pot out of the way, he picked up a tiny white skeleton of a crab and said, 'Eeegaaaaeeee.'

Ginika nodded, wrote *crab* and tried to say, 'Eeegaaaaeeee,' but she couldn't trill the G. Only *R*s made a trilling sound in her mouth.

They repeated this method with *bird*, a *pebble* shimmering pink with quartz and a piece of stringy *seaweed*.

Peri shook his head, open-mouthed at the wonder of this new thing, and Ginika seized her moment. Quickly, she sketched stick figures of a family – a mum, a dad and a child – and tore the page out of the notebook. She pointed to herself, then to the child. She pointed to the parents, then back at the town. (OK, she thought – her grandparents were looking after her in this town, not her parents, but there wasn't any way of telling him that.) She drew a new stick figure with waves around it, said, 'Peri,' and pointed to him. Then she pointed to the sea and asked, 'Where are your family?'

Peri didn't look as though he understood.

She handed him the little drawing and said his name again. Rain was wetting the paper. He frowned and passed it from hand to hand and it began to tear and disintegrate.

'It's OK,' Ginika said. 'Paper falls to bits when it gets wet.'

He looked worried. Disappointed.

'Doesn't matter!' she said, smiling. 'We can do another one. Look.'

He stared at the pieces of paper, smiling blankly. He

couldn't understand that the figures meant people. Years of school meant that Ginika took that for granted, but sea people probably had different methods. She suddenly felt very silly. Their ways were probably just as clever, but totally unknown to her. She grinned back at Peri, but was overtaken by a sinking, frustrated feeling. She was the only one who understood those drawings. The written words had amazed him, but they weren't enough.

His head suddenly snapped seawards, as if he'd sensed a movement. His family? Or a predator? A few seconds passed, and he relaxed again. False alarm.

Ginika frowned, and pointed to the sea. 'Where are the others?' She did some frantic miming: a mother cradling a baby; someone eating; someone sleeping.

Peri went still, and looked like he was thinking. Then suddenly, he grabbed a few of the pink shells he'd given Ginika and laid them out on the sand. He chose four big shells and a smaller one, looked at Ginika pointedly and arranged them in a little group. Then he lifted the smaller shell up to his chest and said, 'Eee-*click*-peri.'

Ginika nodded hard. 'Yes! That's you! I get it!' She reached over and touched the bigger shells. 'And these are your family.'

Peri shuffled the whole shell family further away from where they were sitting and acted out gobbling up shellfish. Then he gathered the family into his open palm and put them in the waves as though they were all swimming away. With his other hand, he plucked the Peri shell away from the family and swam it back to shore, miming a secret and very risky escape stunt. He pawed the air to show the shell family travelling far, far away, on a twisting, complicated route. Then he brought the Peri shell to rest next to Ginika's knee, and they both looked down at it.

Ginika lost her breath. She felt quivery inside, especially in her chest. 'You've run away. They don't know where you are.'

Peri looked lost and a little bit shocked, as though he was only just taking in the hugeness of what he had done. Ginika watched different expressions flit across his face: triumph, fear, even a hint of guilt, but behind it all, she had the feeling that giggles weren't far away. Maybe that's what happened when you got a bit older. Maybe in another six months, she'd be brave enough to do such a scary thing. She took a deep breath.

For the whole of their time together today, he'd kept looking out to sea, so she guessed he was expecting them to come looking for him at any moment. Then she remembered: according to this elaborate mime, *they didn't know exactly where he was*. Worry tightened her chest.

'But why?' Ginika lifted her arms in the air and shrugged her shoulders, hoping this looked like a question.

Peri answered, but in his own language, and Ginika listened with no understanding. This was scary, dangerous and probably stupid. Where was he sleeping? *Could* he look after himself? Her mouth went a little bit dry. The worry in her chest throbbed. Imagine if *she'd* run away when she'd wanted to. If she'd done it as soon as Mum and Dad had left her here like a suitcase ... But Peri had actually *done it*. Maybe his family were also trying to make him do something he didn't want to, and it wasn't just about not being allowed to explore here. Maybe they were too strict. They had looked ultra-tough.

And perhaps that explained something else: when they'd first met, he'd been super shocked to see her. He might have been kept away from *all* land humans, always, and only known about them from legends. He'd never have guessed they came in her size ...

The rain stopped, but all the rainclouds had closed together across the sky now, with no gaps for sunlight, and the sky darkened dramatically, like someone had sent out a filter. Lights came on along the road behind the dunes, and the tops of the prickly grass flared in golden waves.

'Gnka,' Peri said suddenly. 'LiiiTTT. Gnka.' He slapped his chest, said it again and pointed to the lights once more.

From here, they glittered like stars. Maybe he thought they were little stars, come to rest.

Whatever he thought they were, it was easy to see that he was dying to get to them. His eyes told her that, in the same way that someone's eyes might say, *Quick, let's go* or *Help* …

'Me?' she said, touching her chest. 'You want us to go there together?'

The words were useless. She patted both of them lightly on the arm – first Peri, then herself – then pointed to the town.

Perhaps *this* was why he'd run away – to get to those lights.

He smiled. Had he understood? But there was determination in his eyes as they followed a possible route over the wet sand, then the pebbles, then the grassy dunes. He was working out how to get there.

Chapter 13

A strange mixture of dread and excitement took control of Ginika's stomach.

Could she help him? *Should* she? Her heart started beating faster. She'd never seen anyone look quite so *longingly* ... Something about the way he looked at those lights reminded her of her own *aching* yearning. For home. For her old bedroom and the park and the Docklands Light Railway ...

Maybe the octopuses, dolphins and other exciting sea life could wait, for a little while. Peri's turn first. And really, her job was much easier – how hard could it be to show someone silly old Bridleway's Bay and look at a bunch of lights? And later in the day when the huge Ferris wheel lit up too ... being close to that might be a real thrill for him.

But *how* would she take him? It didn't seem as if he

could walk on land at all. And even if he could, she'd never get him far without being seen. Unless she hid him in her bedroom and showed him some electric lights in there … but to get to her room, you had to go through her grandparents' room. So even if she sneaked him in somehow, they'd have to go back through the way they came in if he needed to use the toilet. And actually, would someone who lived in the sea even know how to use a toilet?

Suddenly she felt powerful and purposeful. She was a whirlwind. Her brain did speedy pirouettes and turned in on itself, ablaze with ideas. They'd just have to stick to the town, and be quick. They could get there and back before his parents returned! That's *if* his parents even managed to work out where he was …

But helping him would be risky. He'd need something to travel in. He'd need wheels. But what kind of wheels, and where could they find some? Might a skateboard work? But even if it would, she didn't have one. A trolley? Or there was Grandpa's wheelbarrow; it was an amazing thing to ride in … but really tough to push, and getting him over the pebbles would be crazily hard.

'Travel,' she told him, with a little arms-and-legs-crawling mime. 'Wheels,' she said to herself, spinning her fingers round. 'Where can we find some … ?'

But in the middle of the final word – she was sure her

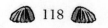

breath hadn't reached the end – Peri disappeared. The movement that took him was a lightning-quick reflex, as if something had sucked him back into the water. He was part of the sea again, just as if he'd never left it.

Then she realised someone was coming.

Someone horribly familiar. Moving closer, carrying her trainers so that she padded soundlessly on the wet sand in her bare feet.

Scarlett.

'Found y*ooou*! So glad, because the Olivias are on a boat trip now. Absolutely everyone's gone – the caravan park's empty. *So* bored. Nearly died of it.'

What was Scarlett doing all the way down here? Had she been spying? 'How did you … ?'

'We saw you running in this direction ages ago – me and the Olivias, before they left,' Scarlett said, slapping her trainers down on the sand and pushing her feet into them. 'What do you do down here? Where do you go all the time?'

'What d'you mean?'

'You're always disappearing off by yourself,' Scarlett said, making her hair swing round to the front. 'Seen you go loads of times. So what d'you do?'

Ginika's heart thudded. 'Nothing.'

Scarlett edged the toe of her trainer close to a jellyfish

stranded on the wet sand. 'Hate these blobby types,' she said.

Ginika didn't know what to say.

'Like, where are its tentacles?' Scarlett said.

Ginika looked at the large, golden-brown splayed-out blob. No way to tell if it was alive or dead. 'They're probably underneath,' she said.

Scarlett bent closer to the jellyfish. 'Ah, something about this kind ... makes me want to prod—'

'*Don't!*'

'Haha, OMG, Ginika, your face! Knew I could make you look like that!'

Ginika felt her cheeks heating up.

'You are absolutely *soaked*,' Scarlett said. Then, before Ginika could reply, she said, 'Right – let's go to the caravan park. We've got something brand new, just finished today. The Olivias will be *so mad* they missed the very first turn ever!'

'On what?'

'Aha – wait and see!'

Ginika scooped up her shells and bag, stepped into her shoes and followed Scarlett gladly, because Peri was surely hiding and waiting right there in the water behind them. Best to get Scarlett as far away as possible. Best to get this over with and satisfy Scarlett so that she wouldn't stay around Ginika and Peri's business. Then Ginika could dash back to him. Then she could quickly show him the town and make that longing turn into fun …

'Come on, let's run,' Scarlett said.

They pelted, flinging themselves at the run like it was a race. Scarlett tried to gabble on about the latest annoying things the Olivias were doing, but the wind took her words and flung her hair in both their faces. The sky was still dark, but the storm must have blown itself out.

The further from Peri they ran, the easier Ginika felt. By the time they reached the dunes – pungent with a fast but powerful stink of something dead – she was feeling lucky. And a tiny bit clever.

At the opposite end of the beach, at the other side of the car park, Scarlett stopped beneath the fancy green iron arches that spelled out BRIDLEWAYS BAY CARAVAN PARK, bent double and puffed out her cheeks.

'Argh!' she gasped. 'Gonna die!' She screwed up her face and forced air from her lungs, watching Ginika doing the same.

A check-in text came from Grandma: *OK, dumpling? Can you get me some bread on your way home, please?*

'Hey –' Scarlett leaned over for a better view of Ginika's phone – 'why have you got a train on your background?'

Heat flooded Ginika's face. 'It's the Docklands Light Railway, from home. It passed right outside my bedroom window all the time and it's total coolness.'

'How come you like smelly old trains when you're into dancing?'

'*That* train isn't smelly and it looks brand new,' Ginika puffed. Her breath wouldn't come back. 'And you can be into lots of stuff at the same time. It would be silly if you couldn't.'

Scarlett made a face. 'Do you like escalators too?'

'No,' Ginika said, although she had when she was very small.

'Why not?'

Ginika shrugged. 'They're just ordinary.'

They reached the trees that fringed the caravan park. Little paths cut through everywhere, some leading to the beach over a grassy bank, others ending nowhere. Mist was coming down in delicate, drifting patches.

'Hah! Do you like vacuum cleaners?'

Ginika kicked a little stone along the path. 'Nope.'

'Fridges? Lawnmowers?'

This was why she hadn't liked Scarlett last year. She was far too annoying. And a worrying thought had struck her: what if Peri couldn't wait and was trying to get to the town *right now*, without her? How far would he even get? There was always broken glass at the tideline. She didn't feel quite so clever now.

'Actually,' Ginika said, standing still, 'maybe I should come with you tomorrow instead. My grandma needs something from the shop.'

'Oh please come! I'm so fed up by myself.'

Ginika tried to arrange her face into a less panicky expression. Her eyebrows almost met in the middle as she tried to think of a way of getting away from Scarlett without making her suspicious all over again. She could see the silver surface of the sea through the trees, looking lonely. Hiding so much. 'Maybe you should have gone on the boat trip too.'

Scarlett breathed out a long, dramatic sigh. 'Been *billions* of times. Text your gran back, say you'll be late for lunch, say you've been kidnapped by a shark. Say anything, go on, I *really* want to show you this now, *please*, please! There are a load of hospital kids staying in the lodges and if they get on the – this special thing – we'll never get a chance.'

'What are hospital kids?' Ginika asked.

'They're families, but with kids that have just come out of hospital, or something. Sometimes nurses have to come too, and they rest in wheelchairs mostly, but some of them can walk a little bit and do stuff.'

'Oh yeah – I think I saw them at the beach.'

'Anyway, we're nearly here. You'll love this, honestly!' Scarlett ducked behind and placed her palms on the middle of Ginika's back, pushing gently until she began walking again. 'Down here. Not far. Trust me.'

Scarlett steered Ginika down a new path to the left where the caravans began appearing again in little clearings amongst the trees. So many. They were identical, each with a little potted tree beside its steps, and blue striped curtains. If only London had these everywhere. Then people could live more cheaply.

Being steered felt strange and wrong, especially when they had to weave out of the way of a teenager circling round the paths annoyingly in a go-kart and using people's legs as obstacle points. And when they narrowly missed a dollop of seagull plop that fell from the sky.

But Scarlett hummed happily. She was enjoying herself. 'We'll go on the bike-pump track tomorrow,' she said from behind, breathing into Ginika's ear. 'Bring your bike.'

'Haven't got one.'

'What? Why not?'

Ginika shrugged and wriggled away.

'Oh yeah,' Scarlett said, 'Mum told me. They had to sell everything, didn't they?'

How did Scarlett's mum know that? The heat came back to Ginika's face.

'But you've, like, still got a phone … that's weird!' Scarlett said, then laughed a wicked, delighted laugh. 'Wait – did you hide it?' She nudged Ginika. 'I bet you did. I can just imagine you doing that! *Excellent!*'

'I didn't,' Ginika snapped. 'Phones are too important to give up.'

There was a silence.

'It doesn't matter, you can use one of the park's bikes,' Scarlett said, smiling kindly. 'Over here.' She ran across the central lawn and Ginika followed. 'They're *supposed* to be for hire, but you can just borrow one! I wouldn't let the Olivias do this, but you're special. Here, choose.' She made a big, kind, generous gesture towards the bike shed. 'Oh – *what? Seriously?* There are normally loads.'

There were only three bikes and two toddler trikes left in the shed, but when Ginika saw one with a little canvas-covered trailer attached, her heart leaped. It had plastic windows and a flag sticking out of the top. She had ridden in one attached to Dad's bike at a holiday camp a couple of years ago. Those little trailers were bumpy, but cool to ride in.

This was the perfect way to get Peri into town secretly!

She skipped over to it and seized the handlebars.

'That one?' Scarlett said. 'Why?'

Wild ideas flashed around Ginika's head. She panicked

for half a second, then said, 'It's for Clawd the cat. He *loves* riding in things!'

'Whoa! Are you allowed?'

'Yeah, it's fine. He follows me all over the place anyway, so this way will be heaps safer.' This was partly true. Last year, Clawd had followed Ginika all the way to the beach. But this year he'd lost interest.

'You'll have to take the trailer off when we do the pump track though.'

Ginika nodded.

'OK. This way.' Scarlett led her on a path through a collection of little bushes that had been shaped into spirals and cubes. Even with the trailer attached, the bike was easier for Ginika to push than she'd expected. Scarlett kept doubling back to smile and pat the seat of the bike, as happy and excited as if she'd been given a gift herself.

It was now twelve fifteen. Ginika thought of Alisha, and a strange pang of sadness rippled through her. It felt like Alisha and Scarlett had suddenly swapped places in her life.

'Park the bike over there,' Scarlett said bossily, pointing to a fence. 'And now – boom!' Scarlett threw her hands in the air then leaned smoothly across the top of a low wall and opened the door of a little metal box set into the outside brickwork. She flicked a switch. 'You're the very first guest to have a go! And you're already wet, so *whee-wooey*! Shoes off!'

It was a mini-splash park. Water bubbled up from shiny metal-plated holes in the ground that Ginika hadn't noticed. A squirt, a tinkle, and then the fountains gushed into life and Ginika and Scarlett were running in and out of spiralling twists of soft water, and jumping at tickles from tiny jets that spurted out at odd angles, making the world tilt when you stood next to them. The air was full of the smell of fresh rain and the sound of their own squealing voices.

'Whee!' Ginika shrieked, wet shorts and T-shirt sloshing. 'This is awesomely amazing!'

Scarlett, shouting at the top of her voice, explained that the tiles beneath their bare feet were smooth enough to run without snagging your toes, but rough enough to stay safe when wet and to slow kids down. 'Because otherwise, little kids could hurt themselves.'

But Ginika wasn't really listening any more. She was imagining being in a fountain like this with Peri. A safe way to be in his watery world, to have fun with water without danger. All water fun should be like this.

Their play was *fast*. It felt so good to screech and scream and jump, to stop and marvel at the liquid jewels that twisted like rope, then dart into the middle where the jets rushed their arms into the air and almost toppled them over. Each time their feet slapped the warm tiles, wet echoes bounced everywhere, like strange but happy music. Ginika tried out some lightning moves and pretended she was part of the water itself – almost invisible. Like Peri.

Scarlett pushed a lever and made the centre jets envelop them like a gentle octopus, glittering silver and white in the sunlight. Ginika's thoughts drifted back to Peri and his glistening rainbow eyes, his silvery echoing voice. She hugged her secret to her heart deliciously.

Chapter 14

'I love the tilting best,' Scarlett bawled, switching the jets back to crazy angles.

Being full of good things made Ginika dizzy and giddy. She sighed and said, 'This whole park is so, so cool! I'd forgotten.'

Scarlett grinned. 'I know. We're really lucky.'

An older girl was striding over in their direction now. She looked a bit like Scarlett, but her light brown hair had pink edges. With shock, Ginika realised it was Scarlett's sister, Eve, looking so different from last year. Older. Almost grown up. Following behind her came a group of mums with kids in prams and wheelchairs, and a couple of nurses. Some of the mums looked worried and their movements were ultra-careful, but the kids chattered excitedly. One of the smaller girls dipped a wand into a tube and blew bubbles that floated in front of her.

'Scarlett – clear out now,' Eve said, and turned the fountains down to a slow corkscrew ripple.

Scarlett stepped free of the fountains and dripped on to the smooth tiles. A wet curl was stuck across her forehead in the shape of a question mark. 'But we've only just—'

'Come *on*, time's up,' Eve said, letting out an exasperated sigh through clenched teeth. 'You're everywhere you shouldn't be the whole time.' She smiled at Ginika, as if she was sure to have more sense than Scarlett, but Ginika knew she was only trying to make Scarlett feel small.

The families gathered closer to the fountains, waiting. Some of the children were in swimming costumes. One boy got out of his wheelchair and stood still, holding on to his mum's arm. The bubble-blowing girl was lifted out of her large pushchair and carefully lowered on to a waterproof seat.

Instead of queueing, another boy circled the group, looping his wheelchair round and round with smooth and skilful speed. It was the boy she'd seen at the beach, staring at the sea. Ginika could now see that he was bit older than her and Scarlett – maybe a year older.

Scarlett and her sister faced each other.

'Well, *obviously* we'll go now,' Scarlett said, 'but you're not in charge of *everything*.'

Her sister laughed. 'Wrong again, Scarlett – as usual! *I'm* coordinating the entertainment for the whole of the hospital group now, so BE TOLD, please, and less of the attitude.'

Scarlett's face blotched pink and Ginika felt bad for her. They stepped away and stood against the wall to dry themselves in the strong sun.

Scarlett dragged her towel across her shoulders and arms roughly then dropped it on the ground without drying her legs. 'But what can they even do in here sitting down?' She spoke to the back of her sister's head. 'What's the point?'

Ginika's chest felt full of rage. 'Scarlett, that's horrible!'

'Why is it horrible? Half of them can walk sometimes anyway.'

Then Ginika became aware of someone staring at them. The blond boy from the beach who had been bombing up and down the path in his wheelchair, looking as if he was ready to make it do wheelies, but now he was closer, and completely still. He must have heard Scarlett.

Ginika flushed, and despite still being damp, felt herself growing hotter. 'What about the other half?' She felt terrible for saying that. It was all still so wrong. She tried again. 'Anyway, it's totally fine to walk as well as using a wheelchair sometimes. Why wouldn't you? And there's plenty to do in the fountains for everyone.'

'Well, it's not my fault, is it?' Scarlett said.

'But you needn't be so nasty!'

Scarlett stared at Ginika, embarrassed, and quickly squashed it by scrunching up her nose, but the boy's stare didn't break. He mouthed something under his breath.

'Sorry,' Ginika said to him, blinking. 'She didn't mean it like that.'

The boy gazed at her, but said nothing. Had any of the other kids heard? The mums were busy and chatty and all the smallest ones had now been lifted out of their pushchairs. 'Ted, come on,' said a mum wearing a swimming hat, and the blond boy transferred himself on to one of the plain waterproof chairs without taking his eyes from Scarlett.

'You should say sorry to that boy,' Ginika said.

'What for? I was talking to Eve, nobody else. She's being mean. It's non-stop now – she treats me like a total pig.'

Ginika wanted to be a thousand miles away. The fountains had been so fantastic … all ruined now. She started walking towards the bike.

'No, Ginika, wait – don't. It's Eve! She's like that all the time now, for no reason. Thinks she knows everything.' Scarlett looked miserable. They must have fallen out.

'I just need to get home,' Ginika said crisply. 'It's time.'

Scarlett followed as Ginika collected the bike and trailer.

They walked side by side now. Ginika didn't know why. It was awkward. Down on the beach, out of sight, the waves would be rolling in and falling away again. She needed to be near them. With Peri.

They came out of the trees and still Scarlett stayed in step at her side. 'I'll come and get you tomorrow,' she said. 'Straight after breakfast—'

'Um, no, I can't.' Ginika scrabbled in her mind for an excuse, but she was too flustered to think. And there was this bike. Scarlett had lent her this fantastic bike. 'Not in the morning anyway. Later on might be better.'

She swung herself over the bike and rode on her wobbly way, leaving Scarlett standing alone by the park gates.

Ginika demonstrated the bike – with difficulty on the sand – and pointed to the town. 'Lights!' she said.

Peri had been waiting for her at the exact spot next to the rocks. He looked eager and ready to go – she'd been right to get back to him straight after stuffing Grandma's lunch into her face. And she'd thought of everything: he could wear the spare dry clothes Grandma forced her to bring to the beach every day. And her pointless floppy sun hat would be perfect to disguise his hair and eyes.

She showed him how to get into the T-shirt and shorts, which made both of them laugh so much she began to worry about having enough strength to control the bike. The shorts were quite long on him, but at least now nobody would be able to see his legs and notice any unusual features. She filled her water bottle with seawater so that he could keep on bathing his eyes. She taught him to be silent when she placed her finger on her lips.

'Zip it,' she said.

'Ship it,' he repeated.

It would be much better for him at night – all those glittering lights! But she wasn't allowed out after dark, and it didn't get dark till quite late in August. Explaining all that to Peri would be hard.

She gestured for him to crawl into the trailer. Ginika could hear his breathless excitement, but he fitted himself into it with ease – a twist, a wriggle and a strong heft on his muscly arms. But he landed heavily on the plastic cushioning. Weight, Ginika realised: he was built for water, not land. But he was in. And grinning.

Ginika pushed the bike back over the sand, then over pebbles, then rode on the tarmac. It was heavier to handle with Peri as passenger. The weight of the trailer leaned to the left, and there were bumpy ruts on Shore Street she'd never noticed on foot. Every couple of minutes she glanced over her shoulder to check he was OK.

The sun came out, shining through gaps in the grey and

purple clouds, making the sky into a huge bruise with a light behind it. Insects buzzed. There was a strong smell of squashed nettles. The road became smoother, and now everything was utterly brilliant. The wet tarmac glittered like a galaxy of stars, and all the stones people had used to decorate their wall-tops shone like gleaming jellies. The street lights were no longer needed, but still they shone, strangely now.

The trailer following behind bounced and squelched. Even the dripping grass in the verges joined in, rippling in an underwater way, as though everything was leading them to the same fun place: The Town.

She was doing it. She was showing him.

There were cars now, so she took a turn along a path she didn't know that cut between the back streets of tall houses, all joined together, and stopped the bike to check on Peri.

'Street,' she said, flinging her arms backwards and forwards to show the length of it.

'Steet,' he repeated. Then, 'Struh-eet.'

The look on his face. Wide eyes. Beaming grin. This was the strangest, most exciting adventure of his life, and he told her that with his eyes, which were drawn again and again to the street lights, even though they were so much weaker now the sun was out.

Ginika pushed the bike now so that she could keep one eye on Peri. That first back street led to another and another, all crowded with houses. She stopped to show him things. She meant them to be unusual things, beautiful things, but in the end, they were just things. Some black iron railings with eagles in the middle of each swirl. A little wall-top rock in the shape of a bird. A shiny bottle top on a heap of scrap metal. One of those bees that just hangs in the air. Dandelions poking through cracks in the pavement. Peri reached out to stroke one, and Ginika taught him its name. Was this the first land plant he'd ever been close to?

The next house had boarded-up windows and a garden gate with jagged edges where something had smashed it. Peri stared as a pair of butterflies flitted through the biggest hole in the gate and suddenly it was a beautiful scene, with a soundtrack: laughter from a garden. A pigeon cooing in the distance. Traffic growling in the next road along.

And then there was a dog carrying its own lead in its mouth – she couldn't begin to think how to explain this to Peri – and its owner wasn't far behind, and now everything changed, because there were people. Someone unloading groceries from a van. A couple of staring girls. And more noises. Humming machinery. Car doors slamming. Steam hissing from a grid outside a little shop. Ginika froze: she hadn't thought about Peri's reaction to people. In the sea, he darted away at top speed. What if he tried to do that now? Scrambled out of the trailer and mud-skippered his way back to the beach? She couldn't believe she'd been so stupid.

'Shh,' she whispered into the trailer, finger on lips. 'No talk,' she said, putting her hand over her mouth. 'Hide.' Her heart raced.

But Peri sat well back in the trailer and just watched everyone from under his hat. The only time he leaned out was when they passed old people. It happened every time. His whole head followed each one until they were out of sight, as though he'd never seen an old face before ... Perhaps he hadn't. Were there no old people in the sea? That idea made her feel strange and sad. She shook her head; she wouldn't think about it any more, for now.

Ginika taught him the words for *car* and *house*. It was obvious what a car was for, and she mimed *sleeping* and *eating* outside a house. After staring at each new object, hearing each new noise and each new word, Peri closed his eyes, just as he had on the beach when memorising words.

They were on a quieter street when the pull to investigate the street lights became too much for Peri.

'Liii-ttt!' he cried, staring up at the nearest lamp-post, moon-eyed with longing.

Ginika parked the bike beside it. He was transfixed. His eyes moved strangely, as if he was watching pieces in a kaleidoscope tumble into each other and turn over. He seemed to be tracking things Ginika couldn't see. If she hadn't known what he was watching, she'd have thought the light was flowing like liquid. He licked his lips – tasting – and sniffed, but what was there to taste or smell? It was only light.

Then he trembled, as if he'd been gathering energy and was now too full. There was no one around.

'Liii-ttt,' he said again, urgently. 'Liii-ttt – marrghh-*click*-hoooh?'

Ginika shook her head. 'I don't understand, Peri.'

He repeated it. He was asking her a question. Bending his neck back, he stared up at the light again. It was as if he *ached* for the light. He didn't just like it. She *loved* the Docklands Light Railway ... but that reminded her of home.

As he continued to stare, she started to see it differently. Bright light. Electric power. It seared into your brain and made your eyes hurt, but it also reminded you of the sun and the stars and the magic of the universe ...

Then Peri mimed something new. He pumped his arms up and down like somebody big and strong, and pretended to wrestle with something inside the trailer, muscles rippling. What did that mean? Power? Strength?

'Liii-ttt,' he said, and repeated the mime.

But light didn't make you strong. Unless ... Did Peri think it did? Then a solid idea burst into her head: perhaps he had totally the wrong idea about light. Maybe this was just like the mistake she'd made with the Docklands Light Railway when she was little! She'd thought it was a railway made of light, rushing and bright, powering the train along. She'd been disappointed when Dad told her the 'Light' part actually meant weight. Peri must have got *this* wrong. Perhaps she was right about his people having legends about land humans, just like humans had legends about sea people. And maybe *their* legends said that our strange, artificial light could make you strong. Last week, his parents had seemed scared of it. Or angry about it—

Suddenly Peri was out of the trailer and climbing the pole. In the time it took Ginika to gulp and scream – 'No! Danger!' – he was already close to the top, gripping the pole with hands and knees, tucking his feet up and up, with strong, nimble legs-together caterpillar movements that seemed to take no effort at all.

Her scream startled him. He looked down and she shook her head quickly. Peri stopped where he was, just under the light, and didn't touch it, but stared into the glare with bare hunger. Ginika's heart thudded. He'd shrivel his eyeballs. Surely the light was too strong to stare at so closely? And didn't these lights get hot, like light bulbs at home? She didn't know. The *click* and the *hoooh* – that must have been Peri asking if this would be OK.

His journey down was harder. He gripped and shuffled, but she could see that his weight was there now, bearing on him in a way that it didn't in the sea.

'No, not safe,' she said, miming frantically with every word. 'People, they'll see. They'll come out. They'll chase you.'

Peri seemed to understand. He climbed back into the trailer and Ginika pushed off, but a man came out of a house whose thin curtains seemed stuck to the inside of the downstairs window, and shouted, 'Oi! What you up to?'

His voice was incredibly loud. Ginika wobbled. Speed wouldn't come. She got the bike going, but it felt like slow motion.

'Come here! What are your names? Where are you from? That's vandalism – you can't just do that and then blow through like a couple of fairies!'

The man didn't stop coming. He moved his arms up and down as if he was herding them like sheep. Ginika's heart skittered.

Three more windows had three more faces behind them. A woman stood in a doorway, staring. Every bump and squeak the bike made seemed far too loud. And every other noise sent shock waves down Ginika's spine – seagulls screeching above, cars crawling past the junction at the end of the road – as she pumped the pedals faster-faster-fastest, with her heart speeding up to match.

Chapter 15

The clouds cleared away and the sun shone even more brightly, low down in the sky. Ginika looked to see what time it was: quarter to four. Even this late, the day was getting hotter. To be on the safe side, she biked down five more streets then came to a halt outside a small church. She dabbed sweat from the back of her neck with her T-shirt and flapped it to get some air moving up her chest, wondering if Peri could even sweat at all. It would be no good if sweat made you cooler if you lived in the sea, because water was always cooling your skin down anyway. She tried to remember what Grandpa had told her about sea mammals ... Was there some special system?

Nobody seemed to have followed them, but she hoped that man didn't call the police. They'd be easy to spot.

A big group of people was heading their way: people

with wheelchairs, buggies and pushchairs. It had to be the holiday group from Scarlett's caravan park. She recognised the stripy red-and-brown hair of one of the nurses. More people on wheels around town could be useful – Ginika and Peri might not stand out quite so much – but she swerved down a side street just in case.

The sun was even stronger now, and the clouds felt closer, as if a thunderstorm was brewing. It made the traffic stinkier. Over her shoulder, she saw Peri bathing his eyes again, and saturating his whole head too. Hopefully that bottle would be enough.

Then, coming round the corner in front of them on Kettle Lane, the nurses and kids from the holiday group arrived again, noisy with babble and laughter and the blowing of little whistles. Ginika crossed the road. Two of the children looked familiar. One of them was the boy who'd overheard Scarlett's rudeness: Ted. The boy who liked to stare at the sea.

They were a big group. Four younger children rode in prams, and a smaller kid operated an amazing trike with his hands, but instead of wheels it had legs that walked like a mechanical caterpillar.

Ginika couldn't help a second glance. Peri too. He leaned right out of the trailer to watch as each pair of legs took turns to lift off and touch the pavement, rippling along like something from a dream. The little boy made it look easy.

The blond boy – Ted – had noticed Peri and looked curious. Before Ginika had time to push the bike off and swing away, he started coming towards them. A nurse said something Ginika couldn't hear, and followed him with a concerned look on her face, squinting her eyes against the sun as she manoeuvred a pram.

Ginika steered the bike away – the last thing Peri needed was nosy adults – but Ted seemed to understand. He turned back and swerved his power chair right in front of the pram the nurse was pushing. He was creating a diversion so that Ginika and Peri could get away! Ted high-fived the child he'd almost collided with, and Ginika took that moment to act: she sped away, pedalling fast.

On Horse Guards' Pass five minutes later, they were slowed down by people traffic. Suddenly, the blond boy was right behind them, chewing gum and staring. He was on his own; he must have broken away from the group. Grandma would have called him a rascal because there was a look in his eyes: a look that said, *No, I won't*. It had been there at the fountains when Scarlett had spoken her worst.

His wheelchair was black, with silver on the insides of the wheels, silver-trimmed controls and musical-note stickers on the footrest. He took out one of his earphones and said, 'Hey. Who are you avoiding?'

Ginika felt herself getting hot and red in the face. 'Nobody,' she said, as if she had no cares in the world. 'Why?'

He grinned and his eyes crinkled up at the corners. 'Every time you see our group coming, you back up and go in a different direction. Bit of a giveaway.'

Ginika stared at her feet.

'Don't blame you. I had to get away from everyone too. Sick of it all, I am.'

'Sick of what?'

'Being babied. Looked after. Fussed.' He pulled a grumpy face, and Ginika was intrigued. She could imagine how that felt.

'You're Ginika,' he said.

He must have heard Scarlett calling her name at the fountains. She smiled. 'You're Ted. This is Peri. He doesn't really talk.'

'Hey, Peri.'

Ginika had meant to end the conversation there, but Peri stared at Ted, all kinds of interest in his gaze. Ginika got between them and made the *zip it* signal, but the floppy hat was doing a good job. The rainbow oils in his eyes were hardly noticeable in its shadow. Sitting down, he just looked like a younger kid wearing baggy clothes.

'So what's the deal?' Ted asked. 'Why d'you need to dodge people?'

Ginika shrugged and shook her head at the same time. 'It's a long story.'

He looked at Peri again, and when Peri just smiled he didn't push it. He simply put his earphones back in. Ginika focused on his ever-so-white eyelashes, and on his freckles. Clippered hair with sides faded to nothing. Neon-yellow earphones. She'd have quite liked some of those.

He took his earphones out and said, 'Coming to the go-karts? I know for a fact the others aren't going there today. They've got a timetable of other pathetic stuff to do.'

'Didn't know there were go-karts here too.'

'Well, whatever you're having to guard him from, he might as well have some fun before he has to go back. These are proper go-karts – not like the scummy ones at the caravan park.' He said this over his shoulder, plugged both earphones back in and rode off down Eastern Lane.

Not bossy, Ginika thought. *Not like Scarlett*. She smiled, got the bike going and caught him up. Soon they were in a hilly place on the edge of town that she didn't know. The ground was even more rutted than the road from the beach, and Ted's wheels kept spinning in mid-air. Every so often, his chair veered to one side and Ginika caught her breath – but Ted corrected it. In smoother places, he rounded corners in a wide, exaggerated way, for extra speed.

Peri was bounced and jolted, but it made him laugh and grip the sides and rock the trailer even more. Ted swiped at everything he passed with a rolled-up piece of paper. Walls, fences, doors, long grass.

The go-kart place was near a main road. There was a small queue, and Ginika noticed a plaster on the back of Ted's hand, attached with sticky tape.

'Won't the nurses get in trouble if you're not with them?' she asked.

He took one of his earphones out. 'Don't need any more nurses. I've been out of hospital two weeks. I'm allowed to walk at home. Doctors say I might be playing football again in a couple of months.'

'So where do they think you are now?'

Ted shrugged. 'Told them I needed the toilet and some privacy,' he said, with a slow half-smile, but as he began to talk about some of their trips, his eyes lit up. On one occasion the group took over the funfair for a whole afternoon, and Ted got to go on the Ferris wheel four times in a row.

Ginika's mouth had dropped open while he was talking. She looked across at the big wheel in the distance, glinting in the sunshine like a slow-motion Catherine wheel, and closed her mouth with a little snap. That wheel was expensive to ride. She had only been on it twice in her life. 'That must have felt like Disneyland.'

'Pretty much,' Ted said. They were now at the front of the queue, so he parked his wheelchair, got out slowly, then explained everything to the go-kart man: he'd just come out of hospital but could easily handle a kart. He spoke with an air about him: he wasn't asking, he was telling, and he wouldn't be waiting to see if he was allowed to ride or not.

Ginika, next in line behind Ted, gestured to Peri, said – 'Same' – and handed over her money for two, then went to help Peri in before the go-kart man could comment. But Peri didn't need any help. A deep breath and his arms walked his body out, legs working nimbly behind.

As she parked her bike beside Ted's wheelchair, Ginika held her breath and used the corner of her eyes to see what the go-kart man was making of Peri's legs. He said nothing, but Peri was having a huge stare at the deep wrinkles on the man's forehead and under his eyes. Ginika climbed in beside him and gave him a quick demonstration of how everything worked by driving for a few minutes. Then they swapped, because it was obvious from Peri's gestures that he wanted to try it. He'd watched every move she made, and all of her reactions. Before trying it, he closed his eyes for a few seconds. His mouth was a straight line of concentration, and his fingers rested on the top of the kart's door, perfectly still.

Ginika kept her feet on the pedals. She took a deep breath and hoped for the best, but there was no need. Peri wasn't just good at go-karting: he was phenomenal. His body might be slower on land, but his reflexes weren't. Even though he flung his body weight in an unusual way on the corners – all elbows like Grandpa – his steering was accurate. He made them spin, then corrected it. Ginika pressed harder on the accelerator and they went faster.

'Slick!' Ted shouted as they passed, and Peri's head wobbled with pleasure, as though he understood.

The world spun. As they roared and charged at each other, it felt like they could spin for hours in any direction – even to the sky – and never hit anything. The go-kart man looked bored, but a slight smile twitched at the corners of his mouth and he turned the music up to thumping, sending Ginika's head speeding even faster than her body travelled. The beats were booming and exciting and convulsing. The go-kart man was a blur, and so were the trees that lined the fence, the houses beyond.

Peri grinned.

Ted hooted and Peri copied him.

Ted roared, 'Legendary!'

Afterwards, when Peri bathed his eyes, Ted watched. As Peri tipped his head back, Ginika reached across to keep the hat on his head. Was she seeing those faint, gleaming rainbow colours because she knew they were there? She bit her lip. She waited for Ted to ask why he was bathing them, but he didn't, so she said, 'His eyes get sore and stingy, so he just bathes them every so often.'

'Yeah,' Ted said, 'I still have to have top-ups.' He pointed to the plaster on the back of his hand. 'For my spine. That's where my op was.' The front of his T-shirt, she noticed for the first time, had a picture of a leopard driving a speed-boat. Then he jumped and hissed, 'The nurses! Quick!'

They scarpered.

Chapter 16

Round the corner, across the road, down the street and out of sight. Ginika was truly zooming now. She'd got used to Peri's weight in the back, could feel that everything was fine without looking, but still, every few minutes, she glanced behind.

'Where's your mum?' Ginika asked when Ted caught up. She was breathing hard. 'Couldn't you just ask your parents to make them let you go where you want?'

Ted had to ask her to repeat it all, as he had both earphones in. 'Mum's gone swimming. The holiday's supposed to be for parents too. I'm supposed to do as I'm told, and I mostly do, but you two …' He looked at Ginika, then Peri. 'You seem to be free.'

Ted looked as if nothing much would ever bother him. A smile kept creeping on to Ginika's lips. He plugged his earphones back in. Dad would have gone mad at that. She giggled to herself. This must be something Ted always did and he didn't care if it annoyed people. It didn't annoy her.

Everyone was sweaty now. Ted said, 'Need ice,' and lifted the front of his T-shirt away from his body. Ginika wished hers had no back so that she could feel the air against her hot skin. Peri sat back in the trailer. Only his knees were visible.

Ted's phone rang, and he ignored it.

'Better answer it,' Ginika said. 'Tell them you're fine and just hanging out for a while. Give them a time when you'll be back.'

Then Ginika's phone rang too. She looked at the screen, saw that it was Grandma, let the call ring out and watched a text materialise: *Where are you?*

This much fun couldn't stop now. *Met some friends*, she typed, smiling down at the phone. *I'll be a little bit late.*

'Not going to speak to them, then?' Ted said, grinning.

'Sorted it.'

Her phone rang again. Ted said, 'Ha!'

Peri leaned out of the trailer to reach for Ginika's phone, and a thought bubbled up in her head. She quickly scrolled the internet for a picture of some fairy lights, and placed the phone in his outstretched hands. 'Lights,' she said. This could be a new world of glittering colours for him.

Ted looked at the screen too. 'He'd love the arcade.'

'Genius!' Ginika said. '*Man!* Can't believe I didn't think of that. We'll catch you up in a minute.'

Ted set off, and Ginika reached down to take the phone from Peri, but his eyes were darting backwards and forwards across the screen extremely quickly, as if the picture just wasn't keeping still. Then he looked at her with his head on one side and questions in his eyes. When he went back to the screen, the green-grey of his eyes blurred into glassiness, like beach pebbles worn smooth.

What was he seeing? And what if this was harming his eyes? Her heart started thudding hard. Those fairy lights were a still image. If she tried a moving one, his eyes might find it harder still. Was this even a picture to him at all? If it wasn't, then … she realised she was holding her breath. Her head felt weirdly dizzy and empty with shock.

Our eyes must be different, she thought. *Or the signals going to our brains, or something.*

But he liked the phone. He held it next to the top of his head and seemed to get more out of that. A huge smile spread across his face. What was he hearing? No sound was coming out of it. Then his eyes rolled back into his head and she quickly snatched the phone from him. Had she permanently messed up his eyes? They came back to normal, slowly, but as she watched, feeling a bit sick, white tears began to stream from them. That was it – she'd definitely ruined him. The sickness rose and her chest tightened.

She reached for the bottled seawater and watched as Peri dribbled it into his eyes again. The streaming stopped.

'Sorry,' she whispered, and gestured for him to sit firmly in the trailer again. He did – so he must be able to see her. Shakily, she biked towards the back of Ted's wheelchair, which had, by now, made its steady way to the end of the street. A bird shrieked, high in the sky. Her heart still thudded.

Long before they reached the arcade they heard it. Music blared and hoots of laughter trickled right across the road. The building was big and square and looked as if it was mostly made of glass – glass doors, mirrored walls and mirrors on the sides of most of the games machines. Fairy lights all over the place. Little flags snapped and rippled in the breeze. Ginika looked at Ted, then at Peri. All three of them were tense and excited.

The doors were open. Ginika wheeled the bike in behind Ted's chair. People saw Ted first and moved out of the way. Inside, everything was loud. Music, excited chatter, squeals. Shouty lads slapped the sides of games machines. Shrieky kids giggled, coconut sun cream smells wafted in the air. The walls bounced the noise around, thickening and churning it.

Ginika bent to check on Peri, but he was OK. In fact, he was more than OK. His eyes told her he couldn't believe yet *another* whole new world was possible. His skin, what she could see of it under the shadow of the trailer, was darkening, like he had the perfect suntan. He studied himself in the mirrors. And then there were the lights. The arcade was full of them: flashing, twirling, sparkling. Long fluorescent ones in tubes, all colours, all bright. This was *the* place for him, and his silence was working: he blended in.

Ted played the grabbing-claw game and won a joke set with itching powder, fake teeth and lips, a miniature plastic hammer and cellophane fish that bent and twisted in the heat of his hand as though they were alive. He shovelled the lot into Peri's lap, then got out of his wheelchair to play on a racing-car game.

Peri passed the hammer from hand to hand as if weighing it, and examined the fish like a scientist. He leaned out of the trailer and reached for shiny coins and jewel-coloured trinkets that fell in a stepped landslide he thought was coming towards him. Ginika couldn't think of a way to show him that they had to be swapped for money, so just shook her head and shrugged and grinned. He dislodged a skittle, which fell off its hook and rolled across the sticky floor, and when he leaned out further to catch it, one of his feet came out of the trailer.

Ginika looked around the arcade. He wasn't the only barefoot person, but he was probably the only one with webbed toes. Ted was now focusing on a skiing game, determinedly, as if it was a job he had to do. The foot tucked itself away again, but Peri kept on closing his eyes and memorising everything, as if he needed to save it, as if this might be a one-time-only event.

A girl bumped into Ted and he flinched.

'Does it still hurt?' Ginika asked. 'Your back?'

'Not really.'

'Do all kids who go into hospital get a holiday afterwards? Would I?'

Ted didn't answer immediately, but was obviously thinking. 'No,' he said. 'I think it has to be sort of ... serious. And the charity who run the group have to know you're in there, and invite you.'

Ginika's mind grabbed on to the word *serious*. Then Ted told her that the charity also sent carers round to his house – and to the houses of some of the other kids who had been in hospital – to help his parents do housework and cooking when all their time was taken up by sitting in the hospital next to Ted, sometimes for weeks. *Serious*, she thought again, and swallowed, wondering what to say next; she might get it wrong.

'What are the other kids from your holiday like?'

'They're all right,' said Ted. 'But they're mostly little ones. Except Keira, but she's too ill to do much.'

'I thought people only came to the caravan park because they were better.'

'Not always.'

Ted turned away and started flipping a pinball machine, beckoning Peri and Ginika to join in. Suddenly, there was a new feeling in the air between the three of them. A breathless feeling, like the seconds before a balloon pops. They threw themselves into it. They lassoed cuddly toys, pressed buttons and yanked on levers, laughed, rolled their eyes, watched kids chase and sweat and scream.

Ginika pulled a metal lever and the spinning symbols behind a glossy window lined up perfectly: four golden keys. A prize fell down into a tray at her knees and she fished out a handful of stickers. 'Space stuff!' she said, showing Ted. 'Stars and planets!'

'Ahhh, whoa, you've got Jupiter! You can see the Great Red Spot really clearly on this one.'

'What's that?'

'It's a gigantic storm bigger than this whole earth!' he said. 'Haven't you heard of it?'

Ginika shook her head.

'It's been swirling on Jupiter for hundreds of years now.'

Ginika let her jaw drop open as wide as possible to show

how astounding this fact was to her. 'Why is it red?'

'I've forgotten. I'll look it up later.' Ted stared at the sticker with admiration, and barely hidden longing.

'Here – you have them,' Ginika said. 'For your chair.'

He murmured his thanks without quite meeting her eyes. His cheeks glowed pink.

Peri fixated on a whizzing ceiling fan, laughing at it and with it. His arms mirrored the motion: round and round. *Yes*, his eyes said. *Show me more!*

It was brilliant. They were being brilliant together, all three of them.

Chapter 17

Near the back entrance of the arcade, Peri was dazzled by a stall laden with all kinds of food.

'Monster treat allowance here,' Ted said, pulling a ten-pound note from his pocket and arching one eyebrow.

'Whoa!' Ginika said, then remembered Peri's natural seafood diet. She looked at the little pots of shrimp. That should be OK, shouldn't it? Fresh from the sea. Ted and Ginika had chips with barbecue sauce.

Ted's phone rang, and this time, he answered it. 'Be back at the caravan park in a minute.'

He cut the call without waiting for a reply, and passed Peri a bottle of pink lemonade before Ginika could intervene.

She held her breath as he drank – he might choke on the fizz. But Peri's expression transformed into dazed, smiley astonishment. He took a larger swig, swilled it around his mouth before swallowing, and grinned. Ginika grinned back and took a long sip of her own bottle. It tasted clean and sharp.

Peri crammed shrimp into his mouth, swallowed, took another swig of lemonade, threw his head back and gargled. Ted laughed. Peri grinned and munched and grinned again, as if he couldn't do both at once.

'Where's he from?' Ted said, stowing his lemonade bottle in the wheelchair's cup holder.

Surprise made Ginika drop a chip. She started to gesture vaguely in the direction of the sea but caught a glimpse of Scarlett. She was waiting for change at the counter, on her own, looking down at her phone.

'No! I can't let her see me,' Ginika hissed and, ducking, grabbed the bike and started pushing it towards the exit.

'Why is she even your friend?' Ted said, but didn't wait for an answer. 'Turn left outside and meet me round the corner.'

As Ginika left the arcade, Ted was approaching Scarlett in his wheelchair.

Pushing the bike out of the arcade and heading for the side street felt like the hugest mistake ever carried out in slow motion, even though Ginika charged and rushed, jerking Peri and the trailer and swaying once she'd pushed off from the pavement. One of the trailer wheels was squeaking now, and a group of lads outside a burger bar watched them go by without trying to hide their stares. If it came to it, she could probably outride Scarlett on these smooth roads. Vanish into the back streets. Find Ted later somehow? She glanced over her shoulder again and again, and that feeling of doubt returned. A crumb of guilt. She tried to push it from her mind. Because Scarlett shouldn't be so … irritating. Maybe Ted was giving her a piece of his mind. Maybe—

Ted caught up with them, and he was carrying three sticks of candyfloss. 'Success!'

Ginika giggled. Peri smiled and gazed at Ted, who held all three sticks as they zoomed off towards the beach, rushing into the last of the sun before it set, the sounds of the arcade fading behind them.

They stopped to eat the candyfloss on a quiet street. Ted shot the gum from his mouth straight into a bin without appearing to try too hard, and Ginika pretended she hadn't noticed.

'I'm not sure it'll agree with him,' she said. 'He's not used to food like that.'

But Peri was watching Ted eat it, and what his eyes were saying was obvious.

'Tiny bit?' Ted offered, handing Peri a stick. 'Can't hurt much,' he said to Ginika.

Peri pulled a small piece away from the cloud of it, copying the way Ted let it melt on his tongue. Within seconds the look on his face settled into confused amazement, and he ate the rest by the fistful.

Ted laughed. Ginika couldn't help laughing too. 'Ha!' Ted said. 'Walloping mouthful.'

'What did you say to Scarlett?'

Ted smiled. 'You don't wanna know.'

A gull swooped from nowhere and snatched a piece of litter from a bulging bin.

Ginika's phone buzzed. It must be past five thirty now, so without even looking, she knew that Grandma would be getting agitated about what time they were eating. 'We have to go home now,' she said.

'I'll ride with you.' Ted patted the arm of his wheelchair. 'I can do seven miles before this needs recharging.'

Ginika took a deep breath, still feeling a bit dizzy from all the sugar. 'Don't you have to get back to the park?'

'I can do what I like. I'm better now.' Ted fished in his pocket for bubblegum and handed it round. Strawberry flavoured. He chewed the new gum faster.

They headed towards the beach. Ginika scrambled a plan together in her mind. They would go to the edge of the sea, where Peri would just appear to be having a last quick dip while she waited. Ted's chair wouldn't work well on the sand and he was surely getting tired now, so he'd say goodbye and it would all be fine. 'This way,' she said.

The sea was calm and flat to the horizon. Rock pools glinted like mirrors embedded in the sand. Dark figures jumped and kicked a ball in the far distance, and Ginika wondered how they could stand to be so energetic in the heat.

'Quick dip first, Peri,' she said, so that Ted would hear. 'Last of the day!'

Peri was pulling a strange face and chewing. A lot. Ginika suddenly remembered the bubblegum.

'Oh! Don't swallow that, Peri.' She did a clumsy chew-but-don't-swallow mime. Peri spat the bubblegum on to the sand and stared at it, baffled.

'Um … not yet, but OK.' Ginika picked it up with a piece of dried seaweed and raced to the nearest bin. Ted was still there, watching from the path. The silver parts of his wheelchair shone in the sun.

'Bye, Ted!'

Ted did not say goodbye.

Ginika pushed, crunched and skidded the bike over the pebbles, parked it next to the water, and Peri climbed out, limbs heavy and laboured. As he ditched Ginika's hat and slipped into the sea in the T-shirt and shorts, Ted was still watching.

Please just go home, she thought. *Please don't notice Peri's relief. Please don't notice how much more at home he is in the sea, or his hair and skin, his eyes.* But within seconds of him entering the water, Peri's weightlessness and comfort and new energy were obvious. Every so often he glanced over the waves to the horizon – checking for signs of his family.

Ginika paddled. She splashed about, covering for Peri and hoping he stayed in the shallows. No disappearing.

Then Ted began to move. He heaved himself out of his wheelchair with ease, but what followed involved lots of sweating and grunting as he walked a few painful steps over the pebbles, collapsed on the sand and inched his way towards them.

'I can get my legs in seawater,' he said, 'but that's all.'

'How come you went in the fountains?'

'That was normal water, and I still had to keep my back dry-ish. Seawater's different. There's all sorts in it. Fish wee, fish poo, octopus wee, octopus poo, dolphin wee, dolphin poo …'

Ginika had to laugh, but her heart was racing. She glanced at Peri, floating on his back, hair transparent like the water. Grandma was calling and calling her muted phone. Ginika texted: *Won't be long, one last thing to do!*

'Aren't you going to get in even bigger trouble if you

don't go back now though?' she said to Ted.

'Gonna be completely grounded after what I've done today anyway. So might as well make the most of this last bit. This is only my second seaside holiday ever.'

This wasn't their usual quiet spot. There was smoke from someone's barbecue. Laughter. Music that sounded like it was trapped in a tin.

Ted and Ginika sat side by side, legs in the water, bottoms on the sand while Peri floated, free, cool and weightless, despite his soaked clothes. His skin! It was getting so much lighter than in the arcade. And greenish. The membranes up his nose! Now that he was in the water again, they might flicker across. She was so used to Peri she'd forgotten about them, but Ted might notice now they were at the same level.

'It's brilliant here after storms,' Ted said. 'The tideline goes scraggy and filthy.'

'Oh that's ... that's exactly it – it does!' Ginika's words tumbled out with a nervous, helter-skelter rhythm. If Ted found out about Peri, what might he do?

Ginika saw that Peri still kept an eye out for his family, but there were no signs. And sometimes he looked back towards the lights of the town they'd just left, where the Ferris wheel, lit up now, towered over everything. He gazed at it with spellbound curiosity, and so Ginika looked at it too, with fresh eyes, watching it lift people high in the air and back down to the ground, over and over, slowly, steadily.

Surreptitiously, Ginika tried to work out what Ted was thinking. She could tell from the movements of his tongue that he was squashing his bubblegum against the back of his front teeth. This close, he smelt of Grandma's first-aid box: plasters and antiseptic cream. And strawberry bubblegum breath.

Tiny flies skimmed the surface of the water. Peri stopped floating and began to move. After being still and quiet and heavy in the trailer for so long, he seemed determined to prove how much of a sea creature he was, almost as if he was intentionally showing them how he could sink to the bottom of the shallows and scoot across the seabed invisibly. And how his body just rippled wherever he wanted to go – he didn't even need to move his arms. When he scooted, those legs moved together in a very stretchy, spongy way, as if his bones weren't even made of bone. It was almost like watching water move. And then the next minute, he'd be floating invisibly with only his nose out of the water, as if he was made of air.

'Brilliant at floating and sinking, isn't he?' Ted said. 'Not many people are that good at *both*.'

Ginika laughed a small, silly, casual laugh, but when she

glanced at Ted he looked like his brain was trying to work something out.

Then Peri got playful and Ted relaxed. The two of them, Ted and Peri, played opposites and copying: Ted's fingers fluttered like anemones – Peri's didn't. Ted waved high in the air at an imaginary person out at sea. Peri ducked under the water, popped up further out and made his toes wave as perfectly as a pair of hands. Peri tasted the air. Ted tasted the air. Ted pretended to look sleepy. Peri closed his eyes and floated on his back.

Ted winced. His eyes looked watery.

'You OK?'

'Yep. Medicine's wearing off.'

'What actually happened to your spine?' Ginika spoke the words without rehearsing them, before she lost her nerve.

'I've got a tumour in it. They've got most of it out, but I have to have more treatment in a couple of months.'

Ginika breathed out a long breath. Her thoughts whirled, then froze in one spot: *a tumour*. It sounded so terrifying. Yet Ted was here, and strong, and funny, and determined. 'How long have you had it?' she asked, once she could trust her voice to work normally again.

'Since I was eight.' He dug his toes into the sand. 'But it's fine. They've got control of it now – that's how the doctors put it. And they're cool, the doctors.' His eyes widened and brightened at the thought of them. 'They say wacky stuff and roll their eyes when my mum and dad aren't looking.'

His words went into a deep place in Ginika's mind. The two of them sat in silence and watched Peri as he skimmed and drifted, floated and dipped.

Chapter 18

Ginika and Peri lay side by side on their stomachs in the waves right at the edge of the sea, resting on their elbows. The retreating water sucked all the sand from beneath them. Ted remained on the sand with only his feet submerged. The sea breathed Ginika and Peri in and out with slurping noises, and it was really hard not to laugh. Ginika's wet clothes made everything feel more ridiculous. They put their heads in the water and let the giggles out that way. Ted looked at them as though they were weird, but his shoulders were shaking too.

Worry and hiding and dodging people all forgotten, the laughter was like something all three caught from each other. Ginika's legs went weak with it and she splayed in the shallow waves like a frog, laughing instead of breathing, laughing instead of thinking about anything else at all. Peri kept his mouth beneath the water. His bubbly laughter was disguised – and it was also a trigger for yet more laughter.

The evening was turning golden, and the sad-happy feeling that always came just before the fishermen arrived was drifting over them, but she didn't care. Laughing had made her too loose and floppy to care about anything, and in any case, she could easily stay here doing this until all three of them were old.

Ted grabbed a discarded balloon and plunged it underwater to make farting noises. Peri drew back and looked wary – maybe he'd been taught to keep away from human plastics. Ted did it again; they all laughed like hyenas, breathing strawberry bubblegum breath on each other.

Peri forgot to keep his face in the water. Then he lost control, bent himself double and released a huge guffaw, with a long, helpless trill at the very end.

Peri's split-bell, two-tone laughter was out in the open.

Ted stopped laughing and stared at Peri without blinking for a long moment.

'Your *laugh*,' he whispered eventually. His bewildered expression was puff-cheeked and frozen, like someone suddenly realising the mouthful they were chewing was far, far too big. 'Your *voice*.'

Ginika's insides turned cold.

Then somebody walked by, and Peri instinctively darted away.

'Whoa. How did he move like that –' Ted stopped to clear his throat and whipped one arm into the air like a lightning streak – '*so* fast? As fast as those tiny fish move when you put your hands in the water. Faster!'

Ginika didn't know what to say. Her finger smoothed over already perfectly smooth, wet sand and she fiddled with her hair.

Peri returned, said 'Hungi,' grabbed Ginika's hat and vanished again, and Ginika knew the game was up. She almost couldn't bear to wait.

Ted started to panic, but she stopped him. 'He's fine. He's gone to eat and he won't be back for a while.'

'But—'

'He won't drown. He can hold his breath for a *really* long time.'

Silence.

Ted chewed furiously for a few seconds, then stopped. 'He hasn't just come out of hospital, has he?'

Ginika shook her head. 'He's from the sea. It's where he lives.'

Ted shook his head too, very slowly. 'Wowzers,' he whispered, staring out to sea.

Everything was so still. The wind turbines in the distance

didn't move a blade. Only the waves still lapped and bobbed.

Ted's eyes, watery again, stared and stared as the sun slid further down, slowly, slowly.

'You better not tell,' Ginika said.

'I won't, but ... how?'

Ginika shrugged and shook her head, stunned by the majesty of the stillness. She was a tiny bit glad to be sharing Peri, and that realisation was also overwhelming. She told him everything.

'I met him here,' she said, after going through the whole story. 'He's run away. His family will be back this way any day now, and they'll collect him. He just wanted a little holiday on land, I think, to see what it's like.'

Ted stared at her. 'Nobody needs to know.'

Biking home hard and fast, Ginika was starving hungry – but she was totally unwilling to stop thinking. Ted finding out was scary, and thrilling, but the feeling was a slippery one, as if everything might yet spill out of her hands. Was it too good to last? Grandma ought to have a word for that.

But in the kitchen, Grandma's words were both extraordinary and shouty. 'You're ruinously late. And where are your shoes?'

'They're full of sand—'

'You need them on because of the lodgers coming and going, bringing goodness-knows-what in on their shoes. It's not like being at home with your mum and dad and I've told you that hundreds of times.'

Grandma had made a chilli, and the delicious hot-tomato-and-spice fumes made Ginika's stomach grumble. Clawd had just eaten his tea. Ginika crouched to stroke his tiger stripes, but he pulled away from her hand to sniff it. And sniff it some more.

'What have you got on your hands?' Grandma's face wore her ultra-alert expression. Knowing when something was going on was definitely her superpower, but something giddy danced behind her words.

'Nothing.'

'It can't be nothing. Clawd doesn't think it's nothing.'

'Just something from the beach then. Or, I know – Scarlett lent me her bike, so it's probably something on the handlebars.'

'Come and wash them right now!'

Ginika took a breath. She was boiling hot now and her damp clothes itched. 'I washed them when I came in.'

'Well, obviously not enough. Do them again. And have you still got this bike? Where have you left it?'

'In the back yard,' Ginika said. Just before putting her hands under the tap, she sniffed them secretly. She couldn't smell anything besides the bits of candyfloss that clung to the neck of her T-shirt. How could Clawd smell Peri through all that soap, when Peri only smelt of salt and sea and new pencil shavings? And maybe of tears – she'd just realised this. Yes, he smelt a little of tears. Could Clawd be smelling his seaweed clothes? But those didn't smell of the smelly seaweed that washed up on the beach, because they were fresh. Clawd's sense of smell was just so much more awesome than hers.

'Oh.' Grandma looked down at Clawd. 'He's just as interested in your legs. What have you been into with those?'

'Nothing.' Ginika took a step away from Clawd's frantic sniffing, but he followed her. 'Stop it, Clawd.'

'Your legs look like someone's painted on a layer of sand with a brush,' Grandma said, studying Ginika carefully all over. 'And there's a streak of lawlessness about you.' Then she smiled, and the smile stayed on her face, as if she was thinking about something far more interesting than cats and handwashing.

'What's going on?' Ginika asked.

Grandma shook her head and turned back to the food she was serving, but she was now clearly in a much better mood.

Secrets hung in the air, and Ginika was no longer quite as certain about which direction they were coming from or heading to.

Chapter 19

The next morning, Ginika got everything ready for another day out with Peri – and maybe even Ted, if he could talk his way out of being grounded. The day stretched ahead, full of wacky, brilliant, funny things, and Grandma was still in her super-good mood. Peri had disappeared with Ginika's hat and clothes, which meant he was likely to emerge from the sea dressed and ready for more action. She felt so light with excitement that when Grandma asked her to hang out the washing, she leaped down the cellar steps to the laundry room, made a turn at the bottom with a low hand-swoop and sprinted to the washing line without emptying the machine.

She messaged Ted: *Are you allowed out? I'll get Peri and we can meet you at the go-karts again. Think he loved them best.*

Ted: *Got in trouble last night for going on go-karts.*

Ginika: *How did they find out?*

Ted: *They got it out of me. No good for my condition. Too much twisting. Gotta stick with their timetable today. Going on a STUPID trip. Back late tonight. Will def escape tomorrow.*

Mr Chihuahua Man came out of the corner behind Grandpa's shed and left the garden hurriedly, on silent feet, bag tucked under his arm. Ginika wondered why there was barely a single yap from that dog. But as she was doubling back to the laundry room to get the washing out, there was a knock at the front door. Ginika had a bad feeling about it – it was a fast, childish knock, and she could hear faint giggling. A message came to her phone at the same time.

Scarlett: *Come out, we've got a MASSIVE adventure!*

Ginika dived upstairs to open the door, and the bad feeling hit the hairs at the back of her neck, which rose.

Scarlett stood on the doorstep and the Olivias balanced on the pavement below her, giggling hysterically, bikes poised for action.

'Quick, Ginika!' Scarlett said. 'Get the bike I lent you, because guess what? Have you heard? There's a boy driving round and round the streets in one of OUR caravan-park go-karts!'

'What?' Her mind was racing. Someone had stolen a go-kart from the caravan park?

'He's quite smallish, looks far too young to be in it by himself, and he's wearing a girl's hat! I've told my dad and he's getting the police, but they're being slow and difficult about it, because it's only one go-kart—'

A sickening, sinking feeling took root in Ginika's stomach. The go-karts were in the bike store next to the beach path, easily reachable from the shoreline.

It had to be Peri.

'—and it's going to run out of charge soon anyway. The plug is trailing along the tarmac! He must have set off without pulling it out of the charging point. So we're all waiting for him to come back this way, because he's going round in big circles. We nearly had him on Eastern Lane, but he zoomed away too fast.'

For a second, Ginika was paralysed with horror. Then she forced herself to move, said, 'I'll get the bike,' and dived back into the house and down the cellar steps.

'This way!' Scarlett said when Ginika and the trailer-bike came out of the back yard.

'No,' Ginika said, 'best to split up. This trailer-bike is slower than yours, so I might as well go in a different direction and catch him that way.'

'Great idea!' Scarlett said. 'Olivia, you go with Ginika.'

'No!' Ginika shrieked. 'You faster ones stay together.' She streaked away before anyone could object.

How had Peri done this? Biking wildly towards the end of Old Boundary Road, she pictured the manicured grass at the caravan park, and the way it sloped gently down to the beach like a green carpet. She imagined the twinkly lights coming on after dark, and Peri waiting till early morning when everything went dead quiet, and then hauling himself out of the water, over the sand and pebbles and up that grassy slope. But how had he found a go-kart? Had somebody left it out? She pictured him charging off into the streets at dawn with the plug trailing behind, scraping the tarmac, setting off sparks ... Could that happen?

She turned on to Fishmarket Street and glanced up and down. He could be anywhere. This direction might be completely wrong, and a crowd might even be following him by now. She wanted to burst out crying – this was too hard, too awful. But it was also too important to give in to tears. If Scarlett and the others found him first ... what would they do? And what would *Peri* do? The police, if they came, would find out he was a child alone, and they'd take him away somewhere safe, and then they'd see how different he looked, and then ... what would happen? Where might they take him? They wouldn't let him stay in Bridleways Bay – that was certain.

She hurried past the Chinese takeaway, whizzed round

the corner of the barbershop, then crossed over to the junction with Kettle Lane, where there was a clear view down the four streets that met at the crossroads. Still no sign of Peri. She biked on, looking in every single direction, but when she turned down Colliers Road, the girls appeared and made straight for her.

'Where can he be?' Scarlett yelled, panting and fizzing with exhilaration. This was probably the best thing to come her way all summer. 'The power's gonna have to run out soon.'

'Better spread out,' Ginika said.

And then she caught a glimpse. Something low to the ground, turning a corner into Backman Alley. There was a pause, and into it Ginika slipped the words, 'There! I saw something!' and pointed in the opposite direction, and a surge of girls raced towards the Fried Chicken Manor end of the street. Gripping the bars of the bike, mouth dry, heart beating fast, Ginika pedalled after them deliberately slowly, then doubled back.

Chapter 20

On Backman Alley, Ginika found the go-kart in the middle of the road in a diagonal position, not far from an overflowing bin buzzing with flies. The kart was stranded, with Peri still inside. The street was deserted, but Dixon the old dog was ambling towards the kart – which was impossible, wasn't it? Ginika had never once seen him walk. He normally just thumped his tail on the ground.

Peri edged back more deeply into the go-kart as Ginika approached, and a hiss shot from his lips. It wasn't the hiss of a cat; it was deep, savage, harsh. Even Ginika jerked away from him instinctively, but then recovered and motioned with her hands, and at the same time, Peri recognised her, said, 'Gnka!' and his whole face changed. It relaxed, lit up into a smile. He was glad to see her, but looked wrecked. Thankfully, he still wore her clothes as well as the hat, but there were scratches and bruises on his arms. His eyes looked wet and sore and scared.

'Quick!' she said, gesturing wildly as she parked the bike. 'Get in the trailer.'

He heaved himself stiffly out of the go-kart and into the trailer, and Ginika frowned. She'd expected him to be gleeful and giggly after such a stunt, even if he'd cut himself getting there, but he just sat in the back of the trailer, exhausted. His chin trembled, and she wondered how long he'd been riding around town. Maybe he hadn't been able to turn the go-kart off? She leaned in to look at its controls. The ones at the go-kart place had been different; all the karts there had smelt of smelly petrol fumes. This one had buttons to push to start the kart, but how did it stop? Ginika didn't know. Peri certainly wouldn't. There were no pedals. And now, as Scarlett predicted, it had run out of power.

As always, Dixon the dog looked like he was smiling at her. 'Good boy,' Ginika said, as she always did. 'You can walk!' But as she made her way back from the trailer to the front of the bike, Dixon nosed his way right through her legs to get to Peri. He rested his chin on the trailer and panted hot breath everywhere. His tail wagged wildly. He whimpered, licked her hand, went into a frenzy of curiosity, pushed his wet nose into the trailer – 'No, Dixon, *sit*!'

Peri leaned out, and in a weary way reached across to pat Dixon's enormous, wiry back. Three quick pats and one slow press. Then again. It was like a pattern he'd used before. Ginika imagined him patting dolphins and seals, playing in the water with them.

'We have to go! Diiiiixon! Get away, please.'

Ginika pushed the bike away slowly, but Dixon followed. 'No, Dixon – go back.' She tussled with him, trying to get his nose out of the way to make room to push the bike off properly, but he wouldn't move. His nose was glued to Peri's hand, and Ginika almost fell over, which would have brought bike, trailer and Peri crashing down with her.

'*Dixon!*'

She pulled the bike away, but he just wagged his tail and carried on, straining, pushing, snorting great nostrils full of Peri, using every atom of energy he had just to stay with him.

Ginika kept pulling and at last, Dixon paused for breath, stumbled, found his feet again and in that moment she swung her leg over the saddle and rode off. When she looked back from the end of the alley, Dixon was panting. He stood exactly where she had left him. She hoped he would be OK.

At the end of Backman Alley, she stopped to make sure the coast was clear before heading on to the beach road.

But the Olivias came speeding around the corner of Woodland Road, hair streaming out behind. Ginika's stomach flipped. A bus was coming. As it passed between them, Ginika turned and biked back the way she'd come, pushing the pedals harder and faster than ever in her life before. The bus blotted everything out, but before it did, she saw half of Scarlett's face.

Ginika didn't look over her shoulder until she was halfway down Old Boundary Road, and almost crashed the bike when a piece of loose pavement dipped, sending her front wheel sideways. She could hear giggles, screams and shouts. That stranded go-kart would be enough to satisfy them for a while, wouldn't it?

She was breathless. She felt like a rat scuttling in shadows. There was only one stupid road to the beach in this whole town, and that went past Backman Alley. If she turned right, then right again and zoomed past as fast as this bike would go, could she get him out of the trailer and into the sea before they caught her up? And actually, was he even fit to go back into the sea yet? He'd looked dazed just now. He might hang about in the shallows, and then Scarlett would call her dad, and he'd get the police …

She had an idea. It was risky, but not as risky as trying for the beach. What if she sneaked Peri into Cormorant Heights through the laundry room in the cellar? He could hide in the trailer. And the trailer – the whole bike – could hide away in the huge cupboard under the stairs, which was more like an extra little room. Grandma never went in there because it was such a jumble of old boxes and tins of paint, and the door was a bit broken – it wouldn't close completely. So everything depended on Peri staying quiet …

She pedalled hard, pictured the girls peering into the empty go-kart, took great gulps of breath and hoped, hoped, hoped.

In the yard at the back of Cormorant Heights, a lodger stood next to the muddy patch, staring into his phone. It was the one with the apologetic eyes and the buzzing machine in his room, and there was no choice any more – she couldn't turn back. She pushed the bike on, but as they passed the twisted, knotty old tree in the middle of the yard, Peri reached out for the lavender in Grandma's pots beneath it, scattering bees into the air. The lodger noticed, in a side-eye kind of way, without moving his head.

Inside the laundry room, Ginika threw the cover of the trailer open and Peri, wide-eyed, took everything in: one of the washing machines was working, tumbling clothes right in front of them. The old freezer was over there; behind it, whitewash peeled from that wall that never quite dried out. But it was a room. Inside a house. Peri looked at it all, and so did Ginika. Then she bent down to him and put her finger to her lips. Lucky he looked so tired.

'Zip it,' she said.

Peri clapped his entire hand over his mouth.

Trembly butterflies fluttered in her stomach. She was probably the first person ever to show a sea person inside a land person's house.

Ginika stood in the middle of the floor and waited for her breath to come back. If that lodger came in again, she would just cover Peri and wheel the bike out. She listened. Cormorant Heights was never quiet. There was always some lodger or other going to a bathroom, or closing a door, or coughing or pulsating.

She peered through the open window. The lodger had gone. There was no sign of the girls. They would be busy with the mystery of the empty go-kart. Maybe they were still looking for the thief. She'd got away with it.

'This isn't where we normally live,' she found herself telling Peri. 'It's just where we wash clothes.' She stretched out her T-shirt to tearing point. 'Clothes.'

'Cloves,' Peri repeated.

'Wash, in water,' she pointed to the clothes rolling around. 'Clean.'

'Ca-leen,' Peri said, drowsily.

This was so hard. Did he even get it? And if you lived in the sea, wasn't everything clean all the time?

His hair, all dried out now, looked crackly. It had taken on all the colours of the laundry room, and changed as he moved his head and reached out to trace his fingers over the writing on Grandma's instructions for lodgers, which was taped to a washing machine:

DO NOT overload. Your clothes will not be clean + machines do not like it

The air smelt of warm, scented steam and the sharp tang of outside, which came in with strips of sunlight through the open window. Peri looked at his reflection in the shiny metal rims of both washing machines, and almost climbed out of the trailer in his effort to touch them. He seemed startled at the difference between the warm window of the one that was washing, and the cool window of the other. Watching him, Ginika felt another pang of uneasiness. And irritation. Running away from your parents wasn't such a brilliant thing if it led to pickles like this. What else might he do?

Then her phone rang. She ignored it – it would be Scarlett, but maybe she could pretend she was at the other side of town, searching for the thief? Then a message arrived.

Scarlett: *Where are you? Found go-kart. Why didn't you stay with it?*

Five minutes later, that fast, Scarlettish knock sounded from upstairs again. Her heart sank. Hiding wouldn't work this time.

Wide-eyed, Ginika pushed the trailer into the cupboard under the stairs – shoving boxes and tins aside until it was fully in – told Peri to *zip it* again, closed the broken door as far as it would go, leaped upstairs to the front door before either grandparent could answer it – and faced her worst fear.

'Ginika, why are you ignoring my calls and messages?' Scarlett leaned her bike against the wall of the house. 'Where's the trailer-bike? Why didn't you come and find us? You must have walked straight past the thief, so what happened to him?'

'Erm … no! He was gone by the time I got there, but my gran wanted me to do an errand. I had to go.' Ginika was so sick of lying. When this was over, she was never going to lie again.

'Whoa,' said the smiley Olivia. 'You totally found the empty go-kart! Dixon the dog was sniffing it to *death*.'

'I rang my dad,' Scarlett told Ginika, 'and he's told the police.'

'Ooh!' Ginika said. 'Epic! Let's go to the beach.'

Scarlett looked baffled. 'What for? We're here now.' She shook her head. 'I'm thirsty, and we haven't seen your room, like, *ever*. Can we have a drink?'

'Lemonade, please,' the smiley Olivia said, abandoning her bike too.

'Me too,' the serious, starey Olivia said.

'Have you got juice?' the fidgety Olivia said.

Grandma arrived in the hallway beside Ginika. 'Hello, girls! Come in, come in! Ginika, what are you playing at? Where are your manners?'

All of the Olivias stood awkwardly in the kitchen while Grandma bustled about organising a tray of biscuits and cold drinks, but Scarlett posed with one leg leaning against the doorframe, bright and pleased, like a satisfied queen. Her curious eyes darted everywhere, lingering over Grandma's huge old-fashioned food mixer with its big shiny beaters and worn-away handle, Grandpa's guitar and his wine-gum jar with its joke lid made of turrets guarded by a plastic wizard.

'Take these up to your room, Ginika,' Grandma said. 'Be hospitable. Be super.'

Chapter 21

Taking the girls through her grandparents' bedroom felt like a dream that was going the wrong way. There was the bed with its layers of velvet and lace. There was Grandma's film-star dressing table and her wardrobe with all the clothes spilling out, bright and wild things from when she was young and had a cool job doing costumes for films. Ginika was leading the way so couldn't see, but all the girls behind her were looking at each other and smirking. She could feel it.

'Woo! It's like a maze,' Scarlett said. 'Bedrooms lead to bedrooms! Is there another room at the end of yours?'

Ginika tried to think of the weather, forced herself to smile, look normal, not panicked, not stomach-cramped and sweating.

'I've never been in a boarding house before,' said the

smiley Olivia, glancing around Ginika's bedroom excitedly. 'Is it like a hotel?'

'It's different from a hotel,' Scarlett said. 'People actually live here. For ages.' She looked at Ginika. 'Are they scary weirdos?'

'Ooh, lodgers!' the smiley Olivia said. 'Can we see some?'

Ginika shook her head and stood in the centre of her bedroom as it filled up with a mood. A feeling of amazement, with politeness on top. It also felt like an invasion mixed with judgement. She folded her arms and unfolded them again, feeling like a kangaroo, except kangaroos probably never had time to feel awkward.

Scarlett's lips twitched. 'Isn't this where people come when they get let out of prison?'

Ginika felt a wave of fury heat her face, but she shook her head briskly. This wouldn't last long. They'd drink, nosy around and then go.

'Nice pictures,' said the smiley Olivia.

'I like your fairy lights,' said the fidgety Olivia, touching Ginika's chair, her mirror, the handles of her drawers, the shells Peri had given her. 'Ah, whoa – these are *so* pink.'

Ginika made her lips smile. 'Thanks.' How long might this take? She tried to imagine what Peri was doing down there, picturing him quiet in the trailer. Not mud-skipping on the floor, exploring …

The room felt full of girls. Squeals. Giggling through covered mouths. Excitement. Her bed looked strange in the middle of it all. Their chatter was dangerous, and she knew she should join in, but couldn't.

'That go-kart!' the smiley Olivia said.

'I know!' Scarlett said. 'Like, *who* can it be?'

'Dunno, but he looked weird,' the fidgety Olivia said. 'Something creepy about him ...'

'How could you even see?' Scarlett said. 'We never got that close.'

'Close enough to see some weirdness,' the fidgety Olivia said. 'Something's not quite right ...' She shuddered.

'Huh,' Scarlett said, and sprawled on Ginika's bed. 'His hat was weird, I'll give you that.' Her hair hung down the side of the bed and she inched closer to the edge until it skimmed the floor. 'Look at my hair. Imagine if I grew it long enough to reach the floor sitting down.'

'Ginika? Like, why are you mad on trains?' It was the fidgety Olivia again. She rocked backwards and forwards on her heels, and all the Olivias looked at each other. They'd been talking about her. Scarlett smirked.

Ginika glared at her, but then felt a tiny nugget of relief. This was a complete change of topic. If they all focused on this instead of the boy in the go-kart ... Scarlett looked surprised.

'Only *certain* trains,' Ginika said. 'Because they remind me of home.'

'Where's your cat?' Scarlett asked, speaking through her hair. 'Shall we give him a ride in the trailer?'

Ginika tried to focus on staying calm, but her voice cracked. 'Um … I don't know where he is.'

The Olivias giggled. Scarlett flicked her hair back dramatically to see what was going on, but was too late to catch the Olivias giving each other looks behind her back. 'He can't be all that far away. You could call him. What's his name?'

Ginika cleared her throat. 'Clawd.'

The fidgety Olivia laughed. 'Oh, I get it! Cats have claws and they claw things, so he *clawed* something, then got his name! And Claude is also an actual name.'

'Oh, Olivia, you're *so* quick,' Scarlett drawled, pulling a mean expression, which slid off her face quickly, as though she was just faking it. For a second, she looked really unhappy.

The smiley Olivia said, 'Some cats think they're human.'

Scarlett smirked. '*You* think you're human.' Then she sat up. 'Let's explore and find *Clawd*—'

'We can't!' Ginika said. 'Because of the lodgers. I'm not allowed to make noise or go snooping around the house.'

'We can do it quietly,' Scarlett said, lowering her voice.

'No,' Ginika said, and her thumping heart made her voice quiver. 'We … can't.'

Suddenly the fidgety Olivia was right behind Ginika. 'Can I feel your hair?'

While Ginika was figuring out how to refuse, the other two Olivias crept over and patted her hair gingerly, one by one.

'So soft!' an Olivia blurted. Ginika couldn't see which one it was, but there was a smell of cooked breakfast about her.

—'And so thick!'—

—'Bouncy!'—

—'I love it! I love Afro hair!'—

Ginika lost track of which Olivia was saying what. Their voices seemed to sink into her wallpaper, her curtains, her duvet cover. There was no echo. Everything was absorbed. Half of her brain listened; the other half panicked, and braced for the shriek from downstairs as Grandma found Peri.

She felt like their pet; a dog or a cat, not a person. She tried to unfreeze herself and remember what Granny Orendu had taught her about how to deal with people touching her hair and making her feel *so*, so different; how to be confident in saying that she didn't like what they were doing and telling them to stop. But Granny Orendu was miles away in Nigeria, and Ginika couldn't remember exactly what she'd said. Tears welled up in her eyes, a ringing sound took over her ears and the room felt smaller and smaller, like it was closing in on her.

Scarlett shouted, 'Olivia!' and all three girls stopped and turned round. 'Don't do that – how would you like it?'

The serious, starey Olivia frowned and spoke into her cupped hand, saying, 'We're only touching it softly.'

Scarlett rolled her eyes and commanded them to feel *her* hair, lowering her head dramatically. One by one, the Olivias did as they were told, but quickly lost interest and started comparing the straps on each other's sandals instead. Straps in a row. Toes in a row. Giggles bubbling over.

'Har *har*,' Scarlett said loudly. None of the Olivias took any notice. 'Feel theirs, Ginika.'

'No thanks.' Ginika sat on her floor, grateful, but cross at feeling grateful, and confused. Now Scarlett had not only lent her the trailer-bike, but here she was, rescuing her from this stupid hair-touching, even if she was doing it nastily. Poor Olivias – Scarlett really wasn't nice to them. And poor Scarlett – the Olivias didn't really like her much at all. It was all so complicated. People like Peri who lived in the sea had none of this rubbish to put up with. But poor Peri, stuck in the laundry room. And poor HER, having to hold all these secrets and lies together in this slippery knot ... A tear rolled down Ginika's cheek, but nobody noticed.

'Go on,' Scarlett said. 'And have a good look down their ears while you're there.'

The Olivias looked up at Scarlett sharply. Scarlett grinned at Ginika, then positioned herself so that she could touch two Olivias' hair at the same time – smiley and fidgety – one with each hand.

Both Olivias flinched and moved away.

'If you don't like it, why did you do it to Ginika?'

'Because I wish I had that hair,' the smiley Olivia said, pointing to Ginika and pouting a little.

Ginika wiped her cheek, and sniffed. She was trembling all over, just slightly, and still none of them noticed.

'It's so thick,' the starey Olivia said.

—'And so dandeliony!'—

—'How do you wash it?'—

—'Can you comb it?'—

—'How long can it grow?'—

This couldn't go on. She needed to get them out of here and away from her and get back to Peri. Anything could be happening to him down there right now …

'Aarrgh, *stop*!' Scarlett shrieked. She jumped to her feet, grabbed hold of the starey Olivia's bag and emptied it out on Ginika's floor. Pieces of paper. A hairband. Glitter pens. A small beach towel. A skull-shaped eraser.

'Hey!' the starey Olivia said. 'Stop it!'

Scarlett twirled the empty bag over her head and dropped it in the middle of the floor. 'Right, fill it again. Everyone!' She picked up a glitter pen and aimed it at the open bag. 'Bet I can hit it from here. Get one in with your foot, Ginika. Kick it.'

Nobody moved except the starey Olivia. She launched herself towards Scarlett as if to give her a shove, but pulled back and dived to retrieve her things instead.

'Come on,' Scarlett said, 'it's only a game! No. Yeah. Here, get this … No! Not like that …'

The fidgety Olivia was hit in the face by a flying hairband. Scarlett threw the final glitter pen in the air and caught it, over and over again. The starey Olivia folded her arms as if she didn't care and was just waiting for it all to stop, but Ginika could see that she cared.

'These Olivias are really something, aren't they, Ginika,' Scarlett said.

At the top of her voice, the starey Olivia screamed, 'We are *not* THE OLIVIAS! We're separate people!'

Scarlett flung herself back on to Ginika's bed and stared at the ceiling.

Downstairs, Scarlett turned in the doorway, letting the Olivias scoot ahead. 'After lunch, just you and me, yeah?'

she whispered to Ginika. 'Zero Olivias! What do you think? We could do the fountains!'

'I'm not really in the mood ...'

'But *why*?' Scarlett peered at Ginika with her head on one side, as though she was something very odd but interesting. 'Everyone wants to hang out, especially since we got the bike-pump track, and now with the fountains. We might even be getting a zip wire next year.'

Ginika could see the Olivias speeding up, looking back over their shoulders at Scarlett, giggling. They were trying to lose her. She felt bad for Scarlett, but blurted, 'I've got to go,' and closed the door. Scarlett's face in that last split-second had been almost heartbreakingly disappointed, but Ginika listened, heard her picking up her bike, and then there was silence.

Alone. The relief was like an avalanche. Ginika leaned against the door for a second and closed her eyes. She felt different. Changed forever. Sick inside at what had almost happened, but giddy too. Scarlett, the Olivias and Peri had all been inside Cormorant Heights at the same time, but she'd kept them apart! And now it was over.

She dashed down to the laundry room, thoughts swirling madly. She was cross with Peri now. He'd done such a stupid, dangerous thing! No wonder he gave his parents the slip. Then as soon as it had arrived, her anger changed to guilt. *She* was the one who had shown him what was possible on land. *She* had put him in a go-kart yesterday, and shown him the controls. There might not be any stopping him now. Tomorrow, or the day after, he might try something else, and then he'd get taken away by the police or social services ...

There was now no choice left at all. Peri *had* to go back to the sea, and stay there until his parents returned.

A big thought struck her, and stopped her halfway down the stairs: the laundry room was going to be the last thing she ever showed him before he returned to the sea for good. His very last adventure was here, now, today. Her eyes filled with tears.

She needed to get braver in the water. Then they could have fun and mess about safely in whatever time he had left. But they'd have to get away from Bridleways Bay. They needed somewhere quieter and more sheltered. Somehow, she had to work out how to tell him his time on land was over.

But when she opened the door to the laundry room, Peri was no longer in the trailer, or even in the cupboard under the stairs. He was sitting on the floor in front of a washing machine, surrounded by magazines and grinning.

Chapter 22

Peri picked up one magazine after another and held each high until the pages flopped over each other, revealing picture after picture. He looked at her. *Another new world,* his eyes told her. *Another playground.*

Not for long, Ginika thought. Swallowing a lump in her throat, she bent to the magazines and showed him how to turn the pages. They were Grandpa's old *National Geographics*; the overspill of a collection he'd kept going for more than forty years. These were the ones Grandma had banished from the sitting room because the tower they made there was getting too high. Peri must have found them stuffed behind somewhere Grandma wouldn't look. Grandpa had similar stashes all over the house.

They were full of photographs from around the world. Seascapes. Mountainous places. Almost everything on the planet was here. But could he even see them properly? If he could …

She tore pictures out greedily, suddenly realising something: these pictures told stories. Could she use them to talk to Peri? Would his eyes understand the images? Could she use pictures to explain that they had to find a new hiding place?

Quickly, her mind whirring, she worked out sequences: a picture of someone sleeping in a bed, using a cooker, eating at a kitchen table, washing in a bath, then a house from the outside. Tapping the images, she pointed to her chest. 'I live like this.'

He seemed to understand. His eyes were wide, amazed, especially at the sight of the bath. All of it must surely look like a world from outer space. She shivered. He whipped through the pages hungrily, drinking in each image. His fingers were so clever at it. Better and faster than hers. But then they were clever at ripping the shells from sea creatures and twisting seaweed clothes together, so it made sense. And he memorised what was on each page in an instant; that was the only explanation of how he was able to quickly find *any* page again when he wanted to show her something.

And what he showed her was absolutely gripping. He found a picture of a bed with someone sleeping on it. Then he flicked to a picture of floating mats of seaweed, laid his head down on the floor and closed his eyes. It was a sentence. Peri had just made a sentence out of pictures.

'This is the way *I* sleep, and this what *you* sleep on!' Ginika said. Excitement rippled up and down her spine. 'Yes! This is *so* brilliant!'

And now it was like a fever. Ginika dived into the images like a superhuman, tearing off what she wanted to say, speeding through sequences in ways she couldn't have imagined minutes ago, and Peri acted just the same. This was a language shortcut. This was *fantastic*. The trailer-bike sat in the cupboard, forgotten.

She found a picture of a ballet onstage and demonstrated dancing on the slippery laundry-room floor. 'Dance,' she told him.

'Dans,' he repeated.

He showed her dolphins. He showed her speedy marlin fish. He showed her octopuses and squid that looked just as curious as people. He found picture after picture, and made mime after mime after mime: he was showing her where he was from.

Soon, Peri created images of sea families in Ginika's mind. When he leaped up from the floor, pretending to catch the wind and take off, Ginika pictured him speeding along in his family group. When he lay on the floor clutching a magazine page showing huge floaty rafts of sargassum seaweed, she pictured him sleeping on it, wrapped up tight. And when he did the same mime with three pictures of sea caves from lots of different countries, and lay there for longer, snoring and snorting from his nose, she decided this must be a BIGGER, longer, safer sleep.

Peri didn't stop. He showed her how they swam *through* the storms at sea, plunging on, using the energy from storm winds to go even faster. And when a storm grew too powerful, they sheltered in sea caves. He showed her an image of jagged fingers of lightning flashing overhead, and put some sea caves next to it. He held those pictures up to her nose for a long time.

'*Click. Click-click. Click-click,*' he said, pointing to the sea cave. '*Click. Click-click. Click-click.*'

'I'll never be able to learn that word,' she said, with a laugh. 'But OK. Sea cave.' There was a sea cave on the other side of the headland, past the caravan park. It was only accessible by sea. She wondered if he'd discovered it.

Peri repeated the whole thing. Sea caves. Storms. Ginika was confused. They headed for the sea caves when there was a storm – that made sense. But he seemed to be saying that it was good to follow storms. Great fun.

'Isn't that dangerous?' she asked, pulling her scared face.

'Liii-ttt,' he said, showing her the sea cave again.

'Sea caves in a storm? All lit up?'

Peri looked frustrated, but as soon as Ginika began to feel bad for failing to understand, he picked a long piece of string off the floor and showed her how sea people use their clever fingers to free dolphins caught in nets. Seconds later, he'd made an intricate plait from the string, and with an image of stars shining on to the sea from a black night sky, he tried to show her something he obviously thought was beautiful and special. Plaiting by starlight? Ginika couldn't make out what he meant, until he found the picture of floating mats of seaweed again. They plaited their beds.

Then he moved on to the main part of what he wanted to say, and for this, he needed lots of images of moving people and animals. Fish swimming, people swimming, everything moving, *everyone* on a journey. This last part was repeated over and over, and always Peri came back to one image: the wide open ocean.

Travelling all over the world. Moving on.

All the time.

So the legend was true. Her heart began to race as his fingers traced the waves. His hands mimed movement. His eyes said: *My home*. He'd run away to *her* slow, still world. How slow the walking land people must have looked to him yesterday in town! Life in slow motion.

Ginika couldn't be absolutely certain she'd understood everything he'd shown her, but within the hour, she'd learned how it was possible to roam the high seas where there was no land or land human, only ever stopping to eat or sleep. Somebody always kept watch. You needed superfast reactions. If anything dangerous was coming, you needed to know about it before it was *anywhere* near, and you needed to outswim absolutely anything. They'd surely need weapons too, she thought, in case there was an attack from something big. She raised her arms to mime it, but changed her mind; perhaps only land humans did things like that.

He showed her only warm-looking seas. Beautiful, tropical places. Scenes of ice-cold seas and icebergs kept coming up in the magazines, but he frowned, shuddered, shook his head and shoulders. *We don't go anywhere cold*, he was saying.

Ginika was still for a moment while she tried to make all the pieces of this settle in her head instead of whirling around. The fairytale sea caves in warm countries made her heart race the most. The pictures he'd found looked pretty safe, at least until high tide – their waters were shallow. Maybe the sea cave around the corner from here was like this. Maybe if she copied his strong, free movements in the water ... He could carry her there to start with, just like he had during the sandbar rescue. And then, when they were safely away from everyone, he could teach her! He could make her a really strong swimmer. Then the water would never be able to harm her again.

She tried out a sentence of her own.

The picture she used showed a sea cave in hot, steamy waters, with inviting golden sand on its floor and aquamarine water up to the level of an adult's waist. 'This is a much better sea cave than our closest one,' she said to herself. 'But it's a sea cave.' She pointed in the direction of the headland. 'Oh, how can I make you understand?' She kept pointing, and held up the sea cave picture at the same time.

'Me,' she said, touching her chest, 'and you –' she touched Peri's chest – 'can go here?' She put her hand on the sea cave and pointed towards the headland again. 'Together?'

Peri smiled, but looked puzzled.

'Now?' Ginika gestured towards the door and made her arms and hands into paws that scurried away.

Peri looked astonished.

Chapter 23

There was a creak on the stairs. A muffled squeak, like a shoe on a step. Someone was coming. Ginika shot a glance at Peri, but he was still leafing through the magazines. He hadn't heard anything. Which made no sense – his reactions were always super aware. The noise stopped. Had she really heard anything? She frowned and dived for the door.

Heavily booted and dropping tiny paper offcuts, the buzzy lodger stood on one of the middle steps with his arms full of papers. He looked fumbly and embarrassed. Dust particles danced in the air between them. 'Oops,' he said with a nervous smile. 'Wrong way.' He turned and went, leaving a faint smell of ink.

Ginika let out a long sigh of relief. Somehow, she'd scared him away. She dived back into the laundry room, closed the door and did a little dance across the floor with her eyes on the magazine pile. 'Let's go now!' she said. 'It'll be so cool. You can show me seahorses on the way, and sunfish and those velvety crabs, and we can *meet seals*, actually in person! And I won't be scared any more, because you're a brilliant lifeguard!'

But Peri looked strange. He gazed straight at her, but it didn't seem as if he saw her properly. His head was straight, but his body slanted sideways.

'Peri, what … ?'

He reached towards the ceiling light, as if trying to get something from it, then reeled over completely, almost hitting his head against the door of a washing machine.

'Peri!'

She leaped to his side. His eyes were red-rimmed and his face was pale. He looked tired and shivery, and when she felt his forehead, it was hot. To make matters worse, Cláwd was scratching and yowling at the cellar door.

'Are you OK, Peri?'

He cradled his stomach in his hands, then pointed to his head. Mimed falling down. Rubbed the back of his neck with a contorted face.

'Where is it? Is it your stomach *and* your head? What's wrong?'

'Meeb-*click*-saahhg-*click-click*.'

The washing machine started to spin. Ginika wished it

wouldn't. Vibrations drummed through the floor and Peri shivered.

Her phone began to ring. It was Dad: 'Hey, Ginki, why don't you come back to Cormorant Heights?'

'I'm there.'

'Oh – you're in your room? Well, why don't you go downstairs. Your gramps might have a surprise for you.'

'How d'you know?'

'You'll see.'

Not now, she thought. She had a very strange feeling in her heart … but she couldn't leave Peri. He was green now, like he was about to throw up.

But if she didn't go up there, they'd come looking for her. She got Peri into the cupboard under the stairs, and put a clean towel on the floor so that he could sit with his back resting against the trailer. His feet could be seen behind the door, but he needed fresh air anyway, so it didn't matter that it wouldn't close. Then she opened the main door enough for Clawd to shoot into the room, grabbed hold of him, put him out through the laundry-room window without saying a word to him, and locked it shut.

Slowly, she climbed the cellar steps, stunned and shaky. Voices came from the kitchen. Familiar. Becoming clearer, yet making no sense, because one of them sounded like

Mum. How was that possible? She couldn't be on speaker-phone – her voice was too close; there was no echo.

She peered round the kitchen doorway. Mum *was* there.

Grandpa, Grandma and Mum stood in a silent *ta-dah* moment, arms outstretched, eyes and mouths overflowing with glee. Ginika shrank from the look on their faces. Normally, she would have screamed 'Mummy!' and flown across the kitchen into Mum's arms like a parachute landing. But her legs felt out of balance and her insides felt empty, so she stayed in the doorway. Mum, grinning, trotted across the floor, gathered Ginika into her arms and pulled her deeper into the kitchen. Everyone began making noise at once. Grandpa sang snatches of a jokey song, Mum said Ginika's name over and over between kisses, and Grandma hooted with laughter at Ginika's expression. 'Where did you pop up from so quickly?' she asked.

'I was close by,' Ginika said, but her heart was beating hard. What if Peri was really, *really* ill? What if someone went into the laundry room and heard him being sick? She felt sick herself. 'Where's Dad?'

'In the bath – he's exhausted. It was a long drive. He had a delivery to do in Lincoln, so I got a free ride!' Mum's voice changed to the breathy whisper that always meant she was excited. 'And we couldn't resist coming up to see our darling.'

The kitchen table began to fill with plates of sliced cheese, bowls of crisps, a big potato salad, a sponge cake. Biscuits. Grandma's special custard tart. Grandpa's overloaded sandwiches. These things must have taken ages. She remembered how giddy Grandma had been last night; they were all in on it. Grandma's hair was even more glamorous than usual: the sides swept up in her best combs; the back loose and swishing. Ginika sat down at the table next to Mum, feeling her stomach tremble.

Grandma started to whisk cream with her tiny-handled whisk. Round and round. The kettle puffed a triangular stream of steam that ran into Grandma's hair and became a misshapen cloud. Flurries of questions pinged around the room. Mum wanted to know everything: Ginika's new life; Ginika's new friends. Ginika mumbled nothing that sounded like much of anything.

'Come on,' Mum said, 'no capers? No escapades? Really?'

'Ooh, Tara, there's not a chance,' Grandma said. 'You'll wait years to get anything out of Miss Secretive Orendu these days.'

Everyone looked at Ginika.

'Tell me about the beach, at least,' Mum said, handing Ginika a plate of sandwiches.

Ginika tried, but her mouth was so dry that the words clicked on her tongue.

Mum was different. Happier. Like she was bursting, and might start humming again like she used to before the eviction. Singing, even. But why? What had changed? Did she *like* living in the campervan now? It almost felt like Ginika could shelter in that humming again. But not today.

Grandma talked about her as if she wasn't there, called her 'poppet', adding annoyance and cringe to the spinning confusion in her head. What on earth was she going to do?

'Ginika?'

She'd missed another question from Mum.

'Um … I don't know.'

Everyone laughed. It couldn't have been that kind of question.

'Well, which do you feel like?' Grandma asked, hovering with a carton of juice in one hand and the teapot in the other. She looked as though she'd quite like to start marching up and down on the spot.

'Juice, please,' Ginika said.

Maybe Peri needed something he wasn't getting on land – something as important as oxygen. Maybe he'd started getting ill the moment he set foot in Ginika's world. Maybe something here was too different, too dangerous, too damaging for Peri's kind. Like those goldfish who are fine one day and then you come downstairs and they're dead in their tank … And then she was furious with herself for thinking such a thing. And he wasn't a fish. But she had to get him back to the sea. Right now.

Pretending to need the toilet, she escaped downstairs.

Peri was worse. He wasn't even squatting on the towel any more. He sprawled, and his breathing was fast. His cheeks were pink now, and when she leaned in close, a pattern of red dots went up into his hairline. He smelt sour.

She dashed out of the cupboard, found a cloth next to the sink, wet it and wiped his forehead and lips.

He felt hot, but his hands were cold.

'Peri, can you get up?'

There was no response.

'Can you get back in the trailer?'

She pulled him to his feet and fed him, clumsily, into the trailer. He was floppy and unbalanced, as if he didn't know where he was, and Ginika's heart raced. Once in there, he was quiet. He clung to the cushion, but made no sound or movement. And his hair wasn't just dried out and crinkly – it no longer changed colour with his surroundings. The inside of the trailer was lined with a sand-coloured fabric, but Peri's hair remained a dull mud colour.

'I'll take you back,' she soothed, 'and then you'll be fine. We shouldn't have come here.'

She pulled the trailer out of the cupboard gently, listening to the hum of electricity. Grandpa had muttered about overloaded plugs in here once, then he'd done some mending. Electricity: that was something very different from living in the sea. She stared up at the light tube and remembered how certain Peri's parents had been about not exploring the town and its lights. Or was it the food from yesterday?

'Ginika? Where are you, darling?' Mum's voice sounded like it came from the top of the cellar steps. Ginika pushed Peri and the trailer back inside the cupboard under the stairs, scrambled out and shut the laundry-room door.

Chapter 24

Back in the kitchen, eating was almost impossible, but Grandma made her. She'd tried telling them she had to do *just one thing first*, which would only take ten minutes, but Grandma saw through the ten-minute lie.

'What? Where? Not now of all times! Your mum and dad have only just arrived. Sit down and eat your lunch.'

It wasn't said in a way that could be argued against. Grandpa and Mum picked up their food and started eating too.

Ginika chewed and chewed on a carrot stick, but it didn't taste of anything. She tried a cupcake. It melted on her tongue, but wasn't much better. Her chewing got slower and slower, which messed up her goal, because the sooner she finished, the sooner she could get back downstairs and get Peri out.

'What's wrong, darling?' Mum asked, glancing at Grandma. 'Are you horribly homesick? Is that it?'

Ginika shook her head and buried her face in her juice cup. Her head hurt from the strain of pretending to be normal. She dipped her tongue into the juice, lapping like Clawd, waiting for Mum's mystified forehead wrinkles to disappear.

When Dad came downstairs after his bath, he looked better than the last time she'd seen him. Not so thin. The lines in his lovely dark brown face had smoothed out a little. He enveloped her in his usual hug – long and slow and happy. His eyes still glanced from doorway to ceiling each time a lodger moved invisibly above them, but he was much less jumpy. Something had changed. Something was better. Her heart lifted, and then Grandma swept Dad into her arms and the two of them got going, and the noise level in the kitchen increased and Ginika wanted to put her hands over her ears.

Her thoughts flew back to Peri. She imagined a lodger taking washing downstairs, finding Peri ... scaring Peri ... Peri suddenly recovering enough to take off through the back door and into the yard ... legs-together mud-skipping down Old Boundary Road. A loud burst of laughter from Dad pinged her ears and she did it – she put her hands over them.

'What's the matter with your ears, sweetheart?' Mum asked. 'And you're a bit pink around the gills ...'

'No I'm not,' Ginika said, feeling herself reddening even more.

'You're not sickening for something, are y—'

'I'm fine!'

Mum frowned at Grandma, who had an *I told you so* look about her that she was trying to squash, like one of her sneezes.

Dad made his fingers into steeples and looked over the top, eyes full of fun. 'She'll be dancing again soon enough.'

'No, Chidi,' Mum said, 'her eyes are all glazed over, see? Are you feeling all right, Ginika?'

'Course she is. Fit as a fiddle, aren't you, Ginki? She's just in shock. The surprise was too much for her – we materialised like magic! Like ghosts!'

Everyone laughed, but Ginika could only think of Peri. Grandma was fantastic at making people better. If only she could ask her. On the other side of her, Grandpa leaned in and winked, smelling of fresh soap. Quick as a flash, he built his meringues into a volcano and dropped peach slices on top, expecting Ginika to do the same, so that he could pretend not to notice hers while making even crazier scenes in his food, expecting her to copy. As she'd done for as long as she could remember. But she couldn't do it. When she picked up her fork to spear a peach, it trembled.

Grandpa sighed cheerfully and lifted the cream jug. He

was about to pour the contents over his volcano to make lava flow from a height, but Grandma stopped him with two words and a sharp shake of her head. 'Table drippage.'

Maybe there was a time limit on being away from the sea and close to electrical things … a time after which sea people *died*, and that was why Peri's family had been so insistent …

'No, she isn't listening,' Grandpa was saying.

Ginika blinked. 'What?'

Grandma swallowed her mouthful and banged the end of her spoon on the table. 'Oh my goodness, Ginika, your mum's asking you about exploring—'

'It doesn't matter, funny girl!' Mum said, laughing. 'I was just talking about how there are rooms in this house that I've never ever seen! Which is so weird when you think about it.'

Grandpa grinned. 'I've seen them all.'

Then Clawd bombed through the cat flap. Ginika ignored him when he trotted over and sniffed her madly, and when his sniffing turned into frantic lip-licking, she tried to distract him with a head stroke. But he angled his head so that his nose was level with her hands, and when she moved those away, he sniffed her legs. When she tucked her legs under her and away from him, he jumped on her lap, sniffing all the time, bristling and determined, as if no smell in his life so far had been as exotic and intriguing as this.

Grandma said, 'What on earth have you been into that Clawd can *still* smell? *Again?*'

'Nothing,' Ginika said, too quickly, making her eyes and mouth still and stiff so that they'd give nothing away.

Grandma folded her arms and continued to stare. The sun shone through the window behind her, catching the very edges of her hair with orange. She looked like a gentle firework. It felt like she was staring the information out of Ginika with her bare eyes.

'It must be something on the beach. I was playing with some seaweed, and ... let's think – what else?' Ginika listed all the sea creatures, and skeletons of sea creatures she'd ever seen. 'Dead seagull with no head – but I didn't touch that. Ugh! Crab skeletons – loads. About twenty jellyfish – blobby ones – but I didn't touch those – ouch! Seaweed. Old rope ...'

Nobody said anything. Clawd looked up from his sniffing into the silence, and met five pairs of eyes staring at him.

Then he sniffed the air and worked his way to the kitchen door in a stalking manner, slowly following his nose. He *scratched* and *scraped* at the door. Everyone except Ginika wailed 'CLAWD!' and Mum jumped up to let him out.

'I'll leave it open,' she said, while Clawd bolted down the cellar steps. 'Then he can come and go as he pleases.'

'He doesn't like to go out the same way he came in though,' Grandma said doubtfully. 'That's his trouble.'

But now Clawd just scratched and caterwauled at the laundry door. They all heard him. Ginika stood. Her heart hammered, but she saw an escape route and seized it. 'I'll see to him,' she said, and dived for the cellar steps.

But Grandma followed, and she was loud. 'CLAWD?' she called. 'Come here, my chubby-faced boy.'

'No, it's fine, Grandma – let me get him. I think I know what it is.'

Ginika was faster than Grandma. She let Clawd into the laundry room. Perhaps if he actually met Peri for a second, he'd calm down, and maybe even love him, like Dixon the dog had? Instantly, Clawd raced across the floor and worked his way into the tiny gap where Peri's cupboard door didn't quite close. He stopped next to Peri's trailer. All the fur along his head and back stood on end. A low warning growl came from his throat. Then he hissed, arched his back and scarpered back the way he'd come so fast he was a blur. Ginika followed.

The bangles on Grandma's wrists were clashing and jangling. She reached the middle of the stairs, saying, 'I'm going to wedge that laundry door open so that whatever he's after, he'll just get it and stop fussing. It's probably a mouse.'

At the beginning of Grandma's sentence, Clawd was hissing at Peri. By the end of it, he'd shot between Grandma's legs on the stairs.

'Clawd? What the blazes—' Grandma reached down to grab him, but she was too late. The cat flap in the front door rattled violently. He was gone. 'What's this?'

There was a pale yellow puddle on the step next to Grandma's legs. Grandma and Ginika looked at it, and Ginika felt her temperature rising again.

'He's wet himself!' Grandma said, horrified. 'How on earth can that have happened?'

'Don't know,' Ginika said, climbing the stairs again so that Grandma would follow her up, away from the laundry room. She wanted to cry for poor Clawd, but there wasn't time. 'He's gone out now, so maybe he couldn't wait? Maybe he forgot he needed a wee, got distracted … ? Anyway, I've *really* got to pop out now—'

'But … what did I tell you at the table before? *Not today*, Ginika!' Grandma turned to follow Ginika back up the stairs, completely perplexed.

'Promised to meet someone. Quick as I can, and when it's over it'll be finished. Tell them I won't be long. Please?'

Chapter 25

Ginika took less than a minute to skip down the front steps, race round the back of Cormorant Heights, skid into the yard and enter the laundry room without anyone seeing.

When she opened the cupboard, Peri was even worse. There was a white mark on his arm where it had been pressing against the side of the trailer. It looked like he'd been crying – there were white streaks on his cheeks. One hand rubbed his chest. The other still clutched the cushion. They didn't have long; Grandma might come looking for disinfectant to clean up after Clawd.

Clawd was nowhere in sight when Ginika pushed the bike and trailer out of the laundry room, but the lodger with the hidden dog came into the yard. He had a nervous smile on his face. Ginika smiled back and they passed each other without a word. It was now two thirty. Big things blew around on Old Boundary Road. Something old and rusted slid further down the wall it had been leaning against, and Ginika pedalled past it hard and fast.

Although she shrank from the thought of leaving Peri alone, she pushed the bike and trailer down the beach – a long way and then further still, to the quietest place possible – and rolled him out and into the shallows. She could hear her own heart beating and the rushing of her blood as she did it all, and the main place it seemed to be gathering and rushing was right next to her ears.

Peri lay with his legs in the water.

'You'll be able to move when the tide changes, won't you, Peri?' she said, to soothe herself.

The sea itself would cure him, wouldn't it? His eyes weren't telling her anything at all now.

'I wish you hadn't run away …'

If he'd never met her, would he even have got so curious about trying out this slower world?

'Get better,' she whispered, and stroked his arm. 'I have to go. I don't want to, but …' Her voice cracked and failed. Leaving him felt so wrong. His fingers burrowed into the wet sand. Clinging on.

Retracing her route along the beach was hard. She looked back at him a dozen times, and as distance made him smaller and smaller, she sobbed.

It was cooler now, and even windier. Along Shore Street,

222

clothes blew out tight and horizontal on washing lines. Branches whipped about wildly. Ginika pedalled hard. The cold grey sky looked clean, ready to blow everything away and start again.

Where Shore Street met Seagrove Passage, Scarlett stepped out of a shop doorway. Without smiling or saying hello, she grabbed the canvas cover on the trailer and flung it wide open. 'Where's your cat?'

'He didn't want to come today—'

'What are you up to?'

'What d'you mean?'

'I know you're hiding something.'

'No I'm not,' Ginika said, feeling her breathing getting raggedy, her heart speeding up.

'Why do you keep trying to dodge me?'

'I don't,' Ginika snapped. 'Why do you keep being *weird*?'

Scarlett's face went pink. 'Weird? *Me*?' She took hold of the bike's handlebars. 'I'll have this back now.'

'Fine.' Ginika turned away, but Scarlett pushed the bike in the same direction.

'Who was in the trailer just before? I saw you talking to someone in there when you rode to the beach. It couldn't have been your cat, otherwise where is he now?'

Ginika stopped walking. She looked at Scarlett's feet.

'You're doing something secret,' Scarlett said, before Ginika could get any words out.

'No, I just like talking to myself.'

Scarlett blinked quickly. 'Yeah, yeah, Ginika. Everyone totally believes you.' She sucked her teeth. And then her words came out fast, tumbling over each other: 'My dad says the far end of the beach is where people go when they're up to no good.'

Ginika walked off without looking back.

'Goodness me – you look as if you're all sharp corners now,' Grandma said in the kitchen doorway. 'What happened?' She reached over and straightened Ginika's top. 'Well, you're in for the treat of all treats now, honey pie!'

Dad was sitting at the kitchen table. Ginika came in properly and looked back at Grandma, who said, 'A night on the beach in the campervan!'

Dad winked. 'Got loads to sort out, Ginki.'

'Isn't that fantastic?' Grandma said.

Ginika nodded and smiled weakly. At almost any other time since she'd been at Cormorant Heights this summer and met Peri, it would have been, but Mum and Dad were crazy about the beach. They'd be in the sea, on the sand, in her face. For the first time in ages, adults would be able to see – easily – exactly where she went and what she did. How was she going to get out of their sight? Peri might need her help for hours … maybe all night.

Chapter 26

The beach. The sea beyond. And the campervan, parked in the special spot for beach camping in Bridleways Bay.

Mum and Dad insisted on making tea before they told her the big news. Cups clinked. Water bubbled. The campervan was still cramped, but that didn't seem to matter to them now. Mum sat down. Dad stayed on his feet. He gave off a bouncy feeling, and Ginika's heart caught it. She scanned Mum's face and saw all kinds of things in her eyes. Excitement was one of them. And plans. The rest were mysteries.

At first, she couldn't understand what they were saying. They were two talking mouths, taking it in turns, telling her a story that would change all their lives.

'Nothing we'd tried worked,' Dad said, 'and we tried so many things.'

Mum nodded sadly, adding, 'Didn't we just.'

'But now ...' Dad bent his knees and stretched both hands out to Mum, as though she was the star performer.

Mum sat up straighter and wriggled excitedly in her seat. 'I've found a new job!' She grinned, wide and toothy and delighted. 'And it comes with a little flat!'

Ginika was astonished. A flat? They couldn't afford a flat. She started to say so, but Dad held his hand up for her to wait. 'This flat is different,' he said. 'It comes with the job.'

Ginika was even more confused. Mum and Dad looked at each other, laughed softly and explained that the flat was included in Mum's wages. And, just like Ginika's bedroom in Cormorant Heights, this flat was called an 'annexe'. It was joined to the main house where Mum would be working. Mum and Ginika could live in this annexe, but not Dad. Dad was going to carry on sleeping in the campervan.

'Missed you far too much anyway, sweet,' Dad said, reaching over to stroke Ginika's head. 'And you weren't really coping at all, were you?' he said to Mum. Mum shook her head.

Ginika's breathing plummeted as Dad took over the telling. She forgot to breathe in and went dizzy. She focused on their mouths. The way the tip of Dad's tongue flashed in and out as he spoke. The way Mum's mouth kept wanting to grin and she stopped it, sometimes with her hands. Ginika was going back to London with them. They were going to turn things around. Everything had been worked out behind the scenes because, Mum said, 'We couldn't risk disappointing you again, Ginika.'

Then they talked about money that was missing and owing and hopeless, but they sounded hopeful. Triumphant. Winning. There had been a race, and they were doing better in it, so now Ginika could come back, join in, right *now*, just at the worst possible time.

Each new fact hit Ginika's brain ... *going back to London* ... and tightened her stomach ... *all of them together* ... but nothing would come out of her mouth.

Mum rubbed her hands together. 'So! We go back tomorrow. The new accommodation is tiny, but it's all set for us to move into – just you and me!'

The campervan fell weirdly silent. Ginika's hands were suddenly hot. 'Tomorrow?'

Dad sat down with a crash. 'We can see that you're not totally thriving here,' he said, squeezing Ginika's arm. 'We got it wrong.'

Mum let out a long, shuddery sigh.

'But now we're going to get it right,' Dad said. 'Your gramps warned us that starting secondary school here would be a struggle for you.'

'So I might be able to start school properly, with everyone else? With *Alisha?*'

'Not just *might*, Ginki – you *will!*'

Ginika focused on the clouds rushing past the window behind Dad's head, billowing in a high wind she couldn't hear. A few weeks ago, this would have been amazing. A dream come true. But now there was Peri. He was ill. He was her friend. And he couldn't come to London with her.

And it wasn't just Peri – it was everything else about Bridleways Bay. It was the beach, the gulls, the sea – swimming looked like it might be just as much fun as dancing, if she could only get brave enough. Suddenly, Ginika saw everything so clearly: Mum and Dad had realised how wrong they were to send her here at the exact moment when *she'd* realised they'd been partly right. Most of her worries and dreads about leaving London just hadn't come true.

She tried to imagine the new London place. A flat joined to a job? How? Would there still be shopping vouchers, and stupid credit cards appearing in the bin, cut straight across their middles? 'But … ?'

They laughed. Mum said, 'Look at her face!' and puckered her lips for a kiss. 'Let's have your hair down,

Ginika.' She unrolled Ginika's bun. 'Wow, it's grown so much! I've missed doing your beautiful hair. Right, so … the job is looking after two little boys. One has just started school and the other is a sweet little one-year-old. It's not far from the beach near Shadwell Basin!'

'Beach?'

'Well, you know – it's still the river, but there are rocks, and it's sandy and smooth. Canary Wharf is just across the water. It's lovely. You'll love it. And I want to hear you start giggling again, Ginika.'

'Giggling?' Dad said. 'She can giggle all right.'

'When did you last hear her giggle?'

Dad said nothing.

Ginika thought of yesterday, in the shallows with Ted and Peri, when they'd just laughed and laughed forever. Suddenly, appallingly, Ginika knew she was going to cry. She tried to block it, but that made a snot bubble shoot from her nose and she scrabbled for a tissue and Mum flapped and stroked and pulled her close for a hug, but she looked close to bursting into tears herself. Dad looked worried and they both soothed and fussed Ginika some more, and that made more ridiculous tears pour from her eyes.

'Does this mean the trouble has all disappeared?' Ginika asked when she was calmer.

They looked at each other. Dad sighed. 'There is still trouble around, but we're managing it.'

'How can you manage trouble?'

'It's debt.' He made the word sound like soupy grey slop you could slip into. Drown in.

Ginika felt dazed. 'Debt? That can't be the whole trouble. Are you … ? Have you done something?'

Dad didn't answer. He stretched out his hands and rubbed them over his whole face.

'What have you done?' Ginika's voice was louder than she'd meant it to be. Her seat was smooth and wooden, the soft cushion slippery if it wasn't positioned properly. It took an effort not to slowly slide right down to the floor.

'It's not like that, Ginki,' Dad said. 'We've made bad choices – but it's mostly me. *I've* done it.'

Mum looked down at the table.

'I knew …' Ginika breathed.

'There are people called loan sharks and I've borrowed money. Not too much at first, but they add interest until your debt gets bigger and bigger.'

Ginika had been fiddling with a teaspoon but stopped when Dad said 'sharks'.

'I'm in over my head and they're hounding me. Us. Trying to take away what little we've got.' Dad and Mum looked at each other in a slightly ashamed way that Ginika recognised. 'We have to move this van to a new spot every single night.'

Ginika said, 'Sharks?'

The word had electrified the room. Everyone held their cup as if hands needed warming, even Ginika with her glass of water.

'Yep,' Dad said. 'Not like the ones in the sea. In fact, this type give the ones in the sea a bad name.'

Ginika's eyes widened. She felt weightless, like she might drift up to the ceiling, and if she went outside, would blow away. So that was the trouble. Debt. Sharks that gave you money, then wanted it back fast.

'Wasn't there anywhere else to get money from?'

Dad looked down. Mum came to his rescue. 'We tried *everything*. These people get you when you're desperate. That's what they feed on.'

Mum looked half amazed, as if something she thought she was handling had just blown up bigger than her wildest dreams. As if this was actually a film, not her life. Sadness washed through Ginika. No wonder they'd been quiet. Lying low. Human sharks had been feeding on their desperation. Eating their sadness. Snapping at their misery with big, knife-edged teeth. She thought of Peri and her stomach turned over.

Dad lifted her chin with his finger. 'You OK?'

Ginika shook her head, then nodded.

Her worry for Peri was growing and growing. She felt like it might burst her. And all the colours everywhere were loud and sharp and shocking.

Chapter 27

Early evening. Ginika slipped out to check on Peri by pretending she had to tell friends her big news.

'Don't be too late then,' Mum said.

Dad came to the door of the campervan and watched her leave. 'Your shoes don't look right.'

Ginika looked down. She'd put her beach shoes on the wrong feet. The big, silly grin she gave Dad felt wrong immediately. It wobbled and slid straight off her face. She quickly stooped to sort out her shoes, but Dad looked curious.

She hurried away, patting all the bottles in her swim buoy nervously. Grandma's liver salts were diluted in one water bottle, another contained plain tap-water and one more was filled with seawater, because she still wasn't sure which was best for Peri. She also carried a long-sleeved T-shirt for him just in case, because things were getting cooler, and the other one might be turning stale. Although the wind had dropped, she was glad of her coat.

But Dad wasn't far behind. She sensed him, looked back, and soon his long, loping strides caught her up. His eyes were thoughtful, but he still looked overjoyed with himself. Keeping secrets from him cramped her insides. She swallowed.

'What's up, Ginki? Got some seagulls to aggravate as well? You look like you're going on night manoeuvres.'

'What are those?'

'Army stuff. Soldiering.' Dad examined her face. 'You look petrified. Is something going on?'

'No, it's … just my friend. They're not very well.'

Dad's eyes widened for a heartbeat. 'Oh dear. Can I help?'

'No, they're shy – I can't …' She panicked, searching her wits for a diversion. 'Are you … ? Will you be able to get another job like your old one now?'

'Who knows?'

Dad's steps matched hers.

'Don't you miss mending all that stuff?' she asked. Her brain wouldn't work. She needed to get away cleanly and innocently.

'I miss the special machines in laboratories,' Dad said. 'I don't miss climbing into ventilation shafts.'

'Oh. Well, at least you get a free van with this job.'

'Huh.'

She stopped talking to see if that worked.

It didn't. He chatted about the move. The new start. Getting on to the motorway early in the morning, beating the traffic, squashing all Ginika's belongings back into the campervan again for the journey.

She stopped beside a twist of wood and a piece of unrecognisable plastic on the tideline and wiggled her legs awkwardly. 'Um … you can't come with me.'

Dad frowned.

'It's top secret!'

He laughed, but carried on walking in stride with her. Suddenly, she knew exactly what to say to lose him. 'What do loan sharks do to people?'

Dad's face changed.

'Do they, like, come to find you like those men in that film where they kidnapped him and beat him up and set traps in his car and—'

'Ginki, I don't want you having nightmares. It's almost all in hand now. And anyway, it's not like that.' But his face made it look as though what she'd said wasn't too crazy.

'Don't be too long, OK?' he said, and doubled back towards the campervan.

Ginika hurried along the beach. A night bird made a soft, sad call in the dunes. She could hear her own breathing, and it was fast. A bit ragged. As she came closer to the waves, their sound made everything a little bit better: in and out, breaking over and over, always.

Slap-slop-slap.

An oystercatcher cheeped, and another answered it. She'd never felt so alone.

He'll be better, she told herself. *The sea will have had time to cure him by now. He'll have needed something from it that he just wasn't getting on land, and now he'll be fine. Back to normal now. Fine-all-fine-all-fine …*

Peri had been moved by the water, but he wasn't better. He didn't even notice her arriving. His reflexes must be really … out of order. And what about his hearing?

'Peri?'

Water seeped into one of his ears and she heaved him further on to the sand. Her hands were shaking. What if his eyesight was next? What if he was permanently damaged? There'd be no more storm swimming. Her head spun.

'Peri, we need to contact your family.'

Peri murmured. His breathing was fast. Every so often, there was a long, deep and shaky breath that sucked his stomach in under his ribs. Then it would start again – short, fast breaths. A long, trembling one. And again, and on and on. His hair wasn't sea-coloured. Its texture was strawlike, the colour still muddy.

He'd been hunched into a tight curve, but now he slackened and the waves pushed him over and dragged him back. Push … and drag, just like when they'd all been in the sea yesterday, but it wasn't soothing or funny any more. A bubble of dread seemed to be lodged in Ginika's throat. What if a predator came?

The sea hadn't cured him. Her mind raced back to her earlier thoughts about electricity, and how living in the sea must be so very different from living on land. She remembered how her phone had affected his eyes. What happened when he looked at the lamp-post up close. Electrical stuff was all over the house. *Especially* in the laundry room. The washing machines. The lights … What if she was right and it really was the electricity itself that had caused this? Then she remembered the sea people swimming through that storm. Lightning didn't hurt them. But maybe our electricity was different; maybe it was toxic.

The waves swirled around him, endlessly overlapping.

'Peri,' she tried again. 'How do we contact your family? How do we do the call?'

She lifted his head and dribbled the liver-salt water over his lips. Some went in his mouth, but not much. There was a faint smell about him now, something that reminded her of turpentine, like the bottle in Grandpa's shed. That couldn't be a good sign. There was a sheen on his forehead too. It didn't look like the normal sweaty forehead of someone ill. It looked bubbly, as though gases were filtering out through his skin.

She had to get him somewhere safer, shallower, where he'd still be in the water, but the tide wouldn't pull him away. She thought of the seagrass meadows beyond the caravan park. He could rest on the seagrass – it would be like a mattress for him – and the plants should anchor him a little. Then he could make that alarm call. Of course! That might be where Peri's family came to feast on all the creatures that hid between the stalks anyway. It made sense to call them from there – she'd have to move him.

Either that or tell Mum. Dad. Hand everything over to them.

But they'd call an ambulance. Then Peri would go to hospital. And hospitals were full of our electricity – he'd get even worse.

She looked at his legs, his poorly skin and reflective hair that wasn't reflecting any more. How would they know what to do with him? How would he ever get back to the sea? But if he was on land any longer, he would die – she was sure of it.

She had to try and get him to the seagrass meadows.

That would mean going past the campervan, which was horrifically risky. If Mum and Dad were looking out to sea … But she had no choice. She'd just have to cling to the hope that they were still inside. Washing up. Making more plans. Her stomach fluttered and cramped.

She called Ted, but he didn't answer, so she messaged him. *Are you back yet? Peri's really ill.*

No reply. She was on her own, but she had to at least try.

She took off her trousers and coat and stuffed them into the swim buoy. Her shoes would be fine in the water. Then she pulled Peri further into the sea to let the water take his weight, and began to push him along, trying not to think of the distance. The swim buoy helped. He clutched her arms, but nothing else about him seemed to know what was going on. It was as if his hands were following a reflex.

Passing through the busy part of the beach was horrible. She had to go deeper into the sea in case anyone saw the state Peri was in. Noise was everywhere, blotting out some of the slap and the slosh of the waves. One boy stared. And three horses were coming – she could see their tails swishing in the distance, and their riders' bright yellow jackets. But as they grew closer, slowed down and started to toss their heads and snort and whinny, the staring boy lost interest in Ginika and Peri, and focused on the horses.

And then there was the campervan. Mum and Dad sat

in front of it on the beach chairs from Grandpa's shed. They held wine glasses. Mum's lips moved, and Dad was looking at her. Their chairs were angled towards each other, not facing the sea, so ... there was a chance. She might be able to slip past. Ginika took a deep breath and did the one thing she hated above most other things: she tucked her head underwater.

At first, visions from the accident rushed at her as the seawater flooded her ears, and she panicked and surfaced immediately. But it was still very shallow. She told herself there was no danger. She tried to focus, gritted her teeth, breathed deeply, took a few more steps and forced herself under. Head pounding, eyes stinging when she opened them, she pushed Peri along from below, so that he looked like someone peacefully floating. He couldn't come down here with her – his breath-holding reflexes might not be working. Greenish light filtered through the water. Other people's legs looked closer than they should, and brighter. Her legs had to bend like a frog's to stay underwater, and that was hard. But being hidden felt good. Safer. Better than she'd feared.

When she surfaced further up the beach, it was emptier. There were cars in the car park, and people in them, but they were quiet. Nobody came out.

She felt like a fizzing mass of trouble and secrets.

Chapter 28

This beach was never-ending. Beyond the wind turbines, it continued down the coast further than she could see using Grandpa's binoculars, and when she was small, that had seemed magical: the edge of the world.

Pushing on. To their right, solid, ripply imprints of the waves had set in the sand. The underwater sand was more like mud now. It oozed over her toes. Another step and her heels sank too. Progress was slow and she felt heavier than she should. Things felt unreal and too real all at once, and when her favourite type of wading bird made its usual call – a sweet clacking sound – she flinched.

Pushing Peri wasn't working any more. *Pull*, she told herself. *Just pull*. She squeezed her eyes shut and did just that, ignoring the pain in her hands, her shoulder.

Then the mud became shallow seagrass meadows. Soft.

Slippery, but luscious against her feet. Mushy submerged sand to burrow down in. She looked around. Further still, things got craggy enough for shipwrecks – the rocks jutted right out into the sea, and you couldn't walk round them, even when the tide was out. She stopped to think. He would be more comfortable here while they made the call.

She let go of Peri and he sank gently on to the velvet-soft plants. The water hissed as it swept through them, releasing an eggy smell. Nearby, wading birds carried out their long-legged business. She emptied the swim buoy out on to the sand, towelled herself dry, pulled on her trousers and shrugged back into her coat. Her soaking T-shirt felt horrible beneath it. Her shoes stuck to her not-quite-dry-enough feet, and rubbed.

Peri's breathing was quieter now. Too quiet? His stillness was worrying. She shook him gently, but he didn't wake.

'Peri!'

She shook him again, leaning over his bone-pale face, sobbing his name. His body went wherever she pushed it without resistance. She sat back on her heels, panic squeezing her lower stomach. Mum. She needed Mum. She stood, ready to run – when Peri's head moved.

His eyes half opened.

'Peri! I've got to get help. I've got to leave you.'

'Meeb-*click*-saahhg …' His voice was throaty, deep. He took hold of her hand weakly.

Ginika looked around. Mum would know what to do, but there would be an ambulance and hospital. 'We need your family, Peri. Your parents.'

Peri groaned.

'They'll know what to do. They'll make you better. Call them, Peri. Make the alarm call.' She did the alarm mime.

Peri licked his lips. The pink dots on his face had joined to form a darker rash. His nose was runny.

He waved his arm towards the headland. He said the word for 'sea cave', the one made mostly from clicks.

'No, *here*. Call from here.' She slapped the sand with the flat of her hand and did the alarm-call mime again. 'Here. Now.'

He shook his head. He waved towards the headland. '*Click. Click-click. Click-click.*' He waved again. Ginika started to wail. 'But you can't get all the way round to the sea cave! Not like this …'

His head slumped back to the sand.

'Not by yourself. I'll have to take you.'

The row of boats bobbed in the shallows back where the seagrass meadows began. All of them wore *Bridleways Bay Caravan Park* nameplates. It wasn't as secret and hidden as she'd have liked. The boats were attached by rope to a big iron thing buried in the sand. She felt as if she ought to know the name of that thing.

It looked easy. The boats were already in the water, so just needed untying. How hard could that be? She set to work. The rope was thick and coiled in some kind of crazy puzzle. When she tried to pull it one way, the whole thing snaked and tightened lower down. All the boats glugged and clinked together, and the boat she wanted bobbed as stubbornly as ever. If she could just cut it free …

She glanced around for something sharp. Back at the campervan there were knives and scissors. And Mum and Dad – they would be fretting about where she'd got to. But she couldn't think about that now. She looked at Peri. No time.

Ted surely had to be home from his trip and back at the caravan park by now? It was almost seven. She phoned again, but there was still no answer. Perhaps his phone was on silent, or he was so grounded that they'd taken it away from him.

Ginika stood up, dithered, and stared at her phone again, close to tears. The panic was now in her chest. Her throat. She pulled at the rope with all her strength, made it worse, kicked it, and sobbed.

A message beeped in and she jumped.

Ted: *Where are you?*

Chapter 29

A trio of gulls swooped from the sky on a tilt, landed close by and went straight into a stalking, confident swagger, looking for food opportunities, as if they always controlled this end of the beach.

Ted had left his chair underneath the wheelchair ramp. He walked across the sand slowly and carefully and was panting by the time he reached Peri, but asked lots of awkward questions about safety and doctors and parents. Questions full of doubt. Questions that made Ginika's heart race and her voice quiver.

'But how d'you know about the parents? How will they know where to find him?'

Ginika explained about all Peri's mimes, the magazines – everything. Ted looked impressed, but super alert, like a hunter. It was strange to see him looking serious. His bottom lip was tense and straight. He kept darting worried glances at Peri.

'How come he's ill? What's he got? What's happened?'

Ginika pulled at her hair. 'I don't know. Maybe I shouldn't have taken him inside the house.'

'Why?'

Ginika shrugged. 'I think the electricity did something to him. Washing machines, the lights, maybe even my phone.'

'Technology wrecks birds' navigation systems,' Ted said. 'We did it at school.'

'He's not a bird.'

'No, but I bet he's got a navigation system. I'd better come with you.'

'No! You're supposed to be recovering.'

'Nah – I'm allowed out of the chair more and more every day. Had hours out this morning. I'm fine.'

Ginika looked at the plaster on his hand, which now had a little tube sticking out of it. 'Do you have to go back to hospital?'

Ted followed her eyes to his hand. 'It's for night-time stuff to go in. Won't be for much longer.'

'But we might get wet.'

'Ha! D'you think? In a *boat*? If you can't get the boat out in the first place, how you gonna get it back, by yourself?'

Ginika swallowed. Doubt washed over her again, as if it had only ever been hiding and waiting. She cleared her throat and mumbled something about managing.

'You look guilty already,' Ted said. 'Act like we're supposed to be here.'

Ginika picked up the rope again. 'How do we get this loose?'

'You don't,' said a horribly familiar voice from the trees. Scarlett. Angry. Flustered. Hair wild from running.

She stopped in front of them. Her rapidly blinking eyes switched between Peri and Ginika, then settled on Peri's strange legs. His cheek was flat to the wet sand. His limp hair covered his face, but didn't match the sand at all now.

'Who's he?' Scarlett spoke through her teeth. They were clenched. Her whole body was clenched. She was like a furious, contained firework.

Ted and Ginika said nothing.

'What do you think you're doing?' She looked at Ted, snapped, 'Wondered where you were going on your own,' then pulled out her phone and began tapping the screen. 'I'm telling my dad, but what gives you the right to just take a boat, after everything I've done for you, everything I've given up for you—'

'*What?*'

Scarlett stuck out her chin. 'I've said no to stuff. I could have gone places with the Olivias, but you weren't invited, so I made space for you instead, and then you just sneak—'

'How is that my fault?' Ginika said. 'Didn't ask you to.'

'I wanted to make things fun so you'd forget you'd all been thrown out of your house, but you were spiky and nothing was ever good enough. Like you'd rather be anywhere else—'

'I was homesick!'

They glared at each other, both breathing hard as the evening air cooled. Ted hunched over Peri, dribbling bottled water over his forehead.

'And you've never been even the tiniest bit grateful for me trying so hard to hang out so you had a friend,' Scarlett continued, pulling at her fingers. 'I don't *do anything* to deserve being left out, but that's all you ever do.' She turned to Ted. '*He's* on holiday in *my* park, so what's he even doing with you?'

Hot anger rushed to Ginika's head. 'Why should I be grateful because you felt *sorry* for me?'

Scarlett echoed Ginika in a mocking way. 'W*oi* should *oi* be grateful.'

'See, that's exactly it! *That's* what you do! You're mean to people!'

'And what about what *you* do to people?'

'I don't do anything,' Ginika said after a deep breath that was supposed to give her strength. Her lips trembled, letting her down.

'Yes you *do*! You're a total dodger, a sneak and a liar. You tell lie after lie after lie.'

'You're exaggerating every single thing—'

'I am *not*! Anyway,' she spat, 'you'll be sorry soon.'

'What do you mean?'

Ted looked up. 'This is stupid,' he said.

Ginika couldn't look at him. Scarlett said, 'Why do you hate me?'

Shocked, Ginika said, 'I don't.' There was a silence, so she said, 'But you've been the most horrible friend I've ever had. You've said *awful* things to me! You've bossed me around all over this town as if you're the queen of the whole place. You only care about yourself and you love making other people feel bad.' Scarlett started to shake her head, and opened her mouth to deny it all, but Ginika jabbed a finger in front of her face to stop her. The unfairness of everything felt like hot needles in her neck and she snapped. 'You're *always* in my face. Always in my business. Ordering me to do whatever you've decided is the law that day. Your law! Your rules! Nobody else is allowed to choose. Everywhere I go, there you are, just—'

Scarlett dipped her head and her hair fell over her face. 'That's what my sister says.'

Ginika had been going to say, *there you are, just like an annoying wasp*, but she listened instead.

'Mum and Dad say Eve's just going through a bad teenage phase and she's got no patience,' Scarlett said, 'but she only speaks to me when she feels like picking on someone.'

Ginika bit her lip.

'We used to do stuff together, but now we don't.'

'Oh.'

'She says I keep pushing and pushing and won't take no for an answer … and so she has to get nasty.' Scarlett's voice was getting higher and louder. 'And I *make* her like that, she says.' She was trying not to cry, and sucked in a great gulp of air. 'And the Olivias are just using me for the park equipment – that's what she says. Every day.'

'What do your mum and dad say?'

Scarlett peered through her hair. 'They used to say it would pass. But it's been months. She laughs at me any chance she gets.'

Ginika thought of Alisha, and the way she seemed to be drifting away now that they were separated by all those miles.

'Don't tell anyone.'

'I won't,' Ginika said. 'I won't.' She said it again because it was better than saying nothing, and Scarlett was really going to cry now. Normally, she'd hug someone who was crying, but Scarlett's tears didn't actually come out. It looked like they were stuck. Behind her, the wild sea beckoned. The sea that Peri needed so much.

Ted murmured something to Peri, but his glances still slid between Ginika and Scarlett. 'His breathing's really raggedy, you know,' he said.

Ginika sagged against the boat and looked at Scarlett. 'But why didn't you tell me any of that?'

Scarlett shrugged. There was another silence. Then Ted said, 'Long breath.'

Ginika crouched close to Peri and Ted, listening to Peri's breathing, and now *she* began to cry, silently. She let the tears fall without wiping them, as though they were just raindrops.

'I'm sorry,' she said to Scarlett. The word still felt wrong in her mouth. She hadn't asked for any of Scarlett's bad behaviour, but she swallowed her feelings down. 'I wish none of it had happened.' Her own voice sounded clogged and throaty. Her tears blurred Scarlett, Ted and even Peri into faceless shapes.

Scarlett picked at the skin around her fingernails. 'You don't really mean it.'

'I do …'

'Yeah, no – you just want me to help you get him out to sea.'

Ginika's heart leaped. 'I mean it. I *am* sorry. But *will* you help us? Could you?'

'Why should I when you've pushed me out of everything all summer?'

Ted cut in: 'We don't have time for this. He looks proper poorly, so decide fast.'

His voice was sharp and Scarlett looked startled. Then her expression turned to curiosity and she looked at Peri. At the hollows under his eyes. At the way his chest moved up and down so quickly. 'Why not just call an ambulance instead?' She looked from Ginika to Ted, her eyes suddenly brimming with suspicion again. 'You two are out of control. My dad could sort out an ambulance for him – this isn't right—'

'They might not know what to do for him,' Ted said quickly. 'His own people are best for that. He's …' He glanced at Ginika, who nodded at him through watery eyes. 'He's not like anyone you've ever known. He just needs his family.'

Scarlett stared. 'So tell me all about him.'

Ginika cleared her throat. While Scarlett scanned her face, she squashed everything she knew about Peri into a few short sentences.

'What? So he's not human?'

'I ... don't really know. I think ... he's another type of human that lives in the sea.'

'Humans can't live in the sea.'

'But sea people can. There are whole families of them out there, hidden. They're camouflaged. They're clever.'

Scarlett let out a disbelieving snort. 'Clever enough to make him better? As clever as doctors? You two are crazy.'

Ted's temper snapped. With a growl of exasperation, he hauled himself up to begin working on the knotted rope himself. 'Look,' he said. 'We *have* to do this. He needs to get back out there *right now* – it's pointless waiting for ambulances and doctors. Things are different when you live in the sea. Stuff gets weird; octopuses have three hearts and blue blood!' He glared at Scarlett. 'We don't know what Peri's like on the inside, so how will any doctor know what they're doing with him? You can either help us, or you can stand there arguing while he gets even worse.'

This seemed to make an impression on Scarlett, because although her mouth remained in a straight, sullen line, her eyes looked more thoughtful and interested. She seemed almost convinced.

The sun was getting lower. The sky glowed orange with streaks of thin white cloud.

For a while, Scarlett fixed her eyes on Ted's determined pulling and untwisting as he wrestled with the rope. Then she crossed her arms and said, 'You could have brought him to the splash park.' Her voice was flat. 'Anyway, you must know more about these sea people than that.'

Ginika jumped on the sand in frustration. 'There isn't *time* now!' Sweaty with panic, she wanted to snatch at Scarlett and pull her hair. 'Please, Scarlett. *Please* help us. I couldn't risk bringing him to your caravan park. You weren't acting like a real friend back then.'

Scarlett looked at Ted, down at Peri, then back to Ginika. 'OK then. I'll help.' Her voice was low and raspy, but full of regret.

Ginika let out a long sigh. This was probably the closest Scarlett would ever come to saying sorry.

Scarlett stood taller and looked out over the sea in a businesslike way. 'But if you're still keeping secrets ...'

Chapter 30

Scarlett was bossy – 'Life jackets on! Yes …' She looked at Peri. 'Him too' – and did baffling things to get the boat free. The rope holding the boats together was as thick as her arm in places, but Scarlett manipulated it as if it was her shoelace.

'You're quick at this,' Ginika said, throwing her coat into the boat.

A wild look flashed on to Scarlett's face, as if she was the only sensible person on a planet of fools. 'We go sea-fishing all the time,' she muttered.

A splintering sound, a small grunt from Scarlett and the boat was free. Gulls called to each other high above. Ted climbed in, and Ginika and Scarlett lifted Peri up to him. The boat went down and stuck.

Scarlett shoved and grunted. 'It'll come right in a sec. This happens.'

Ginika and Scarlett pushed. The boat moved a little. Ginika took a deep breath to calm herself, and started to climb in.

'Hey, not yet!' Scarlett said. 'I can't push all three of you. Wait. Push further.'

They pushed, waded, pushed. The seagrass moved gently against their ankles. The water deepened. Ginika felt a current pulling the boat out of their hands. Her chest was tight and didn't seem to be taking in air properly. She wanted to stop. Go back.

Scarlett said, 'Why are you breathing like that?'

'I don't like the water – I can't ...'

'What? Don't be a freak-out! What's up with you?'

'Had a boat accident. Went upside down in Cornwall when I was eight. Nearly drowned.'

Scarlett looked at her – eyes wide – then looked away. 'What kind of boat?'

'Bigger than this.'

The sea was like a dark blue-grey blanket now. Plants from the seagrass meadows were getting stuck between Ginika's toes. Something wriggled against her heel. She stifled a scream.

'Keep pushing,' Scarlett said. 'We have to get beyond the meadows before we can row.'

Ginika checked Peri. His eyes were still closed. She

shivered. The saltwater was tingly and fizzy on her arms, and her wet trousers were now welded to her legs.

Scarlett was looking at her. 'We're in a millpond,' she said. 'Nothing to be scared of.'

'What's a millpond?'

'She means it's calm as anything,' Ted said. 'Whaa-hey!' he added quietly, looking admiringly at a clear ribbon of water that flowed out to the front and side of the boat with its own definite direction.

Ginika could feel a current pulling the boat out of their hands as the water deepened. It was so strong, darker than ever before, and felt like it might contain things that weren't there earlier. There were definitely shapes, weren't there? Shadows. Something with a sideways movement? The water was like a monster ready to attack. The waves were choppy. Her chin got splashed.

Ginika panicked. The sea crept higher. Soon, it would come for her in great waves and her screams would all be in bubbles. A wave splashed her in the face, and she didn't blink in time. Her eyes stung. There seemed to be no air in her lungs. What if a giant Atlantic roller swelled up out there and rolled them right over? Were those real, or just something Grandma made up to keep her away from danger? She'd never seen one. She asked Scarlett.

'Course! All the time,' Scarlett said. 'They're mega!

They're brilliant, they heave up and then hurl …' Scarlett saw Ginika's expression and stopped. 'But they mostly come in October. We won't see one today.'

Ginika realised the water was still only just over their knees.

'The tide's coming in,' Scarlett said confidently.

'Is that good?' Ginika asked. Her voice sounded like someone else's. Tight. Flattened. In the swim buoy attached to her waist, her phone buzzed. Probably Mum or Dad.

'It means it's gonna be hard as anything to get out there, but we'll be safer. Go on, you first.'

'Out there? How far? Because the sea caves are over there—'

'We can't get there by going around the rocks, you numbskull – we'd get bashed to pieces. Gonna have to row out to sea then come in again.'

'How far?'

Scarlett pointed to the big boat that was always anchored way, *way* out from the beach. Past every single buoy. 'That's as far as I'm allowed.'

Ginika froze. 'But that's miles!'

'It's probably not even *half* a mile. Come on, Ginika!'

Ginika lifted one knee. Lunging, lifting herself off and up and into the boat seemed impossible. She darted a panicked glance at Peri and Ted in the boat. It felt like they could tip out. She let out a little scream, lost her footing and flailed.

Scarlett positioned herself close to Ginika's face and gripped her arm. 'It's fine, it's fine. Just keep trying. It's often like this.'

Ginika's feet slipped again. The sand was too soft; she was sinking. She *knew* how quickly you could be swept away and drowned, she *knew* the pull of the current was unbeatable – and you wouldn't just stay afloat, because people didn't. Couldn't. Grandpa had talked of waves as high as houses and how, if dragged out to sea, it wouldn't be long before you'd *have* to take a breath, and then the water would rush in …

Scarlett was talking. Her face was close and grinning. The talk was of silly things that didn't matter and which Ginika couldn't make sense of anyway. And although Scarlett's hair was now tied back, her ponytail swished constantly, always there, always annoying. Like a clever, sharp-beaked bird, she *kept on* yakking and it didn't matter how frightened Ginika was – Scarlett wouldn't stop. 'Push,' she said, between sentences. 'Push. Now we can get in.'

The fear subsided a little, chased away by Scarlett's chatter. She held the boat steady for Ginika. Balancing was needed. Ginika was a dancer. She could balance. She closed her eyes and leaped aboard.

Chapter 31

Rowing. Oars moving, but getting them nowhere. Scarlett in charge, face strained taut. It was surely impossible. Scarlett's gasping battle with the oars made it seem so.

Peri no longer held on to anything. The reflex in his hands must have disappeared, and they flopped loosely beside his body.

And then suddenly, the sea seemed calmer. They were moving. They were powering the boat themselves. Leaving the oystercatchers behind.

Scarlett began to teach Ted how to row. 'It's gonna be hard,' she said, still out of breath. 'We're rowing against the tide.'

Ted struggled. Grunted. Every single movement took all his strength, as if he was pulling the oars through thick treacle.

'Harder than it looks, isn't it,' Scarlett said. 'And this is a millpond. Imagine what it's like when the sea's normal.'

But Ted was enjoying himself. Rowing must have been straining his back horribly, and Ginika didn't like to think what it might be doing to the part of his spine that was supposed to be healing, yet despite all that, his effortful, concentrating face looked alive and glowing. He wanted to take the risk. Beyond him, two hopeful gulls rode the waves, watching the boat for scraps. Ginika focused on keeping Peri comfortable. His head rested on a plastic sheet she'd found rolled up on the bottom of the boat next to spare oars and life jackets. Her coat was now his blanket. Sometimes his eyes half opened, gleaming darkly like pools of oil.

The sky was huge now. The boat lurched to the left for no reason Ginika could see and as Scarlett leaped to correct it, a surge of fear reared up again. What if this didn't work? What if Scarlett and Ted were risking everything for nothing? She looked at Scarlett, busy watching the waves, checking the boat's direction. Sudden tears sprang into her eyes at the thought of what Scarlett was doing for her, and for Peri, who she hardly even knew. And Ted – what if his back got soaked? What would happen to him?

Scarlett glanced at Peri. Then she fixed her eyes on

Ginika. 'Is he a person or a fish?'

'What are you talking about? He's a person, of course. He just lives in the sea.'

'His feet are like paddles.'

'Not really,' Ginika said, frowning.

'Yeah, that's it,' Scarlett said to Ted. 'You've got it perfect now. Pull that side round more.' She turned back to Ginika. 'Why are his family missing? Where have they been?'

Ginika explained.

'How do they never stop moving? How could anyone even do that?'

Ginika realised she was still being calmed down. Scarlett was never going to stop talking. She sighed. 'I think they stick together. There are lots of them, because he showed me things that meant "lots of eyes". So they keep a look-out all the time. And he's really fast, so maybe their adults are even faster. Anyway, it must work, because there he is.'

'But moving all the time. Waaaa … ! Are you sure you got that right? Ginika, if he doesn't speak English, you could have got everything completely wrong and we don't know if we should even be doing this …'

Ted shook his head. 'They've got a good thing going with mimes and signals. They know what each other means. It's right enough.'

'Yeah? Oh. OK.' Scarlett sucked the ends of her pony-tail. 'Whoa. It's all super freaky!' She sounded like an adult trying to keep things jolly.

'It isn't freaky,' Ginika said firmly. 'It's just another way of living, that's all. And you're being a bit rude again.'

'OK, I didn't mean ...' Scarlett rested her chin in her hands. 'Could be fun, I suppose, when you think about it,' Scarlett said. 'Tiring though. Moving all the time.'

Nobody said anything. The need to make things funny and fizzy was stretched across Scarlett's determined face. 'But then you'd never have trouble getting to sleep,' she said. 'You'd be *weary*.'

Ted whistled long and low. 'Yeah ... whoa. But no pillow!'

Ginika told them about floating on rafts of sargassum seaweed, and the kelp forests and how floaty and comfortable everything sounded, and Scarlett's eyes stretched wide.

There was the big boat – their limit. She hadn't seen it move all summer. The sails – always so brilliant white when viewed from the beach – were splotched with grey stains.

'OK, now your turn, Ginika,' Scarlett said. 'You're going to learn how to row!'

'No, I'm fine—'

 263

'Sit *there*. Hold them like this.'

'But what if I—'

'You can't lose them – that's what the rowlocks are for, see?' Scarlett tapped the brackets that held the oars in place, and Ginika took her deepest breath of all.

Chapter 32

Ginika found that she could make the oars work, and doing that – exactly as Scarlett had shown her – made everything stop churning. It was hard. She needed every ounce of strength from all over her body, and she was soon out of breath. But it felt good, pulling the boat through the water. It was rhythmic, and it felt like real progress.

Ted brought a packet of crisps out of his pocket. 'Cheese and onion?' he said quietly.

Scarlett took one. Ginika rowed without stopping, as though she might never stop. One of the gulls on the water turned its head. Then there were three, then four, but she didn't see where they came from. Scarlett launched into a fishing story about being followed by gulls when she was with her dad, and Ginika half listened, rowed, thought about how her wet bottom couldn't dry off without the warm sun, and rowed and rowed.

Ted carped and teased and picked at Scarlett, but quickly realised that she liked arguing, so gave up. Then Scarlett interrogated him. She found out that he lived near Birmingham, loved music, football and everything to do with space and the universe, hated custard and had one older brother. She asked him why he was using a wheelchair, and why he'd been in hospital, and when he told her about his spinal tumour she asked a dozen more nosy questions about that, easily and without even the tiniest hesitation.

When Ted paused for breath, Scarlett suddenly said, 'No further than this. Stop, Ginika.'

The cave was in sight – a dark hollow tucked inside the rocks – but looked as far away as they had already travelled. Ginika let the oars rest. The wind was getting up again. The crests of some of the waves were foamy with Grandma's white horses. She tapped a text in to Mum, telling her that she had lots more goodbyes to say and would try not to be too late. Her phone signal was hardly there.

'Tide should just carry us back easily, but ... don't know about the currents,' Scarlett said, without looking at Ginika.

A plastic water bottle bobbed in front of them, also

heading for the cave. It was travelling fast. Ginika's heart raced. She tried to tell herself the cave might shelter rare species. Maybe a sunfish had been driven in there by a predator ...

Jagged rocks formed the mouth of the cave. Waves crashed against them, dissolving into froth like saliva dribbling from jaws. '*Sunfish*,' Ginika said to herself.

Ted frowned. 'What?'

Ginika shook her head and licked her lips, tasting salt. She turned to Scarlett. 'Can we really get inside?'

Ted shook his head. 'We'll be splintered.'

'It's wide enough,' Scarlett said, pushing a stray hair out of her eyes. 'If we're careful.'

Another huge wave exploded against the knife-like rocks and the air was drenched. Scarlett let go of one oar and the three of them squinted.

Ginika wiped her eyes. Everyone at home would hate to think of her doing this ...

Then the waves died down. The crashing subsided into *slap, slap, slap*, and a storm petrel arrived at the mouth of the cave. Ginika recognised it because the little bird's webbed feet stepped across the water as though it weighed nothing. If a storm petrel could survive in there then ...

'Let's do it now,' Scarlett said, 'while there's a lull.' She rowed determinedly, eyes fixed ahead. Closer to the cave, the boat was buffeted to the left. Scarlett righted the course, her foot slipping a couple of times with the effort. It was awkward; not smooth.

The storm petrel skittered out of the cave across the water and took flight.

A series of rolling waves took over and the boat was carried forward into the mouth of the cave far faster than any of them expected. Scarlett lost control. Ginika's heart hammered and fluttered. Ted's face couldn't be seen, but his shoulders were braced.

Inside the cave, it was a different world. Out there on the open sea, light from the setting sun had been rippling from the horizon in gently billowing folds, but inside, the cave collected and magnified it. Golden shards beamed between walls already tinted crimson and grey by the centuries, and every movement the water made sent more reflections kaleidoscoping in all directions.

'Waay!' Scarlett said, with a gasp. 'It's huge!'

Ted nodded solemnly. 'We might be the first people to see this. Apart from the sea people.'

The cave extended a long way back. A very short beach sloped steeply, meeting the cave walls and merging with them seamlessly. Ginika's heart flipped over. A cave that you had to sail into was amazing enough; for it to have its own little beach felt almost magical.

Scarlett whistled, and it echoed, reverberated, seeming to cling to the walls. They all looked around, spellbound. Ted tried a whistle of his own, and the sound shivered and bounced from walls to water.

Peri was still. Ginika touched his cheek; it was warm and clammy.

As they moved towards the beach, the smells in the air changed: dead fish, then salty breezes, then a mixture of chalk and metal. The water in the centre of the cave was clear and dazzlingly beautiful. Tiny fish darted through it. But it was very deep, and towards the edges, everything was dark and full of seething currents, shifting shadows. A cloud passed over the sun and the true colour of the lower part of the cave walls was revealed: green-black with patches of slimy wet grey. The cloud disappeared and they were crimson again.

Further in, more chambers led to tunnels. Every few seconds, water slammed and roared from deep within them. This was a labyrinth. The waves continued to take them in, further, further. They were almost at the beach.

'You go ashore with him,' Scarlett said. 'We'll stay in the boat – it's easier.' She chewed her lip, looked around nervously, then pointed to the swim buoy around Ginika's waist. 'Fasten that over his life jacket. Make him super floaty.'

Trying not to think about why Scarlett might be getting jumpy, Ginika put her mouth to Peri's ear and said his name. 'We're here.' She knew he couldn't understand her, but had to continue. 'We need to get out.'

There was no response.

'Peri,' Ginika said, louder, her voice bouncing off the walls. 'You have to wake up.'

He opened his eyes a little and stared at her.

'Time to call,' she said, doing their alarm-call mime.

Peri sagged against her, closed his eyes. Pushing down another wave of worry, she attached the swim buoy to him diagonally, gently, and then all at once, everyone was helping. Ted had Peri's legs; Scarlett took his shoulders. Ginika scrambled out of the boat and into the water – so cold – and kicked out to stay afloat before even trying to find the bottom, but her foot hit a soft surface. Passed through it. A new panic rose, but her footing held. The water was waist high, and warming up.

She took Peri. The swim buoy and life jacket together made him weightless. It was easy to glide him along to the beach and haul him on to the sand – except it wasn't sand.

The beach was made of mud.

'It's like clay,' she told the others, 'and it's warm.'

The mud was the same colour as the walls, and as soon as Peri's skin touched it, he struggled further out of the water and rolled over in it, as though he wanted the mud – needed it. He bathed himself in it, digging out syrupy dollops with his hands and spreading it over the skin of his chest and arms before collapsing, exhausted again.

'You need this?' Ginika asked, mystified. 'On you?' She scooped up handfuls of the warm, watery clay and smeared it on to Peri's back, while the sunset bathed him in its crimson light.

Maybe this was what he'd been trying to tell her with the magazine pictures: sea caves and storms. He'd shown her those over and over, always together. The caves weren't just for big sleeps then. This mud was obviously made out of the same stuff as the walls – dissolved – so perhaps something happened in this type of cave during lightning storms. Something safe and natural. Whatever the lightning did, it was good for the sea people, she thought, not like the electricity in our houses, which must be different, somehow. Or maybe our electricity got mixed up with random chemicals that weren't good?

And the sea people probably thought they could be healed by whatever dribbled down and made this beach, especially when it was almost magically warm. It must be a kind of ritual. A mud bath. She tried to remember which days there had been storms …

Scarlett called out, 'What are you *doing*?'

She tried to explain everything. 'I didn't get it yesterday. Now I do.'

'But what's in it?'

Ginika shrugged. 'I don't know. But it must be special – it's so warm!'

Ted and Scarlett looked at each other.

Ginika nudged Peri gently and made their alarm-call mime again. 'Make the call now.'

Peri opened his mouth, took a deep breath and called. The sound was weak at first, a muted, soggy cry. Then it grew louder. It snaked into her head, deepened and boomed against the walls of the cave. A thrill rippled down her spine as Ginika realised that Peri was calling his own name: 'Eee-*click*-peri.'

Ginika *felt* the sound. It throbbed through her bones, pulling at her, drawing her towards Peri. His voice, already split into two tones, now became three. Four. Five!

Ted shouted, 'Mega acoustics in here!' and Peri slid under the water, still calling, 'Eee-*click*-peri,' but now the sound multiplied again. Ginika would have believed a dozen sea boys were calling, their sound echoing throughout the labyrinth behind them.

Clever to use your own name in an alarm call, she thought. Because then they'd know who was calling, as well as where from.

When Peri came up – nostril membranes quivering – his eyes were bulgy. Ginika was scared for him again. He collapsed into the mud, silent and still, and, not knowing what else to do, she smeared more mud on his back. It felt slippery smooth and good in her hands, but Peri didn't respond.

'Is that enough?' Scarlett asked.

Ginika shrugged.

'Hey,' Ted said, 'let's get going. Bring him back.'

'Maybe we shouldn't wash this off him,' Ginika said. 'Maybe we should stay here till his family arrive and take over.'

'No-no-no,' Ted said. 'Look at the high-tide mark! We've got to get out.'

Ginika squinted at the walls. A straggly line of debris stained the area just below the roof, far above them.

'And look at the levels since we came in!' Scarlett swung herself out of the boat and came towards them. 'Look at the tide! He's right. This cave is filling up fast.'

Ginika looked around. The beach was shrinking. A familiar fear crept into her stomach. 'How long have we got?'

'Don't panic,' Scarlett said. 'Just come. Now.'

Ted and Scarlett were right: they had to go. Even Peri might not be safe here for much longer. But had they done enough to save him?

With Scarlett helping, Ginika pulled Peri back into the water and across to the boat. Lifting him was hard. Their feet were clogged with mud, and the water was now up to their shoulders. If Ted hadn't been in the boat to receive Peri, it would have been impossible. He sat close to the side so that they could roll Peri in and let him fall into Ted's lap. The mud had stuck to Peri's neck and upper back, but the rest had washed off.

Scarlett rowed out to sea again, hard, and single-handed. The boat rose and fell, rose and fell, swaying in almost every direction, and there were the rocks, water churning and lashing them. Ted was wincing so much his eyes were almost closed. Ginika couldn't look at Scarlett, even though they were facing each other, until the boat rolled back into the mouth of the cave for the second time.

Then she lifted her head; their eyes locked for a moment. Scarlett looked determined and scared and brave.

'I'll take the other oar,' Ted said, moving across the boat.

But Scarlett shook her head. 'I need them together in perfect synch,' she said, gasping.

Ginika shivered now the warmth of the mud had faded. She was still wet through.

And then they were clear. The boat bobbed in calm waters. Everyone looked around.

'Now what?' asked Scarlett.

Peri's eyes were fixed on something Ginika couldn't see, but at least they were open now. He felt colder. She wrapped him in her coat again.

'We'll wait,' Ginika said. She turned her head to listen, straining to hear the slightest sound. She imagined his family, rushing to him from the wide open ocean, just under the waves. Perhaps diving through faraway storms, swirling seas, wild winds. She closed her eyes. *Please.*

The boat drifted. Bits of shredded seaweed stems floated on the water, and something fishlike twisted away into the depths beneath.

'What's happening?' asked Scarlett.

Ginika shook her head. 'Nothing.'

'How will they even know where to find him when they come?' Scarlett went on.

'They'll know where the alarm came from,' Ginika said, 'and then just search the whole area, I suppose.'

Minutes went by.

'How long are we waiting?' Scarlett asked again.

'I don't know!' The boat felt hard against Ginika's back.

'Need to keep rowing then,' Scarlett said, taking the oars, 'otherwise the tide will just take us back in.'

Ginika put her arms around Peri and gazed out to sea.

There was nothing but waves and sky and a light wind in their faces.

A long time passed. Ginika guessed it must be getting towards nine o'clock. Her heart didn't stop racing. She kept her arms around Peri, aching for his family to come. Dreading it.

Scarlett said, 'What if they don't come?'

Ginika threw her a baleful look, then turned to face the open sea again, listening for messages on the wind. Wishing she could hear what she was missing, what was happening in the deep.

'Maybe we should row further out again and see if we can meet them,' Scarlett said. 'It's better than doing nothing—'

'No,' Ted said. 'They'll probably know exactly where the call came from and who made it by the shape of the vibrations it made. Like whales – they can tell which direction a sound is coming from really accurately. So his family will know the exact distance and how long it'll take to get here and everything. If we stay around, *they* will find *us*.'

Scarlett had opened her mouth to say something while Ted was talking, but after listening to him, she closed it again. A tiny smile twitched at Ginika's lips and her heart lifted a little.

More time passed. Gulls joined them again, wheeling overhead, then settling on the sea like three living boats. Peri was still motionless. A dead weight against her, he felt as though he was sinking, would sink further yet, and soon.

'Nobody's coming, Ginika,' Scarlett said. 'Nothing's happening.'

'Shush!'

One of the gulls shrieked.

They all listened. Scarlett and Ted looked at each other. Ginika scanned the water.

Chapter 33

When they came, they came silently.

At first, there were only darting shadows, streaks of energy cutting through the water, and all the gulls flew off at once. Then Ginika made out shapes. Human forms, moving at one with the water. Flowing people, flitting underneath the boat and everywhere. All super fast, all furtive and all brilliantly camouflaged. Anyone who didn't know might have thought they were water currents of all sizes and directions. Scarlett twisted and turned so quickly in her efforts to follow the movements that Ted's leg got bashed.

And then they rose out of the water.

There were so many. Strong shoulders. Glittering eyes. Long hair rippling with the waves. They wore much more seaweed than Peri – dark seaweed, close to the colour of the sea. So dark that they looked almost like silhouettes of themselves as they floated effortlessly, as if they weighed nothing at all.

The ones at the back looked fierce. Like guards, their heads whipped this way and that – upwards, to each side and down below the surface – frills of water pouring off them with each movement. Two of them carried something long and sharp and white. A weapon. Made from bone? It looked like bone, and that was the only thing that made sense in the sea.

Changing direction all together as one, they formed a circle around the boat. Ginika thought: *We're surrounded.* She remembered what Peri had mimed: these people were strict. Tough. You probably needed to be like that to survive in the sea, but Ginika began to shake. Scarlett was rooted to her seat, oars in her unmoving hands. Ted was like a statue. Both were pale, staring. Scarlett's mouth was slightly open. 'Do they definitely know he's in here?' she whispered.

'I think so,' said Ginika. She crouched to Peri and spoke into his ear. 'They're here! You have to go, Peri!'

There was no movement from him. Ginika looked at Ted and Scarlett, feeling sick with panic. Ted shook Peri's shoulders gently.

And then came their voices. Deeper than Peri's. Sharp, silvery, like breaking ice.

Peri opened his eyes. He tried to say something, but his voice was weak. His eyes closed again, but one arm lifted, reached for something in mid-air, before flopping back down.

There was a flicker of movement and the sea people disappeared beneath the waves once more. Ginika looked over the side. Movements could be seen, fast and smooth through the black water, converging beneath the boat. A horrible thought struck Ginika: they weren't going to capsize the boat to get Peri, were they? She froze.

'Can you talk to them?' Ted asked.

Ginika shook her head miserably.

And then came the *click*ing sounds. Underwater. Ginika recognised some of the word shapes from Peri's speech, but the water changed the sound. It had a heavy tone, like something dropping through liquid like a stone. Deep. Black. It made her think of long distances, deep waters and bitter cold.

Peri's arm lifted again. His lips parted and another faint sound came out. His eyes opened, and they were like mirrors, as if the sea was already inside them.

'He's just too weak,' Ginika said, emerging from her paralysis. She put a hand beneath each armpit and tried to lift him.

Scarlett helped. 'We gonna just give him to them?'

Ginika nodded quickly.

'What?' Scarlett said. 'Just chuck him over?'

'What else can we do?'

Ted, wincing, shifted into position at Peri's feet, and together they heaved him up and gently rolled him over the side. The boat tilted. There was a splash as he slid beneath the waves and then bobbed up again, buoyed by his life jacket.

There was a flurry of movement, then an underwater booming sound as several shapes ripped the life jacket off Peri, whipped him away from the boat and out to sea. All that was left behind were curved patterns on the surface of the water – graceful, geometrical – and then even those vanished. A faceful of seawater each. Slimy hands from touching the side of the boat. And a wrenching in Ginika's chest as Peri left them and the dark water closed over even the traces he'd left behind.

Nobody said anything. Ginika continued to scour the water for any movement, but the waves just kept coming and coming, as always. 'I didn't think they'd just take him without …'

'Maybe they had to get clear of us,' Scarlett said.

Ginika looked at Scarlett through a blur of tears. 'But I didn't say goodbye.'

Silence. Then Scarlett said, 'I don't think we were exactly … trusted.'

Ginika crumpled into the bottom of the boat. The sun was heading for the horizon.

Scarlett blinked rapidly, over and over again. She took up the dripping oars and began to turn the boat around.

Heading back. The sky was light blue. All the darkness of the coming night was near the ground, like darkness had truly fallen. Ginika was still crying, but now sat up in the boat. Neither Ted nor Scarlett said anything. Scarlett looked like she wanted to hug her, but couldn't quite make the move. She chewed the ends of her hair instead.

The moon appeared, faint in the sky, as though it had been there all along. In the distance, street lights glowed, making the town look twice as tall against the evening sky. Tall and dreamlike. Almost magical, like an enchanted city someone made that way on purpose. But Ginika was completely empty. When they got there, it would just be Bridleways Bay.

The stars were coming out. Rowing was much easier now, because the tide was bringing them in. Ted and Scarlett took turns, but Ted was wincing much more often.

The air was cool on Ginika's skin but not really cold, yet her teeth chattered. The sea felt too close, then too far away. After a while she stopped crying, but couldn't stop sniffing.

She looked up at the stars. 'I wanted to tell him stars aren't how they seem. That every single one is a ball of fire, a sun.'

'They're balls of gas actually, not fire,' Ted said. Scarlett kicked him. 'But it's *not* fire,' he insisted. 'It's really not.'

Silence for a while. Splash after splash as the oars dipped and pulled.

Ted said, 'Well, now you've shown him what lights are close up, maybe he's guessed that stars aren't what they seem either.'

'Yeah,' Scarlett said, nodding vigorously. 'Definitely.'

Ted began to hum softly.

'I never played him any music!' Ginika said. Tears sprang back into her eyes.

'I'm sure they'll have their own music,' Ted said.

'Are you?'

Ted nodded enthusiastically. 'You've got percussion from slapping the water, you've got reed instruments, you've got voices … and whoa, what voices those are!' He paused, then asked, much more quietly, 'What would you have played for him?'

Ginika blinked a couple of times, then let out a long, exhausted breath. 'I don't know. What would you?'

'Something fast and brilliant,' Ted said, 'with mad drums.'

Chapter 34

They were close enough to shore now to make out worrying activity. Searchlights. People. High-vis jackets. Somebody official. Police? And Scarlett's dad, red-faced and angry.

'OMG. OMG,' Scarlett said. 'They came! Didn't think they'd really, actually … come.'

Ginika frowned. 'Who?'

Scarlett's shoulders slumped. She looked away. 'You three were having an adventure and I was left out …'

The beach was only minutes away now. A good swimmer could have reached it in about twenty strokes. Ginika said, 'What have you done?'

'Texted my dad about Peri and this boat. Before I joined you properly … He said he'd phone the coastguard, but … didn't think he'd believe me. Didn't think there'd be an actual coastguard *person*.'

Ted and Ginika looked at each other.

The coastguard's high-vis jacket flapped and snapped in the wind like the sail on a boat; but he wasn't going anywhere. Everyone climbed out. Ted took a long time and Ginika tried to stand steadily while he used her shoulder for support, but the sea was still in her. She swayed and stumbled. The pair of them wobbled to shore, following Scarlett, all three heavy-footed and dripping. They'd returned to a scummy patch of the seagrass meadows, and their feet were stirring up the eggy smell.

Scarlett's dad squinted his eyes at them. 'What are you doing in this boat?' His voice slammed through the air like thunder.

Scarlett began to shout and wail. 'It's not true, it's not true! I made a mistake, I got it all wrong, it wasn't like I said before—'

The coastguard interrupted: 'We're making enquiries about a young boy reported to be living on the beach unaccompanied, and swimming dangerously far out to sea for long periods.'

Ted's feet shuffled on the wet sand. His hand kept going to the base of his spine, but he was silent. Ginika's stomach churned. How were they going to get Ted to his wheelchair quickly now? As soon as he could sit in it, he'd be free to move properly again.

'No, it's all fine now,' Scarlett said. 'He's gone back to his parents. He just needed a lift.'

Scarlett's dad glanced from Ted to Ginika and back to Scarlett. 'Where are his parents? What have you all been playing at? Do you know how dangerous what you have just done is? And illegal? Scarlett? After everything I've taught you.' It was obvious that he really wanted to be shaking his fists. Stamping his feet. His legs moved a little with each word. He turned to the coastguard. 'She hasn't been brought up to do something like this. It's never happened before.'

'An unaccompanied child is of interest to the police and child protection services too,' the coastguard said. He turned to Ginika, stooping a little to fix her with his stern eyes. 'Do you know this boy?'

Choices raced through Ginika's head. Could she lie with all those pairs of eyes staring at her? Her heart was beating far too fast … It was hard enough to get any words out at all, let alone lies. And Peri was gone.

'*She* doesn't know anything,' Scarlett said scornfully, as if Ginika was a nobody who knew nothing. Ginika's heart soared for a second as she realised what Scarlett was doing: she was acting like her old self to make their story more believable. 'She just came with me for the trip. We don't really know the boy, not properly. I've never spoken to him in my life before tonight.'

The last sentence was spoken a bit too truthfully compared to the rest, but Ginika realised that Scarlett was taking the blame for everything. Her heart raced and raced, and Scarlett's dad started again, apoplectic at Scarlett, the utter *recklessness*, what if a *current* had taken them – what if a surge wave had overturned the boat? 'You only *think* you're unstoppable, Scarlett. But in fact you've just proved to me how very, very silly and irresponsible you *are*. You will be *scrubbing* the boats out after every hire for the next month, and that's the *only* time you'll leave the park.'

So many angry breaths puffing from his angry mouth. Ginika wanted to put her hands over her ears, run away, but also didn't much care about anything any more. She shook each foot to get rid of the scum bubbles that clung to her legs. The sand was now copper-coloured.

The coastguard turned to Ted. 'And what do you know about this boy?'

'Not much,' Ted said smoothly, but Ginika could see that he was wilting. Even his eyes looked sore. If nobody had been watching, he might have collapsed on the sand. 'I don't know where he lives.'

'Do you know where his parents were heading? Or what kind of vessel they were in?'

It started spitting with rain. Tiny amounts stopped for a few seconds, started again, stopped.

'No,' Ted said.

And now a noisy crowd was surging down the grassy bank from the caravan park. Nurses. Mums. One dad. Ginika looked at Ted, and Ted looked from Scarlett to Ginika, and all three put their heads down and tried to focus on the sand.

Midnight in the campervan, and Ginika still couldn't sleep. Everything was quiet apart from the rush and sigh of the waves, and the gentle flutter of moths at the windows, trying to get to Dad's little reading light next to his sleeping bag on the floor. She liked their pattering. It sounded like the glass was their drum. Their friend.

That soothing noise finally helped her to pass in and out of something a bit like sleep, but every time she closed her eyes, Peri was there. Slipping into the sea. Going under.

Chapter 35

When morning came, Ginika didn't want it. There was a sound in her dream, but now that she'd opened her eyes, it came again. It was a sound she knew. It was like the call Peri sent out to his parents from the cave, except it was different. This call was strong. This call was full of cheerful notes. She sat up.

Outside, blinking in the early morning light, Ginika found delicate webbing at the campervan door and a tiny money spider spinning it. Still in her pyjamas, she went down the steps. There was another money spider on the outside wall. They'd left a beautiful glimmering maze of silver over the whole van.

The sun had only just risen and hung low in the sky, creeping over the dunes. It seemed strange and magical to see it in that position for the first time. The campervan was parked high up on the beach, well away from the water's edge, but even from this distance, she could see that there was something in the sea.

More than one thing. Heads popped up and bobbed, one after another, but the waves were flowing freely over these heads. They weren't trying to stay above water like ordinary swimmers. These were sea people. One, the smallest of them, was at the front, closest to the shore. Was it … ? She couldn't make out a face. But it had to be – it was, wasn't it?

Walking on air, trembling with a joy that didn't quite dare to believe what she saw, Ginika left the campervan and covered the twenty paces to the water's edge without feeling a single step. She flung herself into the sea and stumbled towards him, and it *was* Peri. He swept through the water, cutting lines in the smooth surface, moving freely. His smile was wide. It was hard to tell exactly how well he was, but at least he was moving.

'Gnka.' He sounded sleepy. His hair was glossy and blue-green, like running water. His eyes were still puffy. There was no rainbow gleam, and at the corner of one eye, his eyelashes were stuck together.

'Are you nearly better?' Ginika said, miming sickness, sleepiness and springing up revived. He pointed to the bladderwrack seaweed tied across his chest, and explained something else that she didn't understand but could guess:

medicine. 'Ha-*click*-duuu,' he said. She recognised the word: those purple snails. She remembered him trying to feed them to her, and chuckled.

His family drew closer. Ten or eleven of them, never fully visible, but always watching. Ginika strained to see more. The expressions of those she could see were different from last night: softer. More curious. What had he told them? The slow, heavy land life with all its machinery had made him ill, but they'd had so much fun too. Would he tell them that? *How cross are they?* she wanted to ask, but she was too overwhelmed to think of a mime.

Instead, she said, 'Peri.'

He grinned. 'Gnka.'

They grasped each other's hands and she moved closer, knees in the water, smelling sea and fish and seaweed and a bit of sea slime and strangeness and tears. Because she had just come from the dry campervan, his wateriness was a shock.

'Dans?' Peri asked.

Ginika laughed. 'Yes! Dance!'

They leaped across the water like a dolphin and a gazelle. Ginika braced herself and gathered every fragment of bravery she had as she worked the waves, but it felt easier this time. And she was fast, electrified with delight, trying out heel turns and watching as Peri, more slowly, scissored the foam to his own rhythm. Then they threw themselves into the waves, letting the water lift them high. Instead of crashing down the other side, Ginika slid into a brave handstand and Peri folded under the surface, rolled and sprang up like a piece of elastic. It was better than the summer dance show could ever have been.

When they stopped and caught their breath on the sand, Peri took longer than Ginika to stop gasping, but said, 'Canifloss.'

Ginika laughed at his lip-smacking, copied it, laughed again at his laughter and wished she could run and get some for him, so he could stuff tuft after tuft of it into his mouth. But even if the candyfloss stall was open this early, there wouldn't be time, because behind him, the family were moving, turning with folding motions, catching the light, ready to leave for the wide open sea. Goodbye was coming, spilling over the waves and pulling at her heart.

More sunshine was seeping through the clouds now, warming, lightening. It shone on his hair, turned it a watery white. It shone on the water, made everything bright, like a miracle. The world looked like someone had made it out of everyone's biggest and strangest wishes. It was all so clear, so definite, as if made of glass. They looked at each other, and at the brightness, and laughed again. They were thinking the same thing.

'Gnka – dans,' Peri said.

She stood and waited for him to join her, but he just said, again: 'Gnka.'

So she danced in the waves again. The power in her legs felt new and revitalising, but tears were building behind her eyes too. At first she copied the way she'd seen Peri move through the water, finding new ways to glide, strike the surface, balance and push the waves away from her. But then the dance turned into something different. Something wild and unruly, a dance with no routine, no rules whatsoever. She flew, and in her mind, the wave she was riding swept her into the centre of a wild sea-storm. It was the best dance she had ever done, and when she came to a zigzagged, drenching halt in front of Peri, the colours of the sky and the sea were almost unbearably vivid and bright.

The fresh morning breeze dried her skin quickly, but her pyjamas dripped and clung to her. And now suddenly, one of the sea people swam up to her with the same invisible surge movement as Peri. Ginika held her breath as the sea lady pushed her warm, wet hands into Ginika's, smiling shyly.

She was smooth-faced, with steady green-grey eyes like Peri's, and a silvery shimmer on her arms and shoulders. Gentle but strong. Breathing quickly. There was a fast, fleeting air about her. This must be Peri's mother.

Ginika looked down at her hands. It was a gift: a handful of smooth green sea-glass. She knew from Grandpa that these were bits of broken bottles turned into polished, beautiful sea jewels by the tumbling action of all the oceans of the world. She had never seen so many in one place.

'Thank you,' Ginika whispered. His mother nodded, smiled again, then zipped away after signalling to Peri with a flick of one graceful hand. Yesterday's hostility must have been fear. And worry over Peri. And Ginika recognised that final hand gesture: *Hurry*.

Peri mimed now. A long one, clear and slow and unmistakeable. He was leaving. His family were waiting. Ginika felt big tears leaving her eyes and dripping into the water without touching her cheeks. Peri held up one trembling hand and skimmed over the waves towards his family. Then he looked back at Ginika, trod water and returned to her. He patted her arm, crying himself now. The sound he made while tears streamed down his cheeks made him seem like a wild creature: it was a howl, long and low, like a whale.

The sea people surged in on seven, eight, nine … ten waves, and fussed around him, and took him into their mass, swam further out to sea and he waved at her. He seemed to be gesturing something. Pointing to the sun in the sky, again and again.

She gasped, waved wildly and then, aware of a presence behind her, she turned and Grandpa was there, looking like he was trying to do a jigsaw puzzle in his head. She turned back to Peri. *The sun*, his gesture was still saying. *The sun!*

'Grandpa! I ...' she said, looking at Peri again. Everything was blurring into blinding tears and bubbles were coming down her nose.

'He means when the sun is in the sky like this next year, you're to come back and he will be here!' Grandpa said. 'Nod, Gini, quickly. Let him know you understand.'

She nodded hard. Again and again.

Would she really get to see Peri again, but not for a whole year?

The last time Ginika saw him, Peri had a big smile on his face. He had always been able to enter the water seamlessly without breaking the surface, but now he made a final enormous splash. The sun shone on the sea, a perfect fiery-ball reflection, which Peri broke up and scattered into a million golden splinters.

She closed her eyes to remember.

Ginika was completely emptied out. The only thing left inside her was water, and that continued to come out of her eyes, but Grandpa looked after her. He had brought milk and bread for their campervan breakfast. He hugged her. He hadn't brushed his teeth yet and his breath still smelt of the night, like something that had been locked away for hours.

Crying felt better with him beside her. The lump in her throat had disappeared – dissolved, she thought, by the tears, which were almost like taking medicine. The lapping waves lulled her too, and as Grandpa began to tell her, quietly and gently, his own little secret, her head felt almost like the moment just before sleep.

Ginika hugged her knees and listened.

Speaking in the extremely quiet voice he rarely used, he told her that he too saw someone who stayed in the sea: a woman, many years ago, when he was in his late teens. Nobody had believed him. It was the event that made him so interested in all things from the sea, and convinced him that the legend of the sea people had some truth to it.

'Do you think she's still out there?' Ginika asked. 'Do you think she came today?'

Grandpa shook his head. 'I suspect they are a *young* community of people, Gini. Life in the sea must be hard.'

Another wave of emotion swept through her, and she squeezed her eyes shut.

'I wish I'd told you in the first place,' Grandpa said, opening his arms wide and reaching across for her.

'Me too,' Ginika said, from inside his hug.

'But this is a beautiful thing,' he said, gesturing at the waves, the sky, the whole bay. 'Peri has his family and you have yours. He knows where to find you. Sea people probably use the sun to navigate and mark their seasons, but we have calendars. So when the sun is in the sky in exactly this position next August, he'll come back to visit. Maybe you can keep meeting year after year. In a funny kind of way, you could grow up together.'

Next year. How might Peri have changed by then? Would she still recognise him? There might be amazing stages of life to go through, when you live in the sea.

Ginika watched the waves arriving in slow ribbons with the rest of the morning. Mum and Dad came out of the campervan, and Grandpa left her to them.

Chapter 36

Ginika was full of eggy toast. As she filled the campervan with her bags – which felt like packing a small ship – voices spilt in through the side window and she looked up to see the buzzy lodger talking to a neighbour. When she wriggled out backwards to get more from the house, they both smiled and nodded at her. She grinned back, feeling oddly weightless. Perhaps it was the weirdness of packing up her things all over again. Or perhaps it was those nods and kind smiles. The whole of Bridleways Bay suddenly seemed shiny and bright, and tears came to her eyes at the thought of leaving it.

Then Grandpa's words from weeks ago played inside her head: *There are several ways to look at it, not just the one.* Not very long ago, going home was all she'd wanted. Now her wish had come true, and wanting to stay here was a ridiculous upside-down, reverse yearning. Peri wasn't even here any more.

But then slowly, another realisation came to her. The last part of it jumped into her brain with the comical speed of something that's suddenly obvious. She *could* have both places – London and Bridleways Bay – just not at the same time. A second home was something different. She thought of Peri. The whole ocean was his home, and he discovered new parts of it every single day.

Last and most carefully of all, she packed the new notebook Grandma had given her, stuffed full of all the *National Geographic* magazine pages Peri had used to describe his world. Tonight, in London, she would glue them all in properly.

London. Parks, pigeons, people, music, noise, that buzzing city feeling, Alisha – and the Docklands Light Railway. By the end of today, she would have it all back.

Mum and Dad were waiting in the van. They'd already said their goodbyes and taken their last big breaths of that warm, syrupy seaside smell.

'Look,' Ginika said to Grandpa, pointing to the sign for Cormorant Heights. The *H* had slipped and hung sideways.

Grandpa and Ginika pressed their foreheads together. 'Not "goodbye",' Grandpa said. 'Just "see you very, very soon".'

'My throat hurts,' she told him. 'It's because of the tears that are coming. But they're not stored there, are they?'

His eyes widened and he shrugged. 'Look at Clawd. His ear has turned inside out, and he's forgotten to put it straight.'

Grandma gathered Clawd into her arms. Ginika tried to smile, but her lips just wobbled, and she was suddenly too hot.

'We're going to miss Ginika, aren't we, Clawdy?' Grandma said.

Clawd shook his head, which set his ear straight. He looked at Grandma as if she'd been responsible for its inside-outness, and struggled down to the ground.

'There you go, sweetheart,' Grandma said. 'Something to laugh about on that long journey.' She grinned, but there were tears in her eyes. When they hugged, Ginika squashed in so tightly that she fit completely into Grandma's stomach. 'You've gone and made a Ginika-shaped indent.'

There were faces at some of the windows of Cormorant Heights. Somebody waved, but they were too high up for Ginika to make out who it was. Mr Chihuahua Man? Whoever it was stood so close to the glass that their nose might as well have been pressing up against it.

Ginika was waving back as Scarlett arrived. They hugged tight. The lump in Ginika's throat was back.

'This is a bit sad,' Scarlett said, sticking her tongue out and wrapping the words in a jokey grin. 'Ted's lot have just set off south too. If you hurry, you could catch him up.'

'I know. We messaged each other after I told you about Peri.' Ginika imagined the campervan following Ted's minibus, and the lump was almost unbearable.

'Don't cry,' Scarlett said. 'Ted'll be back next year too.'

'How d'you know?'

'I can always tell.'

Ginika smiled. 'How are you even allowed out? Aren't you grounded for a century?'

'There's always a way. We should make a group chat on our phones when you get home – you, me and Ted. And hey,' Scarlett said, lifting her arms into a high stretch and faking a serious face. 'When you come next year, there'll be no more secret dogs. Every single person will know every single dog. I'll make sure of it.'

'Scarlett! *Shush!*' Ginika said, but a giggle slipped out.

Scarlett dissolved into snorty snickers too, making Ginika laugh all over again.

The campervan started after Dad did his special pedal-pump and half-key-turn-push-in-and-twist trick. Ginika sat next to the open window, and Mum was in the middle.

'Waving's the worst part,' Mum said, squeezing Ginika's shoulders.

'Why?'

'Highest chance of tears rolling down cheeks.'

Ginika sniffed and kept her eyes on both grandparents as the van pulled away and the cooling breeze teased her hair. They wouldn't stop waving until the campervan was out of sight. After that, Grandma would go back inside Cormorant Heights and start on her next big sewing project. And Grandpa would go and rescue some more houseflies. She pictured him gathering them gently, one by one, and releasing them outside to fly away free.

Mum took a deep breath and said, 'OK, everyone – this is it!'

And now Ginika pictured Peri riding the open ocean waves with his family. Perhaps they were heading back to the warm Indian Ocean. Surging through sapphire-blue water and white foam. Peri would be dipping and surfacing, over and over, then floating in small golden patches of sunlit water.

She closed her eyes and let the vibrations from the campervan's trundling engine lull her. Perhaps Peri was thinking of Bridleways Bay right now. Perhaps he was even smiling as he remembered one of the things they'd laughed at together.

Ginika smiled too.

Author's Note

Here are some of the things Ginika and her grandpa didn't have time to find out:

Peri and his family spend a lot of time underwater, so they need eyes that work for both air and water. This difference between Peri and Ginika's eyes is one of the reasons why he reacted so strongly to artificial light and mobile phones.

And when he gazed so longingly at our artificial lights, I think Ginika was right – Peri really was seeing the spiralling patterns that we can't perceive. It's thought that only mantis shrimp can see spiralling light (circularly polarised light). Patches on their bodies reflect this type of light, which gives them a secret way of communicating, because no other creature or predator can detect it. I've taken a huge liberty in imagining this way of perceiving light in a mammal like Peri, but it's an exciting idea that provided fuel for this book.

Grandpa was partly right when he told Ginika to think about how whales stay underwater for so long, but Peri and the sea people use an extra method that Grandpa hadn't remembered. Like whales and seals, they store oxygen in their blood and muscles, dissolved inside the cells.

Ginika guessed that when a sea creature is changing into its adult form, it might be a bad time to start trying anything new. But Peri was sensible enough to head for that sea cave and use its healing mud. Some good bacteria have the ability to grow in mud and conduct electricity through it. Chemical changes then take place, and I imagined a world in which these changes give the mud special healing properties for sea people, and that's one of the reasons why storms are so important to them, and why Peri isn't hurt in any of the storms that occur.

But for the sea people, natural electricity is very different from the electricity we use in our houses. All our devices produce electromagnetic fields, and these can interfere with birds' navigation systems. Birds have a built-in magnetic compass, which helps them sense the earth's magnetic field, and they use this to find their way during long journeys. I imagined a similar system for the sea people, and Peri's was disrupted by the electromagnetic 'noise' emitted from all of our many electronic devices. Peri's body tried to reject the overstimulation he was receiving from all these household devices and their signals, and that made him very ill. Ironically, the fact that sea people are so well attuned to electricity is the very reason they are so sensitive to the human-generated version, which overloads their environment with magnetic fields. The healing mud calmed everything down and restored Peri's equilibrium.

When wondering how sea people deal with seawater, I looked at marine birds, including gulls, albatrosses and penguins, which have salt glands near their eyes or close to their bills, and these empty excess salt through the nostrils. Sea turtles also have salt glands behind their eyes, but these spill out as tears. Peri does something similar with his white tears, and that's what Ginika noticed, although her phone triggered an overreaction in his system.

Who knows how the sea people make their far-reaching alarm calls? Some whales have a complicated amplification system involving their noses and the air sac at the back of their skulls. Perhaps Peri has a similar system, with differences in the shape of his inner mouth and throat, and he probably has many more vocal folds than Ginika. Lots of people can sing with two different tones at once by changing the positions of their mouths and tongues. This is called polyphonic singing, and I think that once it has vibrated through his unique bone structure, Peri's might sound like an ultra-magnificent polyphonic voice.

What Ginika couldn't possibly have known is perhaps the most amazing aspect of all: Peri's memory is vivid and three-dimensional. Wherever he's been, his memory makes a glittering map, and all he has to do to save it is close his eyes. He only needs to travel any route once to remember every inch, and this forms part of the navigation system Ted mentioned. When he needs to retrieve a journey, he just closes his eyes and the scene replays for him like a video.

It would have been difficult for Peri to imagine how Ginika's memory worked *without* these 3D pictures behind her eyes. It's fascinating to think that they didn't know this about each other. His thoughts and memories aren't abstract like ours; they're vividly visual. So whenever he has a thought, if his eyes are closed, the visual areas of his brain are activated too. This idea sprang from a well-studied phenomenon called synaesthesia, where some people's senses intermingle, so that whenever they hear a certain word or sound, they see a colour too. Other people with synaesthesia get a taste in their mouths or smell a particular smell when hearing words. Peri might even have tasted, smelt or heard artificial light!

I'm indebted to Philip Hoare and his book *Leviathan or, The Whale* (Fourth Estate, 2008) for generating such fabulous inspiration for Peri's natural history.

Acknowledgements

Thanks to my amazing agent, Abi Fellows, to everyone at The Good Literary Agency; and to Salma Begum – what you set in motion rolls on!

Special thanks to Paddy Donnelly for another stunning cover illustration, and to Carla Hutchinson for a phenomenal line edit that lifted the story to yet another level. Thanks for understanding the characters so well, especially Scarlett; I think we must have walked down some of the same streets in life. Thanks to my wonderful duo of developmental editors: Lucy Mackay-Sim and Tilda Johnson. Lucy: thank you for everything, but especially for guiding my misshapen early drafts into an adventure centred in the bay and on the boat. Tilda: I had the sea caves and the boat finale, but only you thought of putting them together.

Thanks to everyone on the Bloomsbury team: Fliss

Stevens, Ellen Holgate, Beatrice Cross, Jade Westwood-Studden, Sarah Baldwin, Veronica Lyons and Anna Swan; and to Philippa Willitts for checking everything made sense for Ted.

Thanks to the children's charity Rainbow Trust, who inspired the idea of holidays for children having hospital treatment (during which Ted enjoyed himself hugely, despite what he'd sometimes have you believe). Between 2005 and 2015, Rainbow Trust gave my family wonderful support, including a fantastic holiday at their respite house in Hexham.

Thanks to my fellow editrixes Lucy Nankivell and Judith Shaw for endless support, and for enduring my moaning. Many thanks to Jo Somerset for reading an early draft. Thanks again to Simon Willan at the Multimedia Shop, who rescued my data from a dying laptop; to the librarians and teachers who have spread the word; to my brother-in-law Mike Bone, who put me on to swim buoys and many other items over the years; to my English teacher Keith Reeves for being a very early supporter, and to Andrew, Peter and Dom for being everything in my world.

Have you read

'I loved this story of intrigue, danger and complicated friendship. Clare Weze is an amazing new voice'
Nizrana Farook, author of *The Girl Who Stole an Elephant*

'A fun, fast-paced fusion of science and imagination … electrifying!'
Sophie Anderson, author of *The House with Chicken Legs*

'Highly original, extremely exciting, and a brilliant adventure'
Katya Balen, author of *October, October*, winner of the Yoto Carnegie Medal 2022

OUT NOW!

Turn the page for a sneak peek …

1

Moth Man

<u>17th July</u>

I'm not sure how you're meant to start journals, but here goes: We moved to Folding Ford in April and now it's July, and maybe it's because we're new here, but to me it's completely obvious that this village is cracked. Today the weirdness got major, which is why I'm going to start writing it all down. If something happens to me, everyone will know the facts, because of this journal.

Here's what happened today:

Only little kids believe in giants, but that's exactly what pounded down the hill, right at me. I was standing on the bridge at the edge of the village. It was dusk and I should have been home already.

He closed in fast, crazy white hair flying out, long string

of a body, big coat swinging with every step, like a cloak. And, OK, so up close I could see he wasn't a giant, but he *was* a ginormously tall man with a creepy face from a nightmare … and butterflies flapping around his shoulders.

The road was empty, the houses quiet and still.

Tried not to stare, but he was too tall, the butterflies were just too strange, and his snarly mouth and angry, darting eyes made him look ready to spring at anyone for any reason. I pretended something had got stuck in the front tyre of my bike, but my eyes were glued.

He scanned my face, a split-second glare that sent chills pulsing down my spine, chills that didn't stop, not even when he marched past me and away. And those weren't butterflies. They were brown, thick-bodied moths. And each one was tied to the man's wrists by a tiny thread.

He was taking them for a walk.

The giant with the moths is just the latest in a whole load of very strange things. Just in case anyone finds this notebook when I'm dead, here's a list of all the weird stuff that's happened since we moved here:

1. *A frozen puddle all by itself on a hot day in June. (Mum thought someone had emptied out their ice box on the pavement, but that was partly my fault. I shouldn't have prodded it before showing her.)*

2. *Thick frost on one branch of one tree near the primary school. Brilliant white, totally arctic and completely impressive (especially for June).*
3. *A whirlwind in one of Dad's beaten-up buckets, bubbling the water into demented spirals, and no wind anywhere else. (A salty smell came off it.)*
4. *A type of cloud I haven't seen in any other place. It's like a stack of pancakes with gaps in between.*
5. *My new best friend Sam's trainers iced up right in front of his eyes. He's been helping me look for clues ever since.*

All those weather freak-outs have *got* to be connected, so Sam and I are on high alert for clues about this weird overload. My new Moth Man discovery is completely different, but he's linked – I'm sure of it. Sam and I will figure it all out and maybe get famous from it, and then this journal will be the official record of how we solve the mystery of Folding Ford.

2

Fight! Fight!

<u>22nd July</u>

A massive day for the investigation! Discovered a HUGE amount of stunning new knowledge. Mum dragged us to a pointless jumble sale in the stupid village hall, and that's how it started, because guess what? The Moth Man was there.

As soon as he walked in, the entire room went quiet. Everyone turned to stare. The same mad hair streamed down his back. The same coat flapped behind like a giant bat had got loose. But no moths.

I grabbed my sister. 'Hey, Lily,' I whispered. 'Who *is* that?'

'How should I know? But whoa – he is so completely gigantic. Imagine how long his innards must be.'

'Remember the man with the moths I told you about?' I pointed at the Moth Man. '*Him!*'

Lily rolled her eyes. 'Give it a rest, Alfie.'

'For real. I swear.'

The hall was so quiet you could hear rain pouring off the roof.

I leaned closer to Lily. 'Look at their faces. Nobody likes him.'

'That lady does,' Lily said.

The Moth Man was rummaging through a stall full of electrical junk run by an old Black lady – the only Black person other than Dad that I've seen since we moved here – with silver beads threaded through her hair and a walking stick. He poked about impatiently, picking up an electrical extension cable without looking at her, even though she was talking nicely to him and smiling her head off.

The jumblers started to murmur again, softly, an up-and-down tune full of questions. Loads of eyes watched him hand money over, and he was every type of awkward a human can be. Kind of cross, but embarrassed, and also maybe in a massive sulk, like he hated the whole world. And he still gave me shivers.

'Ugh – looks like he's getting ready for something deadly. Someone so creepy shouldn't be buying that much cabling,' Lily said, like she was an expert.

'Look at his coat,' I said. 'Looks like it's made of skin.'

The Moth Man was on the move. This time, I had to

follow. He's the best clue I've seen since we moved here: a man who takes moths for a walk on a lead and turns a whole room silent. He *must* be something to do with the weirdness of this village.

'What are you doing?' Lily said, but I ignored her.

The Moth Man's coat still dripped. His hair looked like a dog's fur just before it shakes off the rain, and people made a big gap to let him pass.

I was brave. I got *sooo* close. Could have reached out and touched. The coat wasn't skin after all, but some oily fabric I've never seen before, and it smelt of horsey sawdust. He reminded me of a whopping, untrustworthy spider, and I got all jumpy again. I quite like spiders, but that feeling doesn't seem right for a human.

Mum blocked me. 'Where do you think you're going?'

'Just—'

'Oh no you don't. Mind your own business.' She gave me the stare of destruction.

The Moth Man was stomping off on heavy boots that would probably have liked to kick a few legs on the way out. Slipping away. Soon there was no sign of anyone towering and battishly cloaked.

'Can we just go, then? Home? This is for old people.'

'Nope. We're here to stay, and it won't kill you. We're still the new ones round here. We have to show our faces.'

'As if anyone's even noticed us—'

'Don't argue with me, Alfie Bradley. Stay where I can see you. Don't break anything – in fact, don't *touch* anything. And don't forget to say "please" and "thank you".'

Lily popped up behind her. 'Yeah, Alfie, zero touching. Got it?'

What was I supposed to do? I toured the hall, but there was nothing cool in the entire room, just stinky clothes piled on tables like junk mountains. Bo*ring* – until Lily came up to me, giggling behind her hand.

'There's a full-on shouty-crackers fight in the kitchen,' she said, signalling me to follow. It didn't look like a Lily wind-up, and Mum was bending over a stall.

'They're arguing about your giant,' Lily said. 'He rescues weird animals from abroad and they keep escaping and Mr Fuming says it's dangerous and Mrs Cranky says it isn't.'

'Who? *Who?*'

She took me to a tiny corridor between the main hall and the kitchen. The kitchen door wasn't completely closed, and through the gap we could see the old lady from the electrical-junk stall leaning against the counter. She was the one rowing, and she was doing it with an old man I hadn't seen before, and because the noise from the main hall was like a million murmuring penguins, we were the only ones listening.

This new old man was red in the face and bulgy in the neck, with bristly white side-hair sticking up round the edges of his bald head like a brush. Lily was right – they were having a fantastic blow-up, shouting over each other like we're not supposed to at school. All I understood was, *Don't ever invite him to a parish event again!* (The old man spat that.) And, *Don't you dare tell me who I can and can't invite!* (The old lady yelled this.) And then they stopped and glared at each other.

'You missed the best bits,' Lily said. 'She kept telling him to get knotted.' She put her earbuds back in and skipped away.

I got into perfect secret-listening position, like a detective: body hidden in a corner, head angled round. See without being seen.

The old man started up again. 'This village hasn't been the same since that miscreant came back.'

The lady rapped her fingers along the counter and gave him an impressively fatal scowly look.

'As head of the parish council, I have a duty to police his mess and botching.' His voice was croaky, and deep, like a walrus. 'We've had enough of his marauding animals – they're always escaping. That monstrous bird on the allotments last summer – the damage it did! Spiteful-looking creature. Vermin! Folding Ford is no place for zoo rejects.'

Then he aced it. 'All the children are afraid of him

and it's not the sort of thing we want in this village. Experimental animal breeding, warped hybrids – it's not right. Hellish goings-on at that house.'

The lady made a superb lip-puckered face at him and said, 'Ash House is an animal *sanctuary*, not a—'

'Don't play the innocent,' he snapped. 'We've both seen what's escaped from there. A stampede of giant mutant guinea pigs last spring! Ash House is a charnel house!'

The lady looked at the ceiling and groaned. Whatever a charnel house is, she doesn't like them.

Ash House. The last house in the village. I knew it straight away – we drove past when we were still exploring new places to live, just before we moved here. It's big, white and stands on its own with huge fir trees in the garden. Those trees are the best ever. They sway in the wind, leaning together like they're whispering.

More shouting. More muddle. I couldn't see what was so bad about bringing things into the country from abroad and making wind traps and messing about with stuff and inventing junk – sounded cool to me – but the old man thought it was bad, bad, *baaad*.

'... you name it, he's dragged it back with him like a bagful of Beelzebub's beetles.' He stopped to snigger at his own cleverness, then went on even more spittingly than before. 'Greasy, poisonous things – all those spitting frogs.

And now he's tampering with the electricity supply! All those contraptions of his should be smashed and stopped. Every last one of them.'

'Don't be ridiculous!' the lady said. 'Nathaniel Clemm is harmless. You're the one who needs stopping.'

So the Moth Man was called Nathaniel Clemm.

'Harmless? Spinal cords lying around the place, and you call that harmless?'

Spinal cords!

'Well,' the lady said, 'vultures have to eat.'

'Vultures!'

'Just one vulture,' she said, drumming her fingers again. Her nails flashed silver, like Christmas decorations. 'And she didn't stay long – he was just sheltering her between zoos. He's a conservationist, not a butcher. You want to round up anyone who's not the same as you, don't you? You can't stand people who are different.'

With a ridiculous walrus-like '*Harrumph!*' the old man turned his back on the lady and stomped out of a side door. The lady looked like she might come my way, so I sneaked back into the main hall and blended in like a total spy. The investigation was going better than I could possibly have hoped, but what was the next step?

Suddenly it was obvious: I'd go and look at this spooky old charnel house myself.

Thought I'd got past Mum easy. She was trying to make Lily eat a cupcake, which is just about impossible because Lily hardly eats anything since she got bullied super badly when she moved up into Year Eight last year. (That's why we had to move here, to get Lily a brand-new life.) Anyway, Lily and Mum were in a cupcake stand-off, but Mum must have clocked me, and just as I reached the door, she struck.

'Where do you think you're off to now?'

Never even knew she *could* creep up on people.

'Need fresh air,' I said. Then a brainwave happened. 'And can I meet up with Sam? I've done nearly an hour here.' Sam would freak when I told him about Nathaniel Clemm and Ash House. We could recce the place together.

She looked at me suspiciously.

'It'll give me more exercise ...'

Her mouth stretched into a straight line with dimples at each end, which meant I'd won but she still disapproved. 'Go on then. But you're going nowhere without this.' She pulled out my blue padded monstrosity of a coat from nowhere that made any sense.

'Not that puffy thing! It's hardly even raining now.'

'No coat, no go. You *will* need it, and you *will* take it.'

I grabbed the evil thing and cleared out.

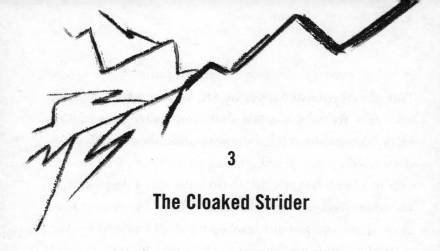

3

The Cloaked Strider

Persuading Sam to come with me was easy – at first. Went home for my bike, then texted, *Meet me at Eggshell Bench. Got intel!*

Sam: *What intel?*
Me: *Too long – tell you in person*

(That sounded professional. I'm getting good at this.)

Eggshell Bench sits at the top of stone steps on a steep grass banking, and you can hide there because it's always overgrown. It's one of our best places. The back of the bench curves over like a smooth plastic eggshell – like it got dropped on the way to a children's playground – and that's how it got its name.

By the time I'd biked there the stupid rain had stopped,

so never even needed my senseless puffer coat. I was tying the horrific thing to the saddle when Sam arrived. I thought he'd be excited, but even when I told him my whole entire intel, he wasn't up for going to Ash House.

'Can't see what it's got to do with the weird weather whatsoever.'

'But, Sam, this is our best clue yet. This might be the source of all Folding Ford's secrets,' I said majestically and watched him thinking. He's in the top set in all subjects at school, and sometimes you can hear his brain working. 'And it's a charnel house.'

'A *what?*'

'Yeah, sounds awful. Needs looking up.'

Sam got it done before I'd taken my next breath and said, 'It's a house full of bodies or bones, or *death*!'

'Whoa. See?'

'Still don't fancy it,' he said. He stared at his front bike wheel, scraping it with the toe of his trainer.

My belly felt like beetles were crawling in it and I went hot all over. 'Why not?'

'He's *well* scary. We call him the Cloaked Strider, because he walks round in that big long coat like a total randomer. Roan used to have nightmares about him.'

Roan is Sam's little brother. 'So the giant on Beggar's

Hill with all those moths – that was the Cloaked Strider?' I said. 'You never told me.'

'You didn't mention any cloak. You were all about a giant with moths on threads – which is impossible, actually. Moths shed scales if you even pretend to touch them.' Sam lives on a farm; he knows the most amazing stuff about any animal. 'If you tried to tie threads on moths, they'd slither away leaving you totally scaled up.'

'Which doesn't stop it from being true that day. I know what I saw.'

He shook his head at me, slowly. 'Anyway, he's *properly* weird. Dodge Cooper's brother says he comes out at night like a bat, and never sleeps. I'm not going near him.'

'But if we just do a little spy work from the road,' I said, rolling my bike down the steps and hoping he'd follow. 'It'll be fine. Come on – he won't even know.'

'There was no Cloaked Strider when my trainers iced up,' Sam said. 'The cold was just suddenly there and I stepped right into it. I'd have seen him.'

'That old guy made it sound like he does things from a distance. We might be able to see his long-range weather-warper machines through the hedge.'

Sam's face went very still and he scanned the village below us, like he was connecting things in his head. Like bits of curiosity were sprouting in his brain. I could almost hear them glooping together.

'We totally need to find out if that old guy's on to something.' I'd reached the road by now. 'Need to find out what a *miscreant* is. Sounds like something worth seeing – probably a deformed monkey, or something.'

'Nope. Not what it means. A miscreant is a kind of villain.'

'Only you would know that,' I said, but he pretended he hadn't heard and let a long sigh bubble out through pressed-together duck lips.

'A villain!' I said. 'Even better. Even more likely to be up to weather-warping business … especially if he's breeding dodgy animal mixtures. Weird goes with weird. Maybe he's planning to whip up a massive storm of mutant clouds that can push through doors and windows and suffocate everyone. Maybe he's lacing them with chemicals. And there are *spinal cords* lying around up there and everything!'

'Spinal cords? Where? How?'

I shrugged. 'Could be anywhere.'

Sam rolled his bike chain forward and back. It didn't need any fiddling, so I knew his brain was chewing through things. Then he bombed to the bottom step, did an excellent wheelie and skidded on to the road.

'Right,' he said. 'Are we going or not?'

About the Author

Clare Weze was raised in London and Yorkshire and has British and Nigerian heritage. Her background is in science research, which she loves to weave into her novels. Her debut middle-grade adventure, *The Lightning Catcher*, was published by Bloomsbury in 2021.